I0691249

Conrad Manké: Black Trons

Richard Mankelow

 New Generation Publishing

Prologue

Time: 5:43am
Date: 21/3/3823
Place: Somewhere in M-Tron, England
M-Trons: 4,015
Black Trons: 16,803
Reason:World war III

"Cry havoc and slip loose the dogs of war" W
Shakespeare

It was a cold morning. Not that march mornings aren't
usually cold, just, this morning seemed colder then
ever. In sixteen minutes the soldiers in this dark hut
were about to get ready for war. No-one wanted to go.
No-one knew what they were fighting for anyway. And
if they had known, they had long forgotten. They had
lost communications a day ago. All they had left was an
order from the President, stating that at six o'clock,
Saturday the twenty first, all M-Tron soldiers from the
special trained units had to secretly penetrate the Black
Tron camp in Scotland, shut down their
communications and then kill all enemy on sight.

The Soldiers have been here for three days. No-one
knew how many Black Trons they had to face. Hell, the
Black-Trons probably know they're there already! All
they have to do is wait for the Sergeant Major to decide
what they have to do, and then follow orders. Such is
the life of a soldier. The Sergeant Major was Conrad
Manké, a man made famous by his father, the late
General Conrad Jacques Manké senior. Of coarse, the
constant streaming of propaganda on the net, TV and
radio had many convinced that Conrad junior was some
kind of super soldier, or even a god. They called him
the Saviour of M-Tron.

3

The men were getting restless, and so, not able to sleep, started to talk to each other. A small group of men in the middle of the hut were talking about the day ahead.

"Ya' know, the Sergt Majors a fool." Opined one weary soldier.

"What you talking about?" Inquired another.

"We're the last M-Tron soldiers left alive. And you know it. The Sergt Maj. wants us to attack the most well guarded building in Scotland."

"What you mean, well guarded? We're not supposed to know it even exists. It'll look a bit suss' wouldn't you think? A large building in the middle of M-Tron provenance, being guarded by Black Tron soldiers. Hmm?"

"They wouldn't be outside now, would they!" Said the first soldier.

"Whatever. This mission is a death-trap."

"Yeah!" Said several soldiers at once.

"So what you reckon Bob?" said a small, blond chap.

"Oh, come on! The way I see it, we'll be marching in...er" He leaned over to see the time. "...forty six minutes, and we'll all be dead in fifty three!"

"Why you think that?" a French man enquired.

"Look. If we had a normal Sergeant Major, we would still be waiting for confirmation from H.Q. But no! We had to have a psycho for a commander that's going to take us to war, with or without knowing if its safe to fucking do so! Come on, what a tit!"

"There probably ain't no HQ."

"Oh, come on guys. The Sergt Maj.'s been good to us. I mean, when was the last time he got one of us killed?" A new voice added.

"Last time? Lets see. How about in fifty three minutes. That'll be the last time for all of us."

"Wow. You really are the optimist Bob." This from a Porte Rican.

"He's right. What makes you think it isn't an enemy HQ?"

"Well, it's in Scotland for one. Every single country around it is M-Tron. How did an enemy base come to be there? How did the enemy get this far into M-Tron occupation without us knowing? And why are they still manning it? Okay, your little United Kingdom is quite lovely, but I doubt this would have happened in the good old U S of A.

"Oh, and here's another thing. How many of us are Scottish?" Then after a lack of hands he added, "Exactly! Why? Because the enemy dropped a fucking nuke on them. Which means the place is radioactive. So where is this HQ everybody keeps talking about?"

"Yeah. That's right. So why we still fighting?"

"Exactly my point. No HQ, no reason to fight. So why the fuck are we still here? Because the Sergt Maj. says so. That brainless idiot is going to send us into a radioactive zone for no fucking reason. The fool needs a smack."

"You going to do it?"

"Yeah. I'll smack that no good, fucking, brainless, piece of shi-"

"Hey!" Interrupted a deep, booming voice "Be careful what you say about Conrad. You never know who's listening."

"Sorry Sergeant, Sir." all the soldiers said at once.

Sergeant Barry Man was Sergeant Major Conrad Manké's best friend, and was built like a brick shit house, so you didn't mess with him. Bob was also very big built and thought he could take Barry on, so...

"You have to admit though, Conrad is a psycho." said Bob.

"I said, you never know who's listening."

"HA! I don't care if you hear me. Conrad Manké is a skinny, useless, psychopathic, cu-uurggg!"

Barry had been laying on his bed with his eye's closed all through this little conversation. But Barry didn't need to look to see why Bob had failed to finish his sentence. He knew as they were talking, Conrad had stepped up from behind Bob and was listening to every word they were saying. He also knew that if he opened his eye's Conrad would have Bob in a very tight, kung-fu style, neck hold and was thinking about breaking his neck. You see, Barry may have amazing strength but, Conrad was trained in many styles of kung-fu and martial arts, which more then made up for his lack of strength.

Barry opened his eye's. Sure enough, Conrad did have Bob in a head lock and was looking daggers at him.

"I told you" said Barry calmly. "You never know who's listening. It could be the one person you *don't* want listening."

"I'm sorry soldier, but I only heard the last bit. Could you slag me off again please." Said Conrad.

All Bob could say was 'uuugh aar uugh' which didn't help much. So Conrad continued,

"Well, if you think I'm so skinny and weak, then you should be able to do more press-ups then me. Yes?"

With this said, Conrad let Bob go. Bob spun round to punch the Sergt Maj.'s lights out but thought better of it.

"Yeah! I could do four times the press-ups you can." Forgetting rank. Bobs first mistake.

"Oh, in that case, drop, and give me six hundred. And if you live through this war I'll get you to do the other six hundred. Although I'll be surprised if you do. The way your going you won't live past latrine duty,

6

which you'll be doing next by the way."

"WHAT!! You telling me you can do three hundred press-ups? Fuck you!" Second mistake.

"Not quite. But we're about to see if you can do six hundred. And you had better, boy, or you'll be on special duties for the rest of your rapidly shortening life you insignificant little worm!"

All of a sudden, Bob forgot about ranks (again) and decided to punch Conrad after all. Last mistake he'll make for quite a while. As Bob punched out to Conrad's nose, Conrad blocked with one hand and then pushed forward, very quickly, with the same hand, into Bobs chest bone. So fast was this movement that Bob didn't realize that his punch hadn't connected until his arse hit the floor. Hard! Conrad just stepped forward and said "Now that could have been fatal. That's six hundred press ups you owe me, but as we're running short on time I'll just settle for fifty, and then to see your sorry arse out on parade in full camo. Oh, and on time." Then to all the soldiers he added. "You lot are with Delta force now! These guys have gone through training most of you wimped out of and the rest of you failed. So, you show them up, or slow them down, I'll turn a blind eye when they bury your sorry arses! You don't screw around with my men! You don't make my men look bad! You don't undermine my authority! If you do, my men will shoot you! Or better yet, I'll shoot you my bloody self!" As Conrad left, one of the other soldiers told Bob,

"I thought you said you were going to slap him. I hope you're better at fighting the Black Trons."

The other soldiers all laughed at this. All Bob could say was, "Shut up!"

***

As with all high ranked officers, Conrad was dressed, showered, armed and waiting for Barry Man to tell him

7

the men were on parade and awaiting Conrad's arrival. As usual, the men were punctual, and so, Conrad didn't have to wait long.

He didn't notice Barry enter at first as his mind was elsewhere. Barry decided to interrupt his thoughts, as time waits for no-one.

"Conrad. The men are ready. Are you day dreaming or just dead?" This was just a joke, but Conrad didn't seem to acknowledge it. In a sad tone Conrad answered,

"Just lost in thought. Am I doing the right thing? or were the men right. Am I just sending the worlds best fighters out to die pointlessly?"

"Oh, don't listen to them. What else can you do? Sit here and wait for confirmation from a President that might be dead? Or we could go home and hope we don't get found out. If we get caught AWOL we'll be up for court martial. Whichever option you chose will be the wrong one, just chose the one that makes the biggest impression and takes the most Black Trons with us."

"Yeah." Conrad got up and walked to the window. "Exactly. But I've just got this bad feeling that I haven't got it right this time. We've always had our backs covered, always known what's around the corner. And even if, like now, we knew fuck; and were pissing into the wind inches from a cliff in the pitch black; I never once gave a damn. We always manage. We could always find some other way. We always had a choice. I always knew the right choice. Now we only have one choice and I don't like it. FUCK." Conrad banged his fist on the table. "It don't feel right. I don't know if I can go through with it. Did Bob do those press-ups?"

Barry looked confused for a moment then, suddenly, remembered which 'Bob' Conrad was referring to.

"Oh! Yeah, then even tidied his sleeping area,

showered and was out on parade, on time and in correct dress." Conrad smiled at this news. He turned round and walked towards the door saying on his way, "Let's get this show on the road."

"OK Conrad." Barry piped. Conrad stopped in his tracks with his hand on the door knob, his face stern.

"That's Sergeant Major to you." He said.

"OK Conrad." Conrad smiles, looks at Barry and say's "Arse-hole!" Anyone else would have been severely beaten. But Conrad and Barry have known each other since they were very young. So Barry can get away with almost anything. Conrad also knows Barry is an exceptional soldier and that he has the up-most respect for Conrad, and would never forget rank in front of the soldiers, so Conrad doesn't mind when Barry 'Lads' about from time to time. Barry leaned forward and opened the door. "You'll get us through. You always do."

"Maybe. But… I still got this bad feeling."

***

The soldiers were waiting as Conrad expected. Four teams of highly trained men. About one thousand men in each team. The worlds most elite fighters. They were arranged in their groups, Alpha, Bravo, Charlie and Delta Teams. From the sky they looked like four perfectly formed squares. They were all facing a large platform with a microphone at front centre. Beside each square was a group Commander, except the last, Delta. Sergeant Barry Man was the group Commander for Delta team and he was fetching Conrad. Delta was Conrad's own team. He had created them, nurtured them and even wrote the Delta's rules. He was the Commander of all four teams, but Delta was his. They were the best of the best, the crème de la crème, the elite of the elite, the dogs bollocks, they were damn good!! All the teams were good but Delta had the edge.

Behind the teams to the left were the ASAU/ASAC hangers and the AUC landing area. To the right were the sleeping huts, canteen and the NCO hut, out of which Conrad had appeared closely followed by Barry. Barry ran ahead and round in front of Delta. At the same time the other three Sergeants stepped out and round in front of their teams. In perfect unison all four Group Commanders yelled, "PLATOON!". The soldiers lifted their heads and dropped their hands lower down their backs (Standing to attention is done in two stages. This is the first.). Then the command "ATTENTION!!!" with the distinctive stretch of the EN in the middle of attENtion. The soldiers brought their feet together and moved their hands to their sides.

Conrad stepped up onto the platform. The Sergeants stepped back to the sides of their teams and stood to attention themselves. Conrad walked up to the microphone and simply said "At ease." The soldiers all moved back to their original position, feet apart, hands behind their backs in the high position, and with a slightly relaxed posture.

Conrad didn't speak for a few moments. Actually for several moments, Barry was about to run up and give the fool a kick, but Conrad started talking as Barry was about to do so. In fact when Conrad spoke, so suddenly, that three quarters of the soldiers flinched (the other quarter was Delta team. They were used to Conrad's idiosyncrasies).

Like all the soldiers that join the MSA (M-Tron Secret Army) Delta Team started as either Alpha, Bravo or Charlie team. It takes a good few years for the best soldiers to be noticed, then they are put through tests that even the old British SAS would wimp out of. But the few that did make it through became Delta Team. It is very unusual for all four teams to be together. Usually Delta team is in a completely different continent then the others, but hard times call for hard measures and so...

"M-TRONS!" Came Conrad's voice over the tannoy. "The time has come. This is it. The final battle. To say that some of you won't see the end of this war is an under-statement. Still, this war must end. We must fight. But, some of you are forgetting why you are fighting and what you are fighting for. LET ME REMIND YOU! Our fathers were only children when the war started. They became soldiers in this war, and when they died, the war continued with their children. US! Will we let it continue with OUR children? No! At least I won't. We are probably the last standing M-Tron Soldiers. Lets make a difference.

"Our children are our future. They are the future of M-Tron and we are the protectors of our children. So M-Tron must live on. We are the last hope for M-Tron. What hope have we if we don't try?" At this point there is another long pause. Only the newest recruits are slightly worried. "We are the best. We are the only. What will we be if we lose. NOTHING! THAT'S WHAT WE'LL BE! So we won't lose will we. We can't lose. For I see before me the worlds greatest men and women. I see the hardest, toughest mother fuckers this world has ever known. Don't let me down, 'Cos I see bravery in all of you... I see the future. And it's red and black. I see M-Tron. M-Tron forever. M-TRON!! M-TRON!!..." The soldiers all pick up the chant with their fists on their hearts. "M-TRON!! M-TRON!! M-TRON!! M-TRON!! M-TRON!!..."

Chapter one

"No-one said war was going to be easy. Some of the most remembered war hero's spent most of their time believing they had lost the war. But they kept going in hope that their effort would somehow make a difference. Usually it did. The rest of the time it just helped them die without fear. This is one of those times." Gen C J Manké

Stars.
Pretty stars.

Conrad was on his back. Someone, or something, had hit him on the back of his head. There was a slight throbbing still, so he hadn't been out long. The fighting sounded like it was in the distance. An ASAU past by, shortly followed by several Octopods. It had been a long war and now it seemed to be over. The Black Trons had known they were coming and had a welcome party ready for them. They were out numbered four to one. They also had plenty of ships. M-Tron ships are much more superior then the Black Trons, but Conrad had hoped for a stealth mission. Stealth is achieved better on foot so only a few ships had been sent. Conrad didn't count on so much trouble.

Conrad looked to his right, which turned out to be quite a painful thing to do. He could see Black Trons running across the brow of a hill away from were he was laying. Just then he glimpsed movement just slightly across from him. It took a couple of seconds for his eyes to adjust. Then he saw them. Just on the edge of his vision were five men with red and black uniforms on. They were crawling over to him. The first was a hulk of a man with a familiar face. He spoke.

"Hey Conrad. You dead?" It was Barry Man. Damn!

That bang on the head must have done some damage. Usually Conrad could tell a familiar face from four hundred yards away in the dark. Barry was just three yards from him. He could now tell who the other four were, Sergeant Aaron Hammond from Bravo team, Private James Rogers from Alpha, Private Charlie Level also from Alpha and Privet Bob Hickery from Bravo. Wait a moment. Bob? BOB! That mouthy shit was still alive, Conrad thought. If he's still alive when we get back to base I'll put him on latrine duty for a year.

"Come on Conrad, wake up." It was Barry again. Conrad must have blacked out again.

"I think he's awake. His eyes are open." said Bob.

"You like stating the bleeding obvious don't you!" Conrad told Bob.

"It's good to have you back old friend." Aaron said. As with Barry, Aaron Hammond was also a school buddy with Conrad. Conrad was always closer to Barry then Aaron though. Some say its because Barry and Conrad share genetic similarities. But the people that know them know that its because Barry's the only person to beat Conrad in a fight. Although Conrad says he lost because he started the fight in anger, which according to the martial-arts teachers is the worst thing you could do in a fight as you're more likely to swing first and think later.

Talking about genetics, I mentioned that Conrad and Barry have genetic similarities. They're not related if that's what your thinking. All M-Trons have genetic enhancements. This is to stop diseases like aids, cancer and the plague (which has threatened to arise on several occasions. Like SARS in the 21st century). In fact, the genetic enhancements were so good that they were used to stop (or as a vaccination against) all known and unknown germs and viruses. No more illness! The genetic modification became more complex as time went by and now it even stops disabilities, mental defects, autism, dyslexia, dyspraxia, physical defects and even premature birth and cot death. You name it, it stopped it. And there were no side affects. In Conrad's and Barry's case the GM (Genetic Modification) was illegal. The M-Tron government decided, so that there were no super humans that would prove difficult to catch if the need arose, they would put a limit to how much modification you can have. This way its fair all round and modifications don't go over the top. Except of course the government themselves could create secret super humans, and inevitably did. General Conrad Jacques Manké wanted his son to take over his job. He wanted Conrad junior to be a super soldier. Conrad was to be the ultimate leader. General Manké wanted a fear factor as well. All Black Trons knew General Manké's face and all feared him. He thought if his son looked identical to him this would make the Black Trons fear him as much. Conrad's ability as a great leader would obviously show in battle and this would add more fear. His leadership skills would be greater then the Generals ever could be. And so Conrad Manké Junior was created in secret. 100% illegal! To aid Conrad in his fight, hundreds of geno-soldiers were to be made. They would be super strong and heal very quickly. However, after the first soldier was created the government pulled the plug on the project. The one and only Geno-soldier was Barry Man. Once again, totally illegal.

"Hey! Are you with us or not?!" Came Barry's voice. Shit! thought Conrad, I blacked out again!

"I Think we had better get him to hospital sir, he don't look good." James said.

"It's alright Jim. You don't have to worry about rank at this time. Hickery, Level, get to that civilian vehicle and start it up. MOVE IT!" Boomed Barry.

"Sir, yes sir." Bob and Charlie jumped to their feet and turned to run towards the vehicle. Suddenly, two blasts of plasma burst through Bob and Charlie's chests. They fell to the floor, dead.

"Hey." came Conrad's voice. "Bob was supposed to do latrine duties. Some shite has just shot 'im! Barry, tell him to get up. He ain't getting away with it that easy."

"Hey man. You OK?" asked Aaron.

"Yeah man, like, the man's dead. How's he s'posed to get up?" added James.

"He's not quite with it." Barry said "We better get him to a medic quick."

"Hey" said Conrad "I'm fine." A burning ship flew by "Ooh looky, a shooting star."

"That's a fucking ASAU Conrad. Shit man he needs help. Quick."

"Right." said Aaron "I see the guy that took Bob and Charlie out. Two man scout, 'bout two hundred yards up, at my twelve."

Barry, Aaron and James sat up and shot in the direction that Aaron indicated (at my twelve meant, directly ahead of were I'm looking.). The two Black Trons dropped instantly.

"We better be quick, someone must have heard those shots. Aaron, help me carry Conrad, that leg looks broken. Jim, grab that car will 'ya."

James gets up and runs for an old Ford that's sitting by a road and starts it up. Barry and Aaron pull Conrad to his feet and drag him to the car. Barry throws Conrad in the back then gets in himself. Aaron jumps in front. James drives of with the tyres screeching as he goes. At the same time six Black Trons appear on the brow of the hill. Barry sees them. "Well, they know we're alive now. We need somewhere to hide."

16

***

After much driving around Conrad sits up and says "Turn right here."

"Conrad, that just takes us to the old Scottish Space Police HQ. It's been empty for years." explains James, as they drive by the turning.

"Not quite. My father was using it before he died. It's were I used to go in the school holidays. I was helping dad with a secret project. If you want somewhere to hide you can't get better then this. The building is half way up a twenty thousand foot high volcano." Said Conrad.

"Yeah!" said Aaron "I heard about that. Went off 'bout two hundred years back. Took the people by complete surprise. Everyone thought the Pennine's were just mountains. Then two of 'em turn out to be volcanoes! Experts say it won't go again for several thousand years, and to prove it they built the cop shop there."

James turns the car around and heads for the turning Conrad pointed out, saying as he does "It ain't gone off since. So I reckon its a damn good bet. Anything to keep those damn Black Trons of our backs."

The volcanoes were about six miles down the road. But about two miles down a couple of stray Black Tron pilots that had gotten shot down were making there way in the opposite direction. As soon as they saw the car they had guns to the ready and stood either side of the road to wave the car down so they could check out the passengers.

"Shit!" exclaimed James "There's no other way through. What do we do?"

"Conrad, any bright ide...Fuck me! Where'd he go?" Conrad had disappeared. As the guys approached the two pilots they were waved at, an indication for them to slow down and stop to be recognised. Not wanting to be recognised the three men pulled their guns out ready to shoot the two pilots and stopped about forty yards from them. The pilots suddenly recognised the M-Tron uniforms and lifted their guns. But as they were about to shoot, the pilot on the right side of the road slaps his hand against his neck in a painful gasp and falls to the floor dead. The other pilot turns towards his fallen comrade, then, shrieks (yes, shrieks like a little girl) while trying to swing his gun round to point in the right direction. The three men in the car could only watch as a large, yellow plasma burst whizzes by, making the second pilots head disappear. Just then, Conrad limps out from behind a rock. He shoots, then shoots again and again. Barry jumps out of the car and grabs the gun off Conrad. "They're dead Conrad, they're dead." Conrad's look was that of a psycho. A shudder runs down Barry's back. This was the first time Barry had seen Conrad lose it, and it freaked him out. The many years of war had finally gotten to him. Barry knew this would happen, ever since they made Conrad a Sergeant Major at nineteen years old. Barry had said many times that it was too much responsibility for him and too soon. But the order had come from the late General Conrad Jacques Manké. Such was the awe inspiring power of the late General, that if a man said that the general had sent an order from the grave the M-Tron soldiers would obey that order. Even if the president himself were to dismiss the idea the soldiers would still obey the dead generals commands over that of the presidents. But for now, they had to find the volcano and hopefully a medic centre on the way. As they get back in the car, James looks back and say's "Nice shot with the ninja star."

"Thanks." Conrad answers, then "WAIT! That fucking star's made of solid platinum. I ain't leaving it in that Black Trons neck to get nicked."

***

As it happens there was a small makeshift hospital, not far from the volcano, that was still in M-Tron occupation. Not very surprising as many makeshift hospitals had been constructed to cope with the amount of radiation victims coming out of infected areas. No-one knew why Scotland had been targeted. The best guess was England had been the real target but the missile went astray.

Conrad had a splint put around his leg. It should have been plastered but it was only a fracture and, because of the war, there was no plaster. The doctors said that Conrad had a large concussion and had to be kept in for observation for a few days. But, Conrad would have none of it, and promptly discharged himself. Barry was told that Conrad was indeed experiencing a breakdown, and that he should be watched for violent mood changes. With that said they were back on the road for the last mile to the volcano base. As they get there it became apparent as to why it was such a good place to hide. There were no signs that there was a building here, except for a small doorway some way around the base of the volcano. The door had no handle or lock that could be seen. Conrad pulls his dog tags out from inside his T-shirt and puts one halfway inside a small slot. The door slides open. As they stepped in the lights came on, revealing a long, long corridor, with another door at the end.

"Bloody hell Conrad. We got to walk all the way down there?" Asks Aaron.

"There used to be some pushbikes here." Conrad answers "So, yes, we got to walk, 'cos some little shit's nicked them! I always got tired cycling down here, so we're going to be knackered walking this."

"Argh, christ man." James whined.

"Stop your whingeing. I've got a fractured leg, and

you don't here me complaining."

They started the long walk down the corridor anyway. Upon reaching the end the men are relieved to find the door was a lift, and it still worked. They walked in but Conrad remained facing the back of the lift. The others thought this was strange but copied anyway. A few minutes later, the back of the lift opens to reveal another short corridor with an open area beyond. As they stepped into the open area they noticed a reception desk in front of them and old Space Police recruitment and anti crime posters on the walls.

"Conrad." Barry started "I thought you said your father was using this as a secret laboratory. It looks like a seventy year old police station."

"Barry." Conrad replies "That's because it *is* a seventy year old police station. Nothing here has been touched. This is the old Reception area. Behind the desk is a corridor. Down the corridor on the left is the old holding cells and on the right are some more holding cells. Just beyond the right holding cells is a lift that takes you down. The floor below is the Space Police changing areas, canteen and sleeping areas. Below that is the two prison cell levels. One with eight blocks, each block holds ten cells; and one with four blocks, four isolation cells, a canteen and another lift to the yard, or recreation area. It's maximum security. But back on this level if you continue down the corridor you will find another lift. That will take you down just one more floor, and out into the centre of the volcano."

"Bugger me! Ain't that dangerous?" asked James.

"No. The volcano's been sealed for years. The government ordered thousands of tons of cement to be poured down to seal the hole. Most of the top of the volcano fell in doing half the job, the cement was poured on top." Conrad answers.

"So what about the secret project?" Aaron asks.

"Ah! Beyond the holding cells on the left is a door. Behind the door used to be some offices. Now, its been hollowed out and a large one floor, three bedroom house has been put in its place. Follow me and I shall show you around."

They proceeded to walk around the reception desk and down the corridor behind. Just were Conrad said it would be a new-ish door stood. Once again there was no door handle, lock or 'open' button. Conrad inserted his dog tag in a small slot and the door opens. They stepped through into a small entrance hall as Conrad resumed speaking.

"Down the corridor on your immediate left are the three bedrooms at the end, and half way down on your right is the living room. At the end of this hall is a corridor to your right, as you can see, this leads to the kitchen on your left and the bathroom on your right." With this said, Conrad began walking down the corridor on the left and opened the door half way down on the right. They stepped into the living room. All the corridors had been white with a blue carpet lining the floors, so it was quite a shock to see the living room had a very modern design. The floors were laminate and the walls were painted a bright pale blue. The ceiling was a traditional white. A huge and very inviting looking, white leather sofa and two arm chairs to match, were the first things to hit the tired soldiers eyes. They immediately dragged themselves over to the chairs and proceeded to collapse in them. In front of the chairs was a fire place with a flat screen TV above. The fire was fake, but it looked the part when Conrad turned it on, and it gave out a constant warmth that caused the soldiers to settle and drift off into a dreamless sleep. All that is except Conrad. Just as Barry was drifting off he managed to ask "So what's the bloody project?" but he fell asleep before Conrad could answer, so, Conrad just said "I'll tell you in the morning."

In the corner of each room there was a small, flat screen on the top of a thin column that stood about four feet high. The screen was mounted on its back on a tilt, so the top (or back at this angle) was higher then the bottom. This meant you didn't have to stand facing directly down at it. It was a type of computer with a touch screen instead of a keyboard or mouse. They were still on. Conrad touched an icon. The screen changed to a plain white background with some more icons, one of which looked like a light bulb. Conrad touched this icon and the lights in the house turned off. With the touch of some more icons, Conrad made all the doors that were open, automatically close, and the two with the dog tag slots, lock. With the fire still going, Conrad put the computer screen on standby (as there was no off function) and made his way to the bedrooms. The last of the three bedrooms was the master bedroom. Conrad entered. The bedroom had a red carpeted floor. The walls had a mural painted all the way around the bedroom. The mural was of mountain peeks with a large, bright blue sky with few clouds. But the main feature were the huge dragons in flight painted in the sky. At least seven dragons were painted on the walls, with one standing as if on the beds headboard. Conrad sat on the end of the bed, pulled a knife out of his pocket and removed the splint from his leg. Conrad got up and moved to the corner of the room. He pulled a small mat out of a cupboard. The cupboard was almost invisible, as it, too, was painted in theme with the mural. Conrad placed the mat at the foot of the bed on the floor and sat on it with legs crossed. He began to meditate. A few minutes later and he was asleep. He started to dream.

⁛

"Junior. Come here. The principal informs me that

22

you've been fighting. Is this true?"

"Yes sir."

"Why?"

"They were causing trouble and picking on the other kids sir."

"You didn't just go and fight them though. You organised an attack with your mates. This is grounds for expulsion."

"Principal! Junior will not be expelled! Leave us so I may talk with my son alone."

-pause-

"Junior. You organised an attack? How?"

"Like we're taught in class sir."

"You mean with military tactics?"

"Yes sir."

"You mean you used M-Tron military war tactics against M-Trons?"

"But..."

"But nothing Junior. You do not use your skill against your own kind. Do I make myself clear?"

"Yes sir."

"I suppose you were just trying to help your friends. Is this true?"

"Yes sir."

"Actually, I already know this. I saw the tapes. What did you just say?"

"I'm sorry sir."

"This is a military school. The kids you are here with are going to be your personal army when you leave. You are the future. You are the future of M-Tron. Don't let M-Tron die with you. You must learn to be the best, NO! the greatest in the world."

"But its so hard sir. I'm afraid."

"No-one said war was going to be easy Junior. Everyone's afraid sometimes. Some of the most remembered war hero's spent most of their time believing they had lost the war. But they kept going in hope that their effort would somehow make a difference. And, usually it did. The rest of the time it just helped them die without fear. This is one of those times, and it will still be one of those times when you go to war."

"But I don't want to go to war. The world is a beautiful place, why do we have to destroy it by killing each other?"

"No matter how beautiful mother nature makes the world, war and human greed always manages to fuck it up. This is the law of man. I'd rather spend my time doing projects with my son then going to the office, thinking up new and better ways of killing people. Then trying to find the best way to win this war without losing to many troops. Its hard you know. I'm not actually there, but I'm afraid. Yes. I'm afraid for them. My orders could lead them to victory, or, sentence them to death. I fear for the latter."

"Yes sir."

"Go on. Back to class."

"Yes sir."

Conrad's dream suddenly changes dramatically. Scenes of previous battles flash in his mind. The battle of Paris. The battle of Texas. Battles in America, Germany, Russia, Britain, Norway, Austria, Australia, Japan, China, India, Africa and many other places. They keep going round in his head. Round and round, scene after scene, faster and faster. Every time he saw himself taking life after life. The blood on his hands seemed to be taunting him, spreading up his arms, across his body and over his face, suffocating him. Then all of a sudden it stopped.

Conrad was looking at his reflection in a mirror. He was six years old. He looked, but the reflection didn't look right. Just then, his reflection motioned for him to follow. His reflection turned round and started to walk away. Conrad just stood there. His reflection turned back. "Come on Conrad. Join me."

"NOOOO! Fuck!" Conrad was awake. He had only been asleep for three minutes. "Nightmare. Shit!"

Conrad closed his eyes and continued to meditate. He did not fall asleep again that night.

Chapter two

Barry opened his eyes. For a moment, he wondered were the hell he was. Then the smell of bacon wafted up his nose. The smell seemed to awaken his senses. The first being that he was hungry. He hadn't eaten since yesterday morning. The second was his memory. He got up and tried to remember were the kitchen was. If he remembered right, it was out the door, turn left, down the corridor, turn left again and then right at the end and it was on the left. Now there were two doors in the living room. Which one was it? Barry went for the first one. It was the right door. He followed the corridor down and found the kitchen. Conrad was at the cooker with a frying pan. Half a loaf of uncut bread was on the counter and some buttered slices on a plate. His splint was gone. Idiot. Conrad looked round and spotted Barry.

"Hey! Come in, sit down. Grab some bread. This bacons nearly done. If you don't want a bacon butty there's cereal in the cupboard over there and milk in the fridge. Or I could do you some eggs, beans, sausages, whatever you want. Just have a look in the fridge. Be careful though, this stuffs been here a while so some of its gone off." As Barry walked in he saw a second door to his left and so asked, "Where does that door lead to?"

"What? Oh! The living room." DAMN! Door number two! Barry realised he could have gone straight through to the kitchen without having to go all the way around the corridors. Never mind though, he wasn't the only one, as Aaron and James came into the kitchen the same way as he had. As they ate they all watched the telly that was on the side counter. The news was on. A young reporter was boasting the Black Trons victory. Conrad suddenly started to listen to what she was saying.

"...Where the last battle took place here in Scotland, England. Just behind me is what our boys were trying to protect. This is the main operations room where most of the battles were commanded from, including the one that happened right here, yesterday. Black Tron have had this base here for most of the war. They felt it would be the last place M-Tron soldiers would look as it's surrounded by a radioactive zone. It proved invaluable. But things could have gone very wrong for us. If the M-Trons had managed to take over this base, it would have rendered us blind to their attacks and, even with the small army they had, they could have won this war. But, thankfully, they didn't. The soldiers have now left this facility. Only a few engineers are left inside, as they do not fear any more attacks. The war is over and we have been victorious. I've been Fatima Sadam reporting for B,T,I,N,A."

Barry, Aaron and James stopped eating. Although the reporter was speaking Kurdish they all understood. It finally sank in. They had lost the war. The Black Trons won. What do they do now? It seemed hopeless. They might as well go to the Black Tron army and surrender. Unfortunately, the word 'surrender' is not in Conrad's vocabulary. Conrad had seen and heard the best news ever. For Conrad, the war was about to start!

"Hey. Do you lot want to see the project?" Conrad asked.

"That's right. I almost forgot. You never did show us this 'project'." Barry said.

"Yeah! So lets see it then." Came Aaron and James both at once.

"Follow me then." They walked out the kitchen and the front door, into the corridor behind the old Space Police reception, and the holding cells. They turned left to walk further down the corridor they came up the day before. About half way down from where they were was a door with no handle or lock. This time when Conrad put his dog tag into the small slot beside the door, a panel opened underneath. Conrad quickly pressed a few buttons and the door opened. As Conrad walked in, a voice said, "Good morning Conrad." Aaron told Conrad that the voice sounded quite sexy. Conrad thought about teasing Aaron by telling him it was a young mans voice, but didn't. Besides, Conrad always assumed it was a females voice, but had never inquired. They all walked in. In front of them was a large, arch shaped desk with two monitors on top and two keyboards and mice. Underneath was a huge, black computer unit with a glass panel on the front. Beside this was a tiny black computer unit, also with a panel door on the front, but plain black plastic. Not glass. A large executive chair sat in front with its back to the four men. In the floor were two half arch shaped panels. Looking down from above, the desk and two floor panels must have made a ring shape, or a circle within a circle. The floor was made from metal sheets (including the two panels). The ceiling was metal sheets. But the walls...From floor to ceiling, along the left and right and the far walls were computer units. The room was small but there could have been nigh three thousand units lining those walls. They were sitting on top of each other like large bricks or building blocks. The only reason you knew the walls were metal was that the walls either side of the doorway were bare. Conrad sat in the large chair and switched the huge black unit under the desk on. The computer started up like a normal computer. When the Door's® operating system came on line, Conrad moved the mouse to an icon and clicked on it. The computer asked for a password. Conrad typed it in. As soon as Conrad clicked on the 'accept password' button, all the three thousand units on the wall started buzzing and the little lights started flashing and the screen went blank. First a block red 'M' appeared on the screen, then the background turned red leaving a thin black line around the 'M', followed by a thin white line around that. Then a tiny black dot appeared behind the 'M' growing larger and larger until it was slightly bigger then the 'M' itself and then three flashes...err...flashed across the screen leaving three black horizontal lines across the 'M'. Like that it stayed. This was the M-Tron 'M', as seen on their flags. All the different countries of M-Tron still kept their original flag, just now they have the M-Tron 'M' in the top left quarter of the flag. America was a bit miffed at losing their stars that were in the same position as where the 'M' was to go, but allowed it anyway.

As the three men stood watching, Conrad pulled a Zip disc out of a drawer and inserted it into the Zip drive that was sitting on the desk between the two monitors. The screen changed back to the original Doors® desktop with the M-Tron 'M' as the background picture. Only this time there was an extra icon. Conrad clicked on the new icon and the computer asked for another password. Conrad typed it in. The screen went blank and all the computers franticly flashed and bleeped. The small black computer that was under the desk with the large one turned on and started the frenzied flashing and bleeping with the others. Although there were just over three thousand computers with six or seven fans inside each, humming quite loudly, the three men could hear another loud hum from below the floor. Then a face appeared on the screen. It was the face of a beautiful young lady. The eyes opened and seemed to look at Conrad. Then all the humming's and bleeping stopped. Although the computers were still on they were just humming quietly to themselves. But apart from the strange humming coming from under the floor it was quiet. The computer face smiled.

"Hello Conrad."

"FUCK!!!" Everybody, bar Conrad, jumped. "SHIT!"

"Damn Conrad! Warn us next time you're going to do things like that! You nearly gave us heart attack."

Conrad laughed. "Sorry mate, but it wasn't me."

"Well who the hell was it then?"

Conrad laughed again. "Gentlemen. I would like you to meet AICS."

"Ace? What sort of name is that?" Aaron asked.

"It's my name." replied the computer. "And it's AICS, not Ace."

"Whoa. She responds to my voice."

"I respond to everybody's voice. Conrad, who are these people?"

"It's been some time since you were last turned on AICS. This is Sergeant Barry Man, Sergeant Aaron Hammond and Private James Rogers."

"Barry Man. Aaron Hammond. I know these names. Forgive me General, my memory is a little off. I need to rerun my memory banks to help me remember quicker." Despite having forty million terabytes of used memory, this only took twenty seconds. "Yes I remember, Barry, Aaron, Martin and Con-Oh! But that would make you...Junior?"

"Yes AICS. I'm a Sergeant Major now."

"Wow. It has been a long time. No wonder I thought you were...Oh yes. I'm sorry to hear about your father. You look just like he did when he was your age."

"It's ok AICS. I understand. I did wonder why you called me General."

"So, where is Martin Sadler? You haven't spoke about him since that last bit of trouble you had at school."

"Err...He died. Just before that bit of, err, trouble we had at school."

"Wait a moment." Came Aaron "How does this computer know us?"

"The computer has a name." Said Conrad. "AICS. Which stands for Actually Intelligent Computer System. So, being she is ACTUALLY intelligent, why don't you ask her?

"Ok." Aaron said. Then in a slow voice asks "Ace. How, do, you, know, Barry Man, and, Aaron Hammond?"

AICS answers in an equally slow voice "Aaron. Conrad Manké, used, to, talk, with, me, about, things, he, did, at, school." then to Conrad "Does he have a speech problem, or is he talking like that to take the piss?" Conrad burst into laughter.

"Hey! Now that ain't funny! Besides, what makes her ACTUALLY intelligent, and not, ARTIFICIALLY intelligent like most computers?" Fumed Aaron. To which AICS replies,

"No matter how life like an AI computer is, its speech, answering capabilities, knowledge and even its learning capabilities are pre-defined by human intervention. Meaning, if a human forgot to write a particular response to something, the computer could not respond. An AI will often give the same reply to a question no matter how the question was put. Or it would randomly select a pre-defined response from a list of suitable responses. But I had to learn from scratch. Just like a human does. Nothing I say or know is pre-defined. My brain is artificial, but my intellect is not. I can choose my responses. I can even make up a response on the spot. I can lie. I can even have some emotional feelings. I can read a book and actually know what's going on in it. Most computers will give a mono-toned reading, or will read with false emotion. When you read a sentence you give it a voice. When a character in a book is sad you read their speech with a sad tone. If they are happy, with a happy tone. You know because you understand the text. So do I. I also call myself 'I'. This is because I am. I quote, 'I think, therefore I am. I am, therefore I think'. An AI would take that for granted, because it is written, therefore it must be true. I on the other hand, think its fucking bollocks. I do have opinions and I can debate them. Also, unlike an AI, which is wrong because its pre-defined answer is wrong, I can genuinely be wrong. I can get the wrong end of the stick. And, I understand jokes, innuendos and double entendres. And, on a last note, unlike an AI, I am self aware."

"Oh, right." Aaron says, gob smacked.

"Yeah, ok, cool. Now how does this help with our little predicament?" Barry said getting a little impatient. "I mean. It's a cool project and all, but, I don't know if you've noticed, but we're in a world of shit right now, and we ain't got time for your little fantasy world. You're a genius Conrad, and we need your intelligence. But I'm starting to think that knock on your head has done some permanent damage."

"What makes you think that, B Man?" Asks Conrad.

"First; You haven't called me B Man since we were at school. Second; The first thing you did this morning was, cook! You made bacon sandwich's. You never cook. You could have spent the time thinking of a way to get us out of this mess we're in. You're too interested in this useless computer. So it can talk with you on an intellectual level. So what?"

Conrad smiles, gives AICS a typed command that no-one, bar Conrad, could read, then gets up and directs himself towards the rear of the desk. Part way round, he stops and turns towards Barry.

"B Man." Conrad begins. "You see that large, curved panel you're standing on. You might want to get off." At this point, Conrad turns and continues his walk around to the rear of the desk. "I don't know if you noticed, but that bread and bacon was well out of date. If I was in a fantasy world, like you said, I would have gone down to the shop to buy fresh food. Did you see a shop of any kind on the way here? No. That's because someone flattened it. That pile of bricks and rubble next to the temp hospital was the mini-market. Oh, and the temp hospital was a small ministry. There used to be a cross, in the space the arse-end of that octopod now occupies. There used to be a roof too but I doubt you guys took the time to notice.

"I can't think on an empty stomach. We have no rations left. So it was either stale bacon butties, or starve. As for my ability to cook, you think I meant the bacon to be that crunchy? No." Conrad suddenly stopped, knelt down and removed a small panel from the back of the desk. He did something that the others couldn't see and then replaced the panel. He got up and returned to the chair. "As for this useless computer, she is the most powerful weapon we could ever have. And you just offended her. By the way, I wasn't kidding when I said you may want to get off that panel." Conrad pressed the enter button on the keyboard. The two half arch shaped panels on the floor started to separate and slide under the main floor. At this point, Barry decided he will get off after all. The strange humming from under the floor was getting stronger. Obviously whatever was making that noise was directly under the desk. Conrad started down a ladder that hung from the circle that he and his chair was on. The arch shaped gap in the floor was about four feet wide. The floor below that was six feet down. Conrad looked up, as he stepped of the bottom rung, at his friends. "There's a ladder your side too. Unless you want to jump." The others found the ladder and proceeded to climb down to join him.

Barry, Aaron and James stood at the bottom of the ladder in a large round room. Behind them, towards the door of the room above, was metal wall. In front was the ladder Conrad had climbed down. But behind the ladder was something that made the men's eyes bulge and their jaws drop. As there was a ladder directly in front of them, they walked around to get a better view of the marvel that bestowed them. For in the centre of this room, on top of a huge podium surrounded with dials, switch's, gages and buttons, was the largest, most complex neuro-brain ever constructed. A neuro-brain is an artificial brain that works exactly like a real brain. Neuro-brains had been built before, but they were only usually a couple of inches big. The human brain is so complex that creating the patterns of electronic pulses that creates our memory was thought to be impossible. Although a small neuro-brain was capable of retaining small amounts of self attained memory, it was never proved that the brain was actually learning. So the idea was abandoned for advances in micro-chip technology. But micro-chips were flawed, they had a limit to their complexity. Micro-chips became so complex, a program had to be written so that a computer could design the next micro-chip technology. But even with computers designing computers, only basic AI technology could be built.

Conrad spoke in a loud, but, far-away voice, as if there were no one else in the room with him. His eye's were fixed on the neuro-brain, as if it were the most fundamentally important and sacred thing on the planet.

"Imagine our combined intelligence, ten-fold, thinking as one mind with one personality, fixed into your own switchboard allowing you to surf the internet, instantaneously and on multiple levels. Not even the most powerful security system in the world could stop you from hacking into whatever you want. You could gain access to any piece of information you want, in an instant. Nothing could stop you. And no one would ever know. Not a trace. All the knowledge in the world." Conrad looks at the other men, as if he'd just remembered they were there. "Imagine. You would have ultimate power." Conrad starts to walk round the neuro-brain towards the other men. "Imagine. What sort of a weapon you would be. Imagine something like that could be built. Well imagine no more. Because its here, its AICS. And we have her. All I have to do is press this button and she's connected to the net. You see, the Black Trons won the physical war, but this is the future lads. Wars can be fought virtually. We can use computers to destroy their communications, radars, all-sorts. We could unleash total havoc. With AICS, we could render the enemy blind, isolated and totally useless against even a small attack. We can still win this war." Conrad smiles, then, starts laughing, a crazed, demonic laugh.

"Ok." says Barry. "So you ain't stupid after all. But you're still a fucking nut case!"

Chapter three

"No matter how beautiful mother nature makes the world, war and human greed always manages to fuck it up." Gen C J Manké

Barry was bored.

For the last two days he had been exploring the volcano. It was a very secure facility. It hadn't been finished yet, however. There was a very large central hanger. Ships could come in and out through the volcano's centre, where lava had once flowed, spilling out and over the top. It looked like someone had began construction on an elaborately designed elevator, designed (Barry assumed) for several ground vehicles. As the Space Police never had ground vehicles, it was obvious that the lifts were a new feature. They were probably added when General Manké was using the complex. There was also a large lift, designed for people only this time, that went up and stopped a hundred feet from the top. Considering the size of the volcano, a hundred feet from the top is a damn long way up. At the top the lift opened on the opposite side leading out. There were several large rock formations around the top of the volcano. As Barry had stepped out he had found a mono-rail station which was hiding, quite neatly, behind one of the larger rock formations. This is where Barry was now. He had walked onto the station and made his way, as far as he could, to the edge of the platform. As there was nothing to stop you from falling off the edge, Barry had sat with his legs dangling. He could see quite far, and most of the view was unspoilt from the actions of war. He was contemplating Conrad's sanity, and was seriously doubting it too. Usually, Conrad would tell you his plans straight up, not beat around the bush. Conrad is the sort of person who would be ten steps ahead of himself. Everything he did was pre-empt. If he was walking to the loo, his mind would have flushed, washed, and walked out of the toilet before he had even undone his flies. As far as Barry could fathom, Conrad was planning to use AICS so he could attack the Black Trons. Ok, the idea was a good one, but, Conrad was missing one thing. A fucking army. Or did he think four of them would suffice. Christ, even if AICS could do what Conrad said she could, a small Black Tron unit that's lost, unaided, and doesn't know there's four M-Tron soldiers about to attack them, would still whip our arses. We would still be outnumbered and outgunned. This was not a good time for Conrad to have a nervous breakdown. Barry remembered that his own father (or the man he called father, as he was a test tube baby) had had a breakdown. It nearly killed him. Conrad was like a brother to Barry, and they all needed him. This was not a good time.

Just then, Barry heard a footstep behind him.

"Barry, Conrad's gone." Barry turns to face Aaron.

"So what? Where's he gonna go?" Barry asks.

"Is there a firing range around here?" Aaron asks back.

"Firing range? No. 'least, not that I know of."

"In that case," Aaron answers "I don't know where he's gone. But he has two plasma rifles, two pistols, a machete and enough C4 to total this place. Considering his present condition, I thought that might be cause for concern."

"Fuck sake Conrad! Why now?!"

＊

Two lousy guards. Pitiful. If only it was like this a few days ago. Conrad was crouched beside a tree. He was looking at a building he, and his army, should have reached three days ago. He had been beside this tree now for eight hours. The others must know that he's missing by now. It was light when he came here. Now he was waiting for the last little bit of light to fade away, and let the darkness surround and suffocate them. Conrad imagined the darkness, actually closing in around the two Black Tron soldiers and, literally, suffocating them. At this, he smiled. He looked at his watch. It showed, half past three. Perfect. That meant, that at half past three, the bloody batteries went dead. Well, Conrad told himself, at least it'll be right twice a day. He looked up. Judging by the height of the moon, and the time of the year, it must be about quarter to eight. It was now pitch black. Time to go.

He ran from the tree, still crouched, up to the wire fence. Oh yes. He was going to get it right this time. This base was once the centre of all Black Tron operations. The last place anyone would look for their main operations. Hidden, smack bang, in the centre of M-Tron. It was a mad, stupid and the most risky idea the Black Trons could ever have dreamt of. But they pulled it off. M-Tron never knew until a week ago, when an M-Tron soldier happened past it and spotted a Black Tron soldier standing outside having a cigarette.

Conrad pulled a small metal stick, with a small 'C' shape on top, out of his pocket. He pressed a button on the object and a tiny laser beamed across the open part of the 'C' shaped piece. He used this to cut the wire fence. He cut a wide, but low hole. He went through. There was a large vent on the side of the building, a short stretch from him. He looked at where the guards were standing. They had their backs to him. NOW. Conrad ran across to the building, used the cutter to open the vent, and slipped inside. There were only four rooms in this building of the complex, (so not very complex then was it! Well, it *was* built in a hurry) the main op's room would be the largest, so Conrad

38

followed the vent at its largest point. Bingo! Conrad found the room. He was above the room looking down through the slits in the vent. It looked like there were a couple of computers still on, but the room was dark and quiet. He cut through and lowered himself down. He looked at the computers. By the looks of it they were still being used. My god! This place was still being used! All the computers were on. Conrad thought they weren't because they were on standby, but he could now see this. The reporter had lied. But why tell everyone the place was being closed if it weren't? That didn't make sense. Never mind, that just means blowing this place up will actually be worth it. But it still seems odd. Conrad walked to one side of the room, slid his pack off and started searched for some C4.

CLICK!

Conrad paused. Why did the lights come on? He looked to his left. There was a large yellow tinted glass cylinder just centimetres from his face. A Black Tron designed DCC (Discharge Compression Chamber). This meant a Black Tron was pointing a plasma gun at him. Oh shit! Conrad drops the bag with the C4 in, and slowly lifts his hands above his head.

"Ah. Hi. Oops." Conrad stutters, a bit confused. The Black Tron with the gun motions for Conrad to turn around and drop his weapons. He does, slowly. Conrad was trying to think of a way to get out of this, but, as he turns he sees the other Black Trons. There must have been nigh forty soldiers. All of Conrad's hopes vanished.

A large Chinese man stepped forward and looked Conrad up and down.

"So, you are the clone of the Manké General. I am so pleased to see you are still alive. But I am surprised that *you* fell for our little trap."

"You going to kill me?" Conrad asks. The china

man grins.

"No. We would not kill the clone of the most powerful M-Tron in history." He pulls up a chair and places it next to Conrad. "Sit." Conrad sits. The china man pulls up another chair and sits himself. "You know, some of the men think you *are* the General. They think you were taken from the past and brought to the future. But I know better. You are no General. You are a fucking clone. Soulless copy of a stupid, dead man. No, I will not kill you. Your precious Delta force needs you so. But you might not be much use to them when you return. So, tell me, how many men are there?"

"Well," Conrad replies casually "Including myself, about four." The china mans grin disappears, and a scowl takes its place.

"Do not make fun of me Manké!" He leans forward. "I know all about you. I have seen all the propaganda filth your precious President sent out. About the son, of the man who saved millions of life's, who will grow up to become the saviour of Utopia. **BULL-SHIT!** If you are alive, then you must have an army somewhere!" He was very angry. He stood up. As he stood, he kicked his chair, and it flew across the room. He stepped forward and grabbed Conrad by the throat, lifting him off his chair, and slammed him against the wall, pinned, with his feet dangling. "Where are THEY!?" He boomed. (By the way, Utopia, is what Black Trons call, M-Tron.)

"They're...all...dead." Conrad choked. The china man, still holding Conrad off the floor, brought his right fist back and swung it at Conrad's face. All of Conrad's martial arts training, snapped into action. He lifted both arms and blocked the china mans attack. Then, instantly, thrust the palm of his right hand into the china mans nose. The china mans nose burst, spewing blood over his face. He let Conrad go. Conrad ploughed a fast fist into the china mans belly, and watched him hit the floor. The Black Tron with the Plasma gun lifted the weapon to firing height, but Conrad was already on him. His fast hands knocked the gun to the side. The Black Tron, despite knowing the gun was pointing in the wrong direction, pulled the trigger anyway. A pulse of plasma shot across the room and hit another Black Tron. The first man only just saw the plasma burst hit when Conrad's palm shot up and broke his nose. The upward force pushed his nose cartilage up into his brain, killing him, instantaneously. Another Black Tron stepped up beside Conrad and thrust a large knife at him. Conrad stepped to one side, avoiding the blade, then jabbed his fingers into the mans throat. The Black Tron backed away, choking. The china man jumped to his feet. Conrad turned. The china man ran at Conrad. Conrad was ready for anything. The china man jumped and pulled his foot up to kick. Conrad braced for a block and positioned himself to step into the china mans attack. But the china man let his kick drop. He landed short, crouched and spun round in an impressive sweeping kick. Conrad's feet disappeared from under him. So, obviously, he wasn't ready, and landed very hard on his back, with his legs, arched above him. They were all over him. Conrad tried to fight back. He struggled, kicked and kept trying to bounce himself up so he could fight better, but there were too many of them. A punch in the face dazed him. He stopped struggling. He was pined on the floor. One soldier placed a foot on Conrad's right arm and placed the DCC of a plasma type, pump action shotgun, on his shoulder.

"You're a fast man. This arm of yours keeps causing trouble for you." He pumped the gun. "Lets see if we can fix that." He pulled the trigger. A small, plasma type pistol would have taken his arm of, quite easily. The shotgun disintegrated most of his upper arm, his whole shoulder, and left a football sized hole in the floor. Conrad yelled in agony.

The china man kicked the man off Conrad.

"HE WANTS HIM ALIVE YOU DAMN IDIOT!" He bellowed. "Bring me my tools." A large case was brought over to him. He opened the case and pulled an electric plug out. He plugged it in a near socket, then, pulled out four wires with long needles attached to the ends. He stuck two needles in each of Conrad's legs. One needle at the top of each leg, and one at the bottom. "You do not need your legs to live." He said. "This *is* going to hurt. A lot." He switched the machine in the case on. A tingling feeling passed through Conrad's legs. Conrad's left leg was still fractured, and the electric pulse was starting to make it hurt. He tried to reach the wires, to pull them out, but another soldier had pinned him down.

"Now, Manké, where are the other Utopian soldiers, and how many are there?" The china man asked.

"I told you once." Conrad answers. The china man turns up the current.

"Then tell me again."

"GO TO HELL!" Conrad yells in defiance.

"You first. And I will meet you there." The china man smiles, and turns up the current again.

Now it was really starting to hurt. Hold on. That don't feel right. Conrad had endured electric-shock torture before. But this felt different. There was a dull pain half way down his right leg. The pain was very similar to that of his left leg. Wait! His right leg was fractured. No, it was his left. Unfortunately there was no x-ray at the makeshift hospital.

"Come on Manké. Tell me were they are and the pain will stop. How many ships are there? Are you here

42

alone? Tell me Manké, tell me." The china man turned the current up again.

"Aaaaaaaaaaaaaaaargh!" Bloody hell, his right leg *was* fractured! But that's impossible, he was running and kicking with that leg. Oh, wait. He was running and kicking with his left leg too, and that was definitely fractured. No wonder it was hurting so much. Conrad knew the china man wouldn't turn the current up too much yet. He wanted Conrad to know it could hurt, so he was only toying with the current. and it was already hurting. He won't toy with it next time though.

"Come on Manké, be a good little clone."

"Bite me! Kiss my arse! Eat my shorts! Go whistle! Take a flying jump!"

"Ok. Have it your way." He turned the current up one last time. This was supposed to hurt like hell, but keep Conrad talking. However, because of Conrad's fractured legs, his bones smashed into hundreds of little pieces. I could not, ever, in words, describe how much pain surged through Conrad's body. It was more then he could take, and so, Conrad passed out.

The china man thought Conrad was pretending. He switched the machine off. As a kind of trade mark, the china man took up the hobby of collecting the eyes of his victims. As he thought Conrad was still conscious, he decided to take only one eye and see if he doesn't scream. The china man took a metal spoon-like tool out of his pocket. He used it to scoop out Conrad's left eye. Conrad didn't make a sound. The china man was now worried.

"I think I killed him." He checked Conrad's vital signs. "Oh, thank god. He is alive. Take him outside the gates and leave him for his friends to find. But do not let him die."

***

Barry was pacing up and down the reception area.

James and Aaron were standing by the desk.

"Where was the last place anybody saw him?" James asks, then adds "I haven't seen him since we were last in the computer room."

"Oh that's just bloody great." Barry retorts. "So no-one's seen him for ten hours. He could be any-bloody-where! Jesus!" He continued to pace.

"Barry, you're gonna wear a hole in that carpet. He thinks we can win this war. Where-ever he's gone, I bet it's part of his plan." Aaron say's, trying to calm Barry down.

"Look, Conrad's stupid plan wouldn't work anyway. But you're right. Whatever Conrad's doing, the stupid idiot thinks he's helping."

They all went quiet for a while. All of a sudden, James had a thought.

"Hey! Barry, why won't Conrad's plan work?" Barry stops pacing.

"The Black Trons main communications don't work through direct link-up. They work with multi-coded digital transmissions, or MDT's if you like. And AICS? Even a computer that powerful would need a few years to figure out a single transmission. By then it would be too late to act upon. Why'd you ask?"

"Well, that means, if we destroyed their MDT transmitters, they would be forced to use direct link-up. Which we can intercept."

"Well, so what?" Barry says, getting frustrated.

"Well, it just so happens, their main operations ain't far from here. I *think* we were supposed to blow it up. They would have the main MDT transmitters for this region, right?" James asks. Barry and Aaron look at each other and both say,

"FUCK ME, CONRAD'S GOT C4!"

"Yep." James adds. "Lots of C4."

***

44

Conrad was in pain. He was half in, and half out of consciousness. He had no idea where he was. His vision was so blurred he couldn't make out a single thing. The throbbing in his head was so severe it felt like his whole body was throbbing in rhythm with it. He closed his eyes as his dream came back to haunt him.

.....

Conrad was outside the principals office. He could hear two voices. The principal, and his father.

"I understand the consequence! I'm a damn General! But you must understand, he is the future of M-Tron."

"General, with due respect, we can't have a pupil causing trouble like this. He had three classes using military tactics in his own personal war. He should be expelled."

"HE WILL NOT BE EXPELLED!! While this is a military school, I still hold jurisdiction."

"Yes sir."

"Send him in."

Conrad was called in. He walks in with his head hung low.

"Junior. Come here. The principal informs me that you've been fighting. Is this true?"

"Yes sir."

"Why?"

"The bullies, they were causing trouble and picking on the other kids sir."

"You didn't just go and fight them though. Did you. You organised an attack with your mates. This is grounds for expulsion."

"Principal! Junior will not be expelled! Leave us so I can talk to my son alone."

"Yes General Manké." The Principal walks out of the room.

"Junior. Look at me. You organised an attack?

How?"

"Like we're taught in class sir."

"You mean with military tactics?"

"Yes sir."

"You mean you used M-Tron military war tactics against M-Trons?"

"But..."

"But nothing Junior. You do not use your skill against your own kind. Do I make myself clear?"

"Yes sir. Are you angry?"

"Angry? I'm livid! Junior, you don't understand how powerful you are. Your skills I mean. Or how important you are to us. What am I to do?"

"I won't do it again."

"No you won't. I suppose you were just trying to help your friends. Is this true?"

"Yes sir."

"Actually, I already know this. I saw the tapes."

Conrad mutters quietly "I'm sorry."

"What did you just say?"

"I'm sorry sir."

"This is a military school. The kids you are here with are going to be your personal army when you leave. You are the future. You are the future of M-Tron. Don't let M-Tron die with you. You must learn to be the best, NO! the greatest in the world."

"But its so hard sir. I'm afraid."

"No-one said war was going to be easy Junior. Everyone's afraid sometimes. Some of the most remembered war hero's spent most of there time believing they had lost the war. But they kept going in hope that their effort would somehow make a difference. And, usually it did. The rest of the time it just helped them die without fear. This is one of those times, and it will still be one of those times when you go to war."

"But I don't wont to go to war. The world is a beautiful place, why do we have to destroy it by killing each other?"

"Oh, Junior. No matter how beautiful mother nature makes the world, war and human greed always manages to fuck it up. This is the law of man. I'd rather spend my time doing projects with my son then going to the office, thinking up new and better ways of killing people. Then trying to find the best way to win this war without losing to many troops. Its hard you know. I'm not actually there, but I'm afraid. Yes. I'm afraid for them. My orders could lead them to victory, or, sentence them to death. I fear for the latter."

"Yes sir."

"Go on. Back to class."

"Yes sir. Thanks dad."

Once again Conrad's dream changes. Those familiar scenes of previous battles flashing in his mind, going round and round in his head. Round and round, scene after scene, faster and faster. Every time he saw himself taking life after life. The blood on his hands taunting him as it spread up his arms, across his body and over his face, suffocating him. Then, as it did before, it stopped. Conrad was looking at his reflection in that same damn mirror again. He looked. The reflection didn't look right. Then his reflection motioned for him to follow, turned round and started to walk away. Conrad just stood there. He knew what was about to happen. His reflection turned back. But this time it said something else. Something that made Conrad's blood turn to ice.

"Come on Conrad, join me.
We can be gods, you and I."

Chapter four

"Conrad. Conrad, can you hear me? Man, you look messed up."

"Aaron! Don't tell him that!"

"Sorry B Man. But you sure he can hear us?"

"No, I'm not sure. The doctor said he might be able to. But no-one knows for sure."

"So why are we talking to him?"

"Just in case. Christ sakes Aaron! We've known the man for Thirty one years. Least you can do is talk to him."

"Yeah, 'suppose you're right. Just freaks me out you know."

"You could always go sit outside with James you know."

"No, I'm cool. Why is James outside?"

"So us old buddies could talk to Conrad alone. Strange man. I told him he could come in, but, he'd rather stay out there."

"Gentlemen. If I could speak to you."

"Sure thing Doc."

"Yeah. Come in Doctor Weng."

"I'm afraid it's not good news. His leg bones are shattered, There's nothing left of his arm, and...and this is the weird bit. It would seem that someone has removed his left eye."

"They cut his eye out?"

"No. That's why it's weird. It's been taken out with a surgical tool. The only thing that was cut was the optic nerves. It's like it was scooped out. I've never seen anything like it. Except in surgery."

"Is there anything you can do for him?"

"No. This is only a temporary hospital. We haven't any equipment. No real surgery. Thanks to the war, we can't transport anything. We can't get body parts delivered. We don't even have the facility to grow new parts for him. I'm sorry Sergeant."

"What about synthetics?"

"We haven't the facility."

"I'm sorry Conrad old friend. I've failed you."

"There is one alternative. But I don't recommend it."

"What?"

"We have a Doctor Edward Julius here."

"What's another Doctor going to do that you ain't done?"

"No Aaron, wrong type of Doctor. Edward is the leading authority on robotics. It's thanks to him we have weapons like the Scout, the M4 Vulcan and the RCFGT. He designed our HC suit's. Everything we have that's got robotic parts was designed by him."

"Cool. Let's get him in here."

"Wait. There's one thing you must know first. To connect robotic parts to a human with all the abilities of the original part, it has to be connected at an atomic level. You can't just strap the thing on and expect it to work. It has to be connected to the nerves. To do this you need to bond the part to the body with Solistic bonding gel. If the stuff works it will be the first step towards cold fusion. But that's 'IF' it works. Solistic has never been tested."

"Ah. In that case I'll think about it. Thank you doctor."

"Hey Conrad. You're going to be the *real* Robocop. We'll have to call you robosoldier."

"AARON! I said I'll think about it."

"Yeah? Well, if that was me lying there, I'd know what I'd want."

"It could kill him."

"And it might not. Would you want to be a cripple for the rest of your life?"

49

-long pause-
"Okay, where is this Edward fellow?"

Chapter five

It was five days after Aaron had found Conrad by the Black Tron base. Conrad had nearly died, but the three of them had got him to the temporary hospital just in time, where Doctor Weng managed to save his life. Since coming around, after his operation, Conrad had been putting the fear of god into the staff.

Doctor Wang was on his rounds early today. He was feeling a little anxious, as his next patient was Sgt Major Conrad Manké. He paused, took a deep breath, and turned into the corridor towards Conrad's room. As he turned, Barry stepped up behind him and put a hand on his shoulder. The doctor yelped.

"Sorry Doctor, I didn't mean to scare you."

"Sergeant Man. I...err...didn't see you, I...I was, just on my way to see your Sergeant Major." He said trying to catch his breath and slow his heart rate down.

"How is Conrad?" Barry asked.

"Well..." He stopped mid sentence. "Sergeant. Walk with me." They headed off down the corridor towards Conrad's room again.

"It's like this," The Doctor continued "Physically, I can't find anything wrong with Conrad. So I give him a clean bill of health, but," They stopped outside Conrad's room. "Psychologically, he's a liability. We would like to run some more tests, but, so far, he hasn't shown any emotion. He doesn't speak. He just stands by that window, looking out. But he can't see anything, as the windows are boarded up. I hate to say it, but, he's psychotic. If rage gets a hold on him, he'll be immensely dangerous. Especially since Doctor Julius has given him a little upgrade."

"Upgrade? What do you mean?"

"Conrad's new arm, eye and legs. They work like

the original body part, and more. I don't exactly know what the *more* is, but I know that, just before he put himself by that window, he flipped out. Threw a male nurse across the room, and wrecked his room. The staff have been afraid of him ever since."

"Oh. I'm sorry doctor. I don't know what to do. Conrad wants to fight the Black Trons. We don't have enough men for a battle. But if it comes to that then, we need him, but, I'm afraid Conrad's going to get himself, and maybe us, killed. You should have seen him take out these two pilots we bumped into. Speaking of which, they must have come past here, did you see them?"

"Who do you think parked that Octopod in our roof? The other mans escape pod landed out back. Those two men took out four of our staff and half of the patients. I'm sorry to say, all the men still able to fight were killed. So I can't help with your soldier shortage. It's quite a shame, as there were almost two whole units in here. All we have left is the weak, the dying and the dead."

Barry sighed, thanked the Doctor, and walked into Conrad's room. The first thing he saw was a digital clock telling time, date and even a simple weather forecast. The date read; 29/3/3823.

"Hey, Conrad. How are you doing old friend?" Sure enough, Conrad was standing by the window staring at the boards on the other side. "Conrad. Come on man, we need you."

Conrad just stood there.

"Hey, Conrad. You with us?" Still no response. "Or are you with the Woolage?" The joke went unheard. The lighting was a little dim since Conrad smashed most of the lights in his rage, but Barry could just see the shape of Conrad's new arm. It looked almost like a normal arm, except there was a slight metallic shine where his fingers were in a light patch.

"Conrad, we can't do this without you. You're supposed to be our saviour remember. I don't know about fate, but I do know you have the most amazing mind ever. You always spot things no-one else ever does. I remember when we tracked a small group of Black Trons across the Sahara. Their footprints were covered with sand from that bloody sand storm. We all thought that was it. We were going to turn back and sod of home. But no. 'Cos Conrad could see a pattern in the dips in the sand. We followed those damn dips for eight miles. We found nothing. But you were convinced that there was an underground bunker and you had us looking for ages. But we found it. You had seen tracks after all. All we could see was sand. Then, when we were searching for a Black Tron base in India, we had to walk across a street, but you stopped us. You said that there were snipers. That Captain Dwight feller used the mobile tracker to find them, but it came up negative. So he took his men across the street. Every last one of them died. We never did work out how you knew. Or how the snipers weren't picked up by the tracker." Barry sat on the edge of the bed.

"The sun." Conrad suddenly said.

"The sun? What do you mean?" asked Barry.

"The sun was shining off one of the snipers sights. That stupid Captain thought it was the glass from the window, but the window was open. As for the mobile tracker, the Indians use a chemical in their bricks that lets off a gas when it gets hot. The chemical is put in to make the bricks red. Its completely harmless, and it smells kind of nice. But it does half fuck with the mobile trackers when its hot."

Conrad turns round. Barry gasps at the sight of his eye. Conrad's new eye was a camera lens about half an inch in diameter. There was no eyelid, and there was a small gap down either side of the lens. Conrad stepped into the light. The sight of Conrad's new arm and eye put Barry on edge.

"Freaky isn't it." Conrad said. "I've been playing with my new sight. It would seem I now have infra red imaging and night vision. Also I have an eight hundred times optical zoom. Cool hey?"

"Yeah, cool." Barry said getting a little worried.

"NO ITS NOT FUCKING COOL! SOME CUNT'S GIVEN ME A FUCKING DIGITAL CAMERA FOR AN EYE! Oh, but its ok, because it has auto focus. Don't tell me, if I push the button on my bum cheek a fucking gloss print comes out my arse! Or do you have to drop me into Boots for processing!?"

"Chill out Conrad. There was no other way to give you your arm and eye back."

"CHILL OUT!? CHILL OUT!? I HAVE CCTV FOR AN EYEBALL!" Conrad spun round and punched the wall, knocking a brick loose.

"OK. Next time you go without."

"What? You ever heard of plastic surgery?" Conrad asked.

"Yeah. You still remember that we be in the middle of a FUCKING WAR!?" Barry stood up. "I s'pose we could have cut the arm and eye from one of the other patients. Or maybe you prefer a corpse. The only plastic surgeon here is a trainee, and he don't know naught 'bout bones. Or did no-one tell you that the biggest piece of bone removed from your legs were 'bout the size of a golf ball?"

"You know, you do half talk common when your wound up. S'pose, naught, 'bout. You've been around Aaron and James too much."

"What?" Barry was confused. "Look, Conrad. It was either that, or nothing." Conrad turned to face the window again.

"Conrad? Don't do this to me again. If I have to come over there and deck you, I will."

"You lied to me." Conrad said in a sad tone.

"What d'ya mean? How?"

"You told me I was doing the right thing. I've done the one thing my father never did. I sent my troops to die. I sent **my** men into a trap because you said I was doing the right thing." Barry walked up to Conrad as if he was going to give him a hug. Then he gave Conrad the hardest left hook he had. Conrad spun round from the force, and collapsed onto his knees. Conrad spat out a tooth. "Ow!" Barry put his face next to Conrad's and spoke through clenched teeth.

"You are not going to put this on me! You sent the men to die!" Barry sat back down on the bed. "What you don't understand is, your father would have made the same choice you did. 'Cos there weren't any other choice." Conrad turned and walked towards Barry. Then he put his hand around Barry's throat. Barry tried to stop him, but Conrad's robotic arm was too powerful. Barry tried to punch Conrad again, but Conrad's reach was just too long.

"My father NEVER makes mistakes. And I'll kill any man who says otherwise." Barry's feet were now off the floor.

"Yes he did. Many of them. And if you have to kill me to figure this out, then so be it." Barry lifted both his fists and crashed them down on Conrad's arm. Now this must have hurt somewhere down Conrad's body, because he grimaced as his robotic arm was forced away from Barry's throat. Barry threw another punch, but Conrad caught it with his robotic arm.

"Remember when we were children B Man? I fought you once before. I was very angry that you won, and thought about killing you. But I couldn't. I couldn't then, and I can't now." Conrad let go of Barry's fist.

55

Barry punched Conrad round the head, very hard, and knocked Conrad out.

"I thought about killing you once. I can't do it either."

Chapter six

All was not well in the office of President J Moon. He had been getting phone calls all day from the leaders of the IC (Independent Countries). Every last one of them asked the same question; 'Are we in danger of another attack?'. Jason was getting fed up with it. Since the news was sent that the clone of 'The Manké General' was still alive, mass panic spread through the IC like wildfire. Jason didn't even know if the man that General Kil Spree captured actually was Conrad Manké. It didn't seem right. Jason had called a meeting with all the IC leaders, which was due to start in five minutes. But for now, President Jason Moon just wanted to take the phones off the hook, and put his feet up. Since the war began, the leaders of the IC had agreed to work together as a united force. This union was called the Bureau of Lands And Countries of Khan. Khan was a universal depiction of leader, king or ruler. The 'Khan' being Jason Moon. The word 'Tron' was placed after the abbreviation, as a kind of taunt, making the united IC codename, BLACK Tron. And President J Moon was the Black Trons Khan. He is the leader of Black Tron, and soon the IC leaders will give him full control over their countries. He will rule the world, and the IC leaders will make it so.

A young receptionist put her head inside the door and, gingerly, told Jason that it was time for the meeting. With that, she was gone. No-one ever came in his office. Except the IC leaders, of coarse. Since Jason returned from his operation, everyone noticed that Jason had become very ruthless. He started spreading a lot of propaganda through the IC leaders. This propaganda was then, in turn, spread through the countries they were running. The Muslim leaders were the easiest to convince, as they hated the west more then any other IC country. Then he tried with China and Japan. China wouldn't believe it and promptly joined the M-Tron society. But Japan. Oh Japan. They took the propaganda as if it were gospel. Jason managed to turn all the countries, that remained independent, against M-Tron. Once he had them singing his tune, he united them. Black Tron was born. Being the leader of Black Tron, Jason was, effectively, in control of all the Independent Countries. He had the monopoly on it all, and they don't even know it.

"Ahem. Sir. The meeting is in progress." The young receptionist had returned.

"I'm on my way."

***

The IC leaders were waiting patiently. A few of them had started talking to each other. The others were quietly sitting around the huge horseshoe shaped table. It would seem that the Black Tron president was being fashionably late again. The IC leaders, that had started chatting, were talking about, just that.

"I think he may be with that receptionist. If you know what I mean."

"No. I think he is assessing the situation. You must remember *who* this meeting is about."

"I don't think so. I'm sure he does it by purpose."

"Maybe, he won't turn up at all. Given the nature of this meeting."

"You think there will be another attack by the Utopians?"

"If the Manké clone is still alive, then yes. He's already proved to be quite the aggressor."

"What should we do then? We lost almost three quarters of our armies. We have no reinforcements left."

"We all used our reinforcements. We have *no* men left."

58

"Then something *has* to be done!"

"THEN SOMETHING **WILL** BE DONE!" Jason Moon had entered the room. "Good evening gentlemen. Please be seated." Everyone took their seats. "I have had my best men looking into the situation, and they have found out some interesting facts. To start with, the Manké clone is **not** alive. Secondly, there will **not** be any attacks from the Utopians. BUT! We have not found the Manké clones body. Therefore, I vote that we keep Black Tron running. This way, we will be independent and benefit from unity at the same time. You have witnessed how powerful we can be in union. I vote that we have a World President, that will control Black Tron, and will help keep order between our lands and peoples. So that we can unite as one if ever our way of life is threatened again."

"Yes. But we must have a say in who is World President." One IC leader called out.

"Of coarse. There will be regular elections, so you can vote for the man you want as World President. In fact, we will start the ballot in six months time. All those in favour, say aye."

There were a few 'nays' but the 'ayes' had it. Now all that Jason needed was to be elected, and he would have it all. The meeting was over. Jason was happy. The meeting went quite well. Once again those fools believed every word he said. Now he just has to remove a certain Sgt Major from the world of the living. But for now he was happy.

Jason was still smiling when he entered the briefing room and joined his Generals. They were sitting around a long table in a small room. Jason promptly sat at the far end of the table. His men just sat there.

"Good evening gentlemen. Please be seated. Oh, you already are. I have had my best men looking into the situation, and they have found out some interesting facts. To start with, what the fuck is Conrad doing alive? Secondly, there **will** be another attack from the Utopians, because some idiot let Conrad go after they, somehow, managed to capture him. Choo Lou. How did this happen?" Chou Lou stood up. It was the china man who took out Conrad's eye. He looked a little worried.

"Sir. I...I...I take full responsibility sir."

"Why was Conrad let free?" Jason asked.

"I gave the order sir. He was not in good shape sir." Two soldiers, who were standing near the wall behind Lou, stepped forward and stood directly behind him.

"So you let him go."

"Y...Y...Yes s...s...sir." Lou was really getting worried.

"You failed me. I don't except failure." The two soldiers grabbed Lou and, pulling out a knife, slashed at his throat. Lou managed to pull his sidearm out and shoot at Jason. The bullet ricocheted off Jason's head. His face twisted and scrunched. He put his hands to his face. But when he removed his hands, his face looked normal. No marks. No blood. The two soldiers pulled Lou's body out of the room. No-one said a word. Until Jason spoke again.

"Anyone else want to fail me? No? In that case, could someone tell me why that, fucking clone of the Manké General, is still alive? No answers eh? then I'll just say this. Next time one of you fucking idiots capture him, bring him to me. Alive."

He pressed a button on the table. A hologram of Conrad appears.

"Sergeant Major Conrad Manké. Caucasian male, English. Five feet and ten inches tall. Weighs eleven stone. Slim built. Thirty one years of age. Gray eyes, dark brown hair. See the way his hair is cut? Grade one down the sides and a two inch thick strip of very long hair across the top and down the back. He could make one hell of a Mohican with that, but instead he ties it up near the top of his head in a ponytail. Always wears black leather boots, black jeans, black belt, T-shirt with the M-Tron logo upon it, black shirt. When he's in the field he wears a camouflage jacket, sometimes, and plenty of weapons. Favourite weapons are his samurai sword and twin, custom made, platinum Glock F17s. Martial artist, weapons expert and pilot. Oh, and he has his very own army picked from the best soldiers M-Tron has to offer. His Officers are," the hologram changes to Barry "Sergeant Barry Man. African-American male, USA. Six foot four, sixteen stone, very big built, muscular. Also thirty one years of age. Blue eyes. Bald. Usually wears army issue black boots, camouflage trousers, belt. Also he wears a black muscle shirt and camouflage body warmer. Favourite weapons are two plasma guns or his bare hands. Boxer. Mechanic, engineer and heavy weapons specialist." the hologram changes again, this time to Aaron "And Sergeant Aaron Hammond. Caucasian male, English. Five foot three, twelve stone two pound, muscular. Thirty one years old again. Brown eyes, short blond hair. Wears army issue black boots, camouflage trousers, belt, shirt and jacket. Only his black fingerless leather gloves and black sleeveless T-shirt are not army issue. Favourite weapons are, plasma rifle, Walther PPX hand gun, large knife. Kick boxer. Ex F1 racer, so he makes a great getaway driver. Any of these men are dangerous on their own, and devastating as a team. Find them. Kill them. But bring Conrad alive."

***

General Chou Wong was angry. His little brother was dead. And it was all the clone of the Manké General's fault. He went to Jason Moons office and entered.

"Sir. Permission to speak sir."

"Go ahead my old comrade."

"I wish to lead the search for the Manké clone sir."

"Why?"

"Because it just got personal. Chou Lou was my brother, sir."

"Then you have permission to lead the search. Take your revenge on any M-Tron you find. But I want Conrad alive. After I get to talk with him, if things haven't changed, you can kill him. But I want to talk to him first. Am I understood?"

"Yes sir. Thank you sir."

"General Spree here will join you. But for now, take a seat and join us in a drink. We have a world to control. And things are going in my favour."

Chapter seven

Conrad was meditating in his room at the volcano base when Barry entered.

"Conrad. Chow down."

"What?" Conrad asked.

"Grubs up. Foods ready. Eat. You do remember how to eat?"

"Don't take the piss. It doesn't suit you."

"Yeah, well, come and get some food then."

"I'm not hungry. Besides, I seem to be missing some teeth."

"Well whose fault is that?"

"Yours! You bloody hit me remember!?"

"You were being an arse remember?" Conrad didn't answer. "There we go then. Psych out on me again and I'll bloody well knock you into next week."

"You dare talk to a senior officer in that tone? Don't forget I out rank you."

"Oh, Conrad. The war is over." Barry sat on the bed. "We don't hold ranks any more. You're my friend Conrad, and I'm trying so hard to help you, but everything I do you throw back in my face. So fuck your rank." Conrad opened his eyes. Barry recognised the look in his eyes. It was the same look he had when he killed those two Black Tron pilots and when he grabbed Barry by the throat in the hospital. Conrad stood up and, without even looking at Barry, walked out of the bedroom. Conrad walked all the way to the aircraft landing area in the centre of the volcano, and towards a large metal container, which he proceeded to beat the living shit out of. Barry decided to let him cool off.

When Conrad finally returned, they were all in the living room. Conrad entered quietly. His left hand was dripping with blood. He went to his favourite chair and sat down. Barry looked at him. There was no expression on his face. Barry offered to patch the cuts on his hand up, but Conrad waved it away. They were watching TV. There was a report about a general election for a World President. Hmm, Conrad thought, they oppose M-Tron for their unity, but want to unify themselves. These people are fucked up.

"...The elections will be held on Saturday the eighteenth. I'll be voting. You should too. This is Mohanned Kalif reporting for B.T.I.N.A."

"And those headlines again. A man was..."

"Oh, my, god." Conrad suddenly exclaimed. "What a twat! What an idiot! Why didn't I think of it before?" The others were confused.

"Conrad. What you going on about?" Aaron asked.

"They won't kill a president. Not their own."

"We don't get it." James said.

"Let me put it like this. I've got a plan."

***

They were all in the computer room. Conrad was holding a red Zip disc with the words 'Top Secret' and 'AICS internet connection codes and drivers' written on it. Conrad looked at it as if it were a very difficult task. He sat there with the thing in his hand, not moving. Aaron decided to interrupt his thoughts.

"Conrad? Are you alright?"

"Yeah." James added. "You going to put the thing in or what?"

"I'm sorry." Conrad said. "It's just that, my father never finished this project. If I put this disc in, I'll be finishing his work." Conrad lowered his eyes. "It just reminded me of how this project was so important to him. And to me." Conrad looked at his friends. "It was the only way I could get close to my father."

Barry put a hand on Conrad's shoulder.

"In your own time. General Manké would be proud

64

of you."

"Ha! I don't think so! Dad hated me finishing off his work. But thanks for the thought though B Man." Conrad put the disc in. He started the program on the disc running and sat back.

"Why can't Ace program herself?" James asked.

"Well, all computers need drivers. This lets them know where ports, devices, drives and other pieces of hardware are. Inside this computer alone there must be billions of different connections all leading to another billion different connections of their own. How is AICS supposed to know the right combinations to connect to the modem? Or how to use the modem when she finds it? So she needs a driver. Her human thinking will let her program herself, but she still needs the drivers. Anything that's plug and play she can sort out herself. Imagine having a jigsaw puzzle with a million pieces and no picture on it. All the driver does is draw the picture. Basically, when this program is finished, she will be connected to the internet. But once she has a basic driver installed, she can change them to run with any computer hardware. Well, of the same type. She can't use a video driver for a sound card, but she can use a video driver for *any* video card. This means she can control everything and anything. 'Cos she's got every driver going installed." The computer bleeped to let Conrad know the driver had finished installing. "Including modem drivers now." Conrad added. The computers started doing their frenzied flashings again and AICS appeared smiling as usual.

"Good afternoon gentlemen."

"AICS. I have a job for you. I want you to intercept the Black Trons MDT transmissions." Conrad told her.

"But I can't decipher MDTs Conrad. You know that."

"I don't want to know what they say, I just don't

want anyone to receive them."

"Oh. You mean jam their signal right?" Conrad nodded. "OK. Will do." Aaron was puzzled.

"How did Ace know that you nodded?" He asked.

"Easy. See that camera over there?" Conrad pointed over to the far end of the room. Sure enough, there was a CCTV camera in the corner. "See the one above your head? And the web cam on the monitors? There's a camera, or two, in every room. She can use them like we use our eyes."

"Cor, must be hard to see lots of different places at the same time." Said James.

"Not for a super computer. AICS. After you've jammed their signals, send a ghost virus and kill their systems." Conrad said.

"I need to know their security codes. I'm afraid they work by a rotating combination, so I need to know the combination sequence."

"Funny you should mention that." Conrad typed in a code sequence. "I see this when I was in the Black Tron communication rooms." Then he had a thought. "AICS. Can you get a satellite view of the Black Tron base?"

"Of coarse Conrad. It'll take twenty seconds for the satellite to be in position. Their communications are jammed and the ghost virus is sent." AICS told them.

"What's a ghost virus Conrad?" asked Aaron.

"It's an untraceable virus." Conrad answered.

"Ah. Nothing exciting then?"

"It's a virus that works without any one knowing it's there. Usually a virus does something that you can see happening. A ghost virus doesn't."

"Conrad. Satellite is in position. Up-link complete." A window opened, and inside a live view of the Black Trons communication base in Scotland appeared. Conrad pulled a detonation device out of his pocket. "Forgot about this." He said, then pressed the detonation button. Nothing happened. Conrad stared at the screen and waited, but still nothing happened.

"Bugger. They must have removed the trigger. Never mind, it was worth the try." Conrad typed a command which AICS followed. Then to the others he said "In a few hours their systems will be down. For Black Tron to send communications to this region they will have to use Direct link-up. When they do, we will see it. Now let us prepare. We have a ballot to fix."

***

Conrad got the information he was hoping for two days later. The information he had asked AICS to provide was from a message she had intercepted telling the location of where the Black Tron election was to be held. In this election, as there are many countries involved, the votes were first conducted in each individual country, and then the IC leaders have to meet with the name of their highest voted candidate and the final vote will then be conducted. The final vote was to be held in Moscow. This is what Conrad wanted to know.

He prepares be putting as much weapons about his body as he can. First, his samurai sword, long with a thick wooden handle and chrome finishing. The blade shone in the light. This he put in a wooden scabbard, with matching chrome finishing, and tied to his belt on his left-hand side. He tied a large sheathed knife around his lower right leg, put his twin Glock F17s in their holsters behind his back and a shotgun over his shoulder. Then in his hands he held a large chain gun. This had been left by the cops when the volcano was still a police station. Conrad had restored it to its original, deadly, state. He had a couple of hand grenades tied to his belt as well as his shurikens (ninja stars) in a small leather pouch. Then, tying his long hair back in a pony tail, near the top of his head, he walked out the door. The hair at the sides of his head had grown long over the many months he had been at war, it was due a cut, but he tied it back with the rest of his hair for now. The haircut can wait.

Conrad met with Barry. Barry was wearing his usual armoury. Twin Plasma guns, the MK 1 type PEEP (Plasma Enhanced Energy Projectile), a hunting knife attached to his belt (a present from Conrad, it had 'happy birthday B Man' engraved in Chinese along one side of the blade) next to a black Glock F17. Aaron approached them. He was dressed in his favourite arsenal. A Walther PPX was tucked into his trousers. A large lock-knife was on his belt in a pouch and a MK 1 PEEP rifle (Plasma rifle for short) in his hands. James was sporting a PERL, a Plasma Enhanced Rocket Launcher (the most powerful PEEP invented. They only made the one type, so no 'MK' number was given), a Plasma gun (MK 1 PEEP) and a solid alloy baseball bat sticking out of a rucksack on his back.

"Ready? Who's got the C4?" Conrad asked.

"In the bag." James answered with a shrug of his shoulders to make the rucksack shake.

"Then we're ready. Lets go. And remember men, this is a stealth mission, so no ruddy talking or I'll shoot you myself."

Barry, Aaron and James looked at each other and said.

"Conrad's back."

***

To get to Moscow, Conrad needed a ship. Only a Black Tron ship would do though, as he had to get past the Black Tron boarders. An M-Tron ship would stand out like a sore thumb. But Conrad didn't have a clue where to find a Black Tron ship, especially one big enough to fit four men. They were near the beach when Conrad had an idea. Unaware of Conrad's plan, Barry decided to ask where they were going.

"If I'm right, there's an old fishing harbour just a little south of here. But it's a long shot." Conrad answered.

"What's a long shot?" Aaron asked "That the harbour's still there, or that the Black Trons have ships there?"

"As far as I know, the Black Trons have never been there." Conrad replied.

"So why is there Black Tron ships there?" James enquired.

"There isn't."

The walk was long, but no one complained. They finally reached the harbour. It was quite gloomy and the old, rusty building next to the harbour looked like it was going to collapse at any moment. Conrad walked up to the jetty that was beside the main harbour area. Barry looked across and saw a large boat. Suddenly, a thought crossed his mind.

"We're not crossing the sea in that are we?" He protested.

"Yes B-Man. We are." Conrad said without emotion.

"But it's a shitty old fishing boat! It probably has more holes then Swiss cheese, more leaks then a green grocers. It's got more rust then-"

"Yeah, alright already!" Conrad interrupted. "I get the bloody point. The thing is, these boats are built to last. So it won't have any sodding leaks! Also, they're undetectable."

"What? How?" Came the obvious reply.

"We don't use naval ships any more since they're a sitting target for Octopods, and neither do the Black Trons. So no one ever looks out for them. Water vehicles are too slow so no one ever uses them except for leisure, commercial or fishing purposes. It would be very easy to pass this boat off as a Black Tron fishing boat, as it has a very old analogue radio. The brains at M-Tron once thought of this idea, but dumped the idea as they realised it would only work once."

"Mate, can't we use a ship?" Aaron whined.

"Aaron. This is a ship. Not a flying ship I grant you, but a ship none the less. It has large, twin motors, a spacious lower deck with sleeping quarters and a kitchen and canteen area. There's also a working loo." Conrad said.

"Oh! A working loo? That's it. When can we move in? You've sold it to us." Aaron joked.

"Just get on the bloody thing." Conrad snapped back.

"How do you know the loo's working?" James asked.

"I don't. Hell, I don't even know where the cockpit is." Conrad confessed. Aaron overheard this.

"Cockpit!? It's a bloody boat! There ain't no cockpit. That there is the bridge." Aaron pointed at the front section of the boats upper half. "The helm is in there. That's the bit that makes it steer and speed up, slow down. Starboard is the right side, port the left, stern is the back and bow the front. The engine room is usually between mid-ship and stern, for this size of boat. The sleeping quarters and eating area is near the bow below the bridge and the hold is mid-ship. There is one loo and it's a chemical loo. No kitchen as such, just a gas stove and a fridge if your lucky. This thing only has *one* motor, and can do about twelve and a half knots."

"Aaron. I didn't know you knew so much about boats." Barry said.

"Yeah. My dad and me went sailing every summer when we were kids. But I thought you guys knew that." Conrad and Barry were staring at Aaron. "What?"

70

Aaron asked. "What you staring at? Wait a minute. You want me to sail that boat. No way! My father and me sailed on a yacht, not a full sized, deep sea fishing boat."

"Oh, come on Captain Hammond. You know you want to." Conrad jeered. "And you know I can make you a Captain."

"You going to bribe me with a higher rank? Look, I'll do it, but only 'cos none of y'all can sail to save ya' lives. You can't can ya' Jim?"

"Oh, no. Actually, I hate boats." James answered.

"Damn! Looks like I'm sailing then. We can't sail to Russia though, that'll take days, and we only have a few to spare."

"I know. Land this thing somewhere near the top of Norway. We can work our way from there."

"Dock. You 'land' things that fly, you 'dock' things that sail!"

"Just do it."

So they all took the boat to Norway. The trip was uneventful. James was telling the truth when he said he hated boats. He spent most the trip with his head over the side spilling his guts.

The Black Tron base in Norway assumed them to be an IC fishing boat, and let them pass, just as Conrad predicted. On the trip, while James was throwing up over the side, Conrad had sat with him trying to get him to drink some fluids. Conrad struck up a conversation by asking James why he had joined the army.

"Oh. My father said it would be good for me." He had replied.

"Yeah, mine said the same. Mind you, I didn't get much of a choice did I. I 's'pose you could say I was born into it, literally."

"Yeah, I see what you mean." James turned to hurl some more of his last meal over the side of the boat.

71

"Never thought about joining the navy then?" Conrad asked. James smiled.

"Yeah, right. I've never liked boats. Never been fond of the sea much either."

"Can you swim?" Conrad enquired.

"Why? You ain't going to throw me overboard are ya?"

"No, just curious."

"Well, no. I'm afraid of water. My best friend drowned when I was young. I guess I never got over it." They were silent for a bit, then Conrad asked

"How come you've stuck with us for so long?"

"What, you mean since the war..." Even now, none of them could say the war was over. It brought back too many sad thoughts.

"Yeah, since then."

"I see. You **are** trying to get rid of me." James joked. "No, I stayed for the excitement. And it's definitely been exciting."

"Yeah, well, we try our best. No, really. I would have thought you'd run a mile by now. Not many people can put up with me, especially with my antics lately. Even when I think back on it I find it all a bit weird."

"I've been finding lots of things weird lately. I stayed 'cos, I got nowhere else to go. Besides, your Conrad Manké. I knew if I stayed with you I'd be alright. I know you'll get us through this, I have faith in you, we all do. Even Aaron, but I doubt he'd admit it. I 's'pose you're kind of my idol. Sorry."

"Wow. I have a fan. How old are you?"

"Actually, you have more fans then you could ever know. Over four billion to be precise. From sixty year olds down to two year olds. And I'm eighteen today." Conrad was stunned. No-one in the special force was younger then twenty five. When the war became

72

critical a handful of soldiers were fast tracked into Alpha team, but Conrad thought they were all around twenty two. This kid was just, a kid. He wasn't genetically enhanced like Conrad, Aaron and Barry were. He was just a normal kid, who had a normal childhood and chose to join the army. Even Aaron had been forced into the army. Aaron was genetically enhanced by a black market doctor. Somehow the authorities found out and had Aaron scheduled for termination, but his parents pleaded with the courts and Aarons life was saved. But he had to attend military school, and when he was sixteen he had to be recruited into the army. All three men, Conrad, Barry and Aaron, when at school, were given different classes to the rest of the children. They had to deal with tuff teachers and very strict rules. Aaron found it hard at first. To see the other kids getting the easy life. They were forced to watch live animal killings. They were isolated, which meant when they were allowed to play with the other kids they were bullied. There was a fourth kid that attended with them. His story was similar to Aarons. His name was Martin Sadler. The bullying got so bad at one stage that Martin was killed by three other kids that had ganged up on him. Conrad had his first taste of blood when he found Martins body and then killed the three kids. Conrad remembers very little of his childhood except what they were taught.

But James had been allowed to be creative. He could even be naughty and only get told off. Conrad had never been told off. None of the four had. They had only ever been court martialled. Can you imagine being court martialled at five years old?

"When I was younger, I only had three people I could turn to. I never did, although they always turned to me for guidance, but I knew I could. One of those people aren't with us any more, but there are still three people here that I know I can turn to. That I can trust. That I can count on."

"Thanks Conrad."

"And happy birthday. I would make you a cake, but you'll only throw it over the side." Aaron laughed until he stopped himself by throwing up again. He would have started laughing again but he suddenly made a worrying observation. All through that conversation Conrad never showed any emotion, even when he made that joke about the cake. Conrad was far from being alright, but once again, like in his childhood, he had to be the strong one. No emotion. No feelings. Just eat, sleep, kill and give orders. You'd think the guy giving the orders would have it easy. And you'd be wrong.

Chapter eight

Jason was pondering. If Conrad was still alive, what would he try to do? What would I do, he thought. At this moment Conrad should be trying to gather as many soldiers together as possible. Conrad always has a large army with him. Mind you, he isn't easy to kill when he's on his own either. Damn it! Conrad should have been given a desk job by now. But, typical Conrad, he just couldn't leave his precious Delta team. If he had, he'd be dead already. There couldn't be many M-Tron soldiers left. Maybe he's on his own. No. Barry and Aaron would be with him. Those three are inseparable. Well, if they are alive, Jason knew his men would find them. But it didn't matter now. The war was over. Black Tron won. All Jason had to do now was to win the elections and rule the world. Jason had been slowly gaining control of all the IC countries. Now that he has them working together as Black Tron all he needed was to be named World President and he would officially be in control of Black Tron. Jason formed Black Tron. He nurtured it and made it what it is today, but if the IC leaders knew he had full control from the start they would have dismissed the idea. So Jason had let the IC leaders have an equal say in the Black Tron committee. Jason took control by tricking the leaders into agreeing with his ideas. Now that he was about to be the World President, this meant he would control Black Tron alone. But the IC leaders underestimated Black Trons hold over the IC. Because Black Tron was in control of the IC. So Jason would also be in control of the IC. The only people who could stop him were either dead, or soon will be. Except Conrad. With Conrad by his side, Jason would never have to worry about being voted out of his position. Jason could stay in power as long as he could keep manipulating the IC leaders votes. But with

Conrad he wouldn't have to. However, if Conrad wouldn't cooperate, Chou Wong would be more than happy to take his revenge on him. All the movies Jason had seen, made 'taking over the world' look easy, but it's not. The sucking up, arse kissing, manipulating; always from the shadows, with some other guy thinking he's in charge. In the movies, the villain would be the guy making all the decisions, giving all the orders and generally making a lot of people dead. Jason had to convince eight people just to kill one man. Jason decided, since the IC leaders were too slow, he should have his own private army. Now all he had to do was give an order and anything he wanted would be done. But still he has to keep himself in the background. Sure, he currently has more soldiers loyal to him then all the IC leaders have together. Taking the Independent Countries by force would be easy, but they do still have a large army between them. Much better if he could send them to do his bidding, and leave his own, huge army to mop up what's left. M-Tron has already fallen. Now is time for the rise of Black Tron.

"Sir, the voting will take place in four days. If you do not leave now you may be late. I have a car ready. Do you not want to be there?" It was General Chou Wong.

"No. I'll let the IC scum tell me. Then I can act surprised when they proclaim me as World President." Jason told him.

"I got word from General Spree that four men in a fishing boat landed in Norway last week."

"So? So what?"

"They are Utopian soldiers."

"So go and kill them then!"

"I thought you might like to know, the Manké clone is one of them."

"What? And the others?"

76

"Barry Man, Aaron Hammond and some other guy."

"Find out all you can on the fourth man. I want to know who he is!"

"Yes Sir."

***

Since landing, Barry had found a family estate with a German registered number-plate. As Germany was an independent country, the car would be allowed to pass all the IC borders under Black Tron guard. There were a few M-Tron borders to cross, but the soldiers guarding them would be Black Tron. They got to Moscow two days before the final elections. Just time to set their trap. Thanks to the advancements in explosive technology (things that go BOOM!), C4 could be used in small amounts with great effect. A piece of C4 (or plastique) the size of a crayon could easily render a car 'written off'. Half that amount would be sufficient to kill, or seriously maim, a person. The elections were being held in a large, new office block in the east-end of Moscow. Conrad told the men to find some food for the next few days as they still had two days to wait. Barry, Aaron and James still weren't sure what Conrad was trying to do, but they had faith in him. Conrad had been doing some strange things lately, so he wasn't quite reliable, but his mind was amazing, so if he had a plan, it would surely be a good one.

That night, after a feast of pizza and vodka, Barry started thinking about his family. This is something none of the three friends ever did. Thinking about your family distracts you from what you're doing, so it wasn't done. But Barry couldn't stop the thought creeping into his mind. Since the Black Trons launched the first nuke, the M-Tron government decided to put the people in underground bunkers. There they could survive for ten years, until the radiation and nuclear fallout had passed. Only the army and a few presidential personal stayed above ground. That *was* ten years ago. And still they had to remain. Barry had a wife somewhere underground, and now, more then ever, he wanted to be with her. He hadn't any parents, but wished he had. Barry was a test tube baby, designed for the army by the army. The only people he had ever known were hard, strict military officers. The only four people he had ever loved were his three friends that he considered his brothers, and his wife. He had lost one of his friends when they were young, and lost his wife to the underground cities. Barry thought he may never see his wife again. He spent that night fighting back tears.

He wasn't alone. Aaron was thinking about his parents and three younger sisters, faces he hadn't seen since he was taken by the military and put into military school. In fact, he had never seen his sisters, only heard them through the telephone when he was allowed to call home. This pleasure was seldom permitted, but Aaron made the most of it.

James too was thinking about his parents, last seen going into the underground bunkers.

Conrad.

Conrad was thinking about death. The death of the Black Trons, and his plan to bring this about. He was grinning from ear to ear, pleased with how well it was going. Conrad fell asleep with that stupid grin still plastered on his face, though it may be because he drank too many bottles of Russian vodka. Conrad had the best nights sleep ever.

***

General Chou Wong was busy with paperwork when he got a call from the manager of a liquor store in Russia. How he got this number, Chou Wong will never know, but when he heard what the man had to say, he was very happy that he did. Wong thanked the man and rushed to his car. At this time, Jason would be in Iraq, just across the border from where Wong was. The sun was just starting to make an appearance when Wong drove his car out the parking lot. If he kept driving at a hundred miles an hour, he would get to Jason in two hours. So he put his foot down and spun the wheels as he pulled away.

***

Jason was still asleep when General Wong started banging on his door. Reluctantly, he got out of bed. If this was someone doing another door to door mugging, I'll rip the little fuckers head of, Jason thought. Putting a shirt on Jason ran down the stairs as Wong banged the door again.

"I'm fucking coming! Shut up!" He shouted as he fumbled for the right key.

"Sir. I have some great news for you." Wong said as Jason opened the door.

"This had better be good, come in." Wong stepped into the small apartment and followed Jason into the living room. "Brandy? Bourbon?" He asked.

"No thank you sir. I have word that a man brought six bottles of vodka last night."

"Ah! Vodka. I have some here. But why should this concern me?"

"Because it was brought with a Utopian credit card."

"Ah. Do you suspect Conrad Manké to be in that area? And where was it purchased?"

"The card belongs to a Private James Rogers, Utopian army. General Kil Spree has identified the man as the fourth member of the Manké clones group. And they are in Moscow."

"I don't understand why Conrad hasn't more men with him. Why should them being in Moscow concern me?"

"Sir? The election is being held tomorrow. What if

the Manké clone were to blow the building up or something?"

"As long as the IC leaders get to vote, blowing the building up will only be in my favour." Jason handed a glass of vodka to Wong. Although he hadn't asked for it Wong took the drink anyway.

"How would that be?"

"If the IC leaders are killed, there won't be any one to stop me taking world domination. I'll be the World President remember."

"What if they do not vote?"

"Then I'll be World President by default. Either way, I win. We will not be held back any longer. They keep us out of Utopia. Some of us were once Utopian but were thrown out for silly misdemeanours. They refuse to give us the genetically modified DNA sequence that they give to all their people. They live without disease, while we die of it. They turned their backs on us. Four Utopian soldiers aren't going to stop us. I said Utopia would fall and it has. It doesn't matter what they do, because Utopia has fallen. M-Tron is dead. We won. So let them do what they want. They can't stop us now. Just get me Conrad Manké!"

"I'll have General Kil Spree intercept them tomorrow. The Manké clone will be brought to you."

"Good. Now drink your drink. We have a big day tomorrow."

***

Waiting. The job of a sniper. Sitting in a dark room, staring out of the window for the slightest hint of movement. Waiting. Just waiting. Patience is the key to a successful kill. His targets were probably asleep, but just in case, he had to stay awake on the off chance that one of them would step out of the building. Watching. He won't be getting any sleep tonight. If he had to wait until the middle of the next day, he would. Breathing.

The room he rented was old and damp. His bed was covered in mildew, but he wouldn't be needing it. Forever watching. In silence, he kept an ever watchful eye on the only exit in the building opposite. His only companion, his trusty Snype 100 Pro. The latest weapon of choice is the new Snype 800 XT. But since he can out shoot anyone with his 100 Pro, he decided not to upgrade his gun. Waiting. The other weapon of choice is the Laser series MK I plasma rifle, but this was more like an old pump action rifle then a highly accurate sniper rifle, and had too wide a spread for the professionals liking. So he had opted to stick with his 100 Pro. Watching. The Pro version had a better shaped butt, it didn't dig in like the original did. Also, unlike the Snype 100, it had a professional style scope, a five centimetre longer muzzle and a drop-down stand to rest the muzzle on. The 800 XT has a laser sight, thirty shell magazine (the 100/100 Pro was side loading, only holding nine shells at a time.), automatic firing, green plastic coverings, but a crap scope. Fighting back the tiredness, he yawned, took a sip of water and pissed in a bottle without ever taking his eyes off the exit. Sitting. Breathing. Watching. Waiting. His kill would come. He had three targets to kill, and one to capture. But a sniper never kills more then one target at a time. So it would be first come, first served. In the dark he sat, watching, waiting, always waiting.

**

"Ooh. Don't ever give me alcohol again." Conrad was hung over. His head felt like someone was hitting it with a heavy, foam hammer. "What's the percentage?" He asked.

"Forty percent by volume." Came the reply.

"Really?" Conrad was confused. "But that's standard. You sure? 'cos my head's pounding. I've got a hang-over for gods sake." The morning gloom was making it hard to see. Conrad had to strain his eyes to see who it was he was talking to. Not easy with a hang-over.

"Conrad, mate. You drank eight bottles of the stuff. I'm not surprised you got a hang-over." Barry said, his face hardly showing in the morning light. Conrad got up and decided to do some cooking. As well as pizza and vodka, Barry and Aaron also brought bacon and bread. The bread was the uncut type made the Russian way. It didn't look any different, a bit browner maybe, but it had a slightly different taste, which complimented the bacon quite well. While cooking, Conrad noticed a hole in the mortar. I thought it was a bit chilly, he said to himself, bloody hole goes straight through. Conrad took a closer inspection and noticed he could see the building across the street. Conrad grabbed some kitchen towel and ran it under the tap, after which, he promptly stuck it in the hole. That'll fix it. Conrad finished making the bacon sandwiches and put them on the table.

"Grubs up lads!" He shouted at the others. "Hey, Aaron. Where did you get the money for the food? I didn't think we had much money and this stuff ain't cheap."

"Yeah, I know." Aaron answered. "But luckily, Jim had his credit card with him." Conrad froze. He dropped his sandwich back on his plate and stared at Aaron.

"Why? What's up?" Aaron said confused. Conrad started, slowly, to shake his head. Aaron was, by now, very confused. "I don't understand. What's up?"

"Aaron." Conrad finally said. "We don't have money in M-Tron. All the cash we have is marked with the Black Tron 'B' so we can buy stuff in the IC without people knowing that we are M-Tron. So when you use an M-Tron credit card, since we don't have money, the credit is taken from the M-Tron trading account."

"Yeah, I know all this. What about it?"

"None of these Independent Countries can take money out of the M-Tron trading account without authorisation from the IC council. And Black Tron owns the IC council, so they now know we are here. There's probably an army on the way to meet us right now. Which means we have to leave these premises ASAP, and lay low for a while. Not good when we have to be somewhere tomorrow." Conrad glared at Aaron.

"Oh. Sorry Conrad." Aaron said sheepishly

"And the big, red 'M' on the front of the card is a bit of a giveaway too. So thanks guy's."

"Well, it ain't that bad." James cut in. "The card's in my name, so, they're only looking for me."

"Let's hope so!"

After they had finished their breakfast, they gathered their gear, and got ready to go. But Conrad was feeling a little uneasy. Since mentioning the M-Tron 'M', he kept thinking about the colour red. He couldn't shake the feeling. They walked down the stairs and Conrad opened the door leading out. He stopped. Conrad was standing in the doorway, the others behind him. There was a small van across the road. Something wasn't right. Barry asked Conrad what the hold up was, But Conrad's mind was working overtime. Conrad looked at the vans number plate. It read: K1L 5PR33. Across the bottom of the plate were the words: Custom made by TaeTec China. Conrad thought back to a previous mission. A file he had read contained information about the Tae Wong Technology Corporation. Tae Wong was the biggest company in the IC, and it was funded by Jason Moon. But his mission had been to bring the corporation down. Was Tae Wong Technology Corporation revived as TaeTec? If so, then TaeTec would be owned by Jason Moon, as Tae Wong was shot by his cousin Chou Wong. Which means Black Tron owns TaeTec. So the car has a Black Tron number plate. Red. RED! Something red! Conrad thought back to the scene with the hole in the kitchen wall. He played the scene back in his mind, slowly, so he could take notice of the detail that he might not have noticed at the time. In his mind he could see the building opposite. Red. Something red was in the window of the building opposite. But what? Conrad forced his mind to replay the whole scene: *While cooking, Conrad noticed a hole in the mortar. 'I thought it was a bit chilly,' he said to himself, 'bloody hole goes straight through.' Conrad took a closer inspection and noticed he could see the building across the street.* There! Conrad stared through the hole. There was a window just a little to the left of his view. The window was boarded up, and looked like it had been for some time. But there was a faint red glow coming from that room. Conrad forced his mind to look closer. He could just see the source of the light, two small red circles. He had seen something like that before, but what was it? NIGHT VISION GOGGLES!

"SNIPER!" Conrad yelled at the top of his voice, just a split second after Barry had asked what the hold up was. He stepped back away from the doorway and let the door close. He pulled his hand guns from their holsters on the small of his back and flicked the safety switch's off. "There's a sniper in the building opposite." He told the others.

"How do you know that?" Aaron asked.

"Look, I worked it out in my head in less then a second, but the time it'll take me to explain it to you guy's, we'll be dead. So get ready to shoot and run like fuck!"

"Where do we run to?" Barry asked.

"The sniper left his car over there. Get behind it as fast as possible." Conrad told Barry. Then he held the door open and yelled 'GO!' Barry ran as fast as he could to the car, shooting towards the other building as he ran. As soon as Barry had made it, Conrad told Aaron to go next and pushed him out the door. Once he was safe, it was James's turn. Conrad watched and waited for his turn. Just as he was about to go a shot skimmed his knee. "Fuck!" Conrad fell back. Clever Mr sniper, Conrad thought, he knew someone was holding the door open and shot through the door where he thought my leg would be. Conrad checked his leg. Just a scratch, so the snipers shot wasn't that good after all. Conrad got up and tried to run to the car again. This time, as he swung the door open, the shot just missed his nose.

"Ooh. I hate this guy. Hey! Give me some bloody cover will'ya!" He shouted at the others. Barry sat up and sat, promptly back down again as a bullet ricocheted off the roof of the car. Conrad thought that the sound was familiar, but couldn't quite place it. The bullet made a sort of 'pitow' sound as it left the gun. Conrad knew the sound was made by the silencer, but was different to a normal silencer. He started searching his memory, trying to place that specific sound. Obviously, it was some kind of rifle, as it was too accurate to be anything else. Considering the task the gun was being used for, it had to be a sniper rifle, obvious also. Conrad, gingerly, reached out and ran his finger over one of the bullet holes in the door. Had to be a 22. No, the width was wrong for a 22, so it must be a 24. That didn't seem right also, think Conrad, think.

Just then, another shot took out a window on the car. Conrad didn't see this happen, but the sound of breaking glass was a giveaway. Unless he hit one of the windows on the building, but that was just silly. The nearest window was on the next floor, so if he had, it would have been a stray shot, and he was too good a shot for that to happen. Besides, he would only shoot at moving targets, and nothing was moving on the next floor, as that was the room next to the one they were staying in, and it had been empty.

Conrad thought back to the sound, and tried to match it to the size of the hole made by the bullet. The sound said 20, and the hole said 22 or 24. What type of bullet does that? Unless it was double compression. This would mean the shell was narrower then usual, giving the bullet extra push when fired. When the small gunpowder filled cap on the rear of a shell is struck by the firing pin, the gunpowder ignites causing a small explosion. The force from the explosion is directed into the shell causing the bullet to break away and is propelled forward at great speed. If the shell is narrower, the compression inside the shell is greater, causing the bullet to be propelled faster. This would explain the larger hole, but by Conrad's calculation, that would mean the bullet was a 21. But that's a custom size bullet, and damn expensive. M-Trons don't use money, so Conrad couldn't say how expensive, but he knew they were. Wait, wasn't there a report some years back about the 21's becoming more available to the Black Trons? Yes, Conrad suddenly recalled the report. 21's became more available because a company called N.M.E. ltd started mass producing them for their new range of rifles. The bloody Snype series! Conrad remembered them. He couldn't see a red dot bouncing around, so no laser sight, and it wasn't a plasma rifle. In that case, considering this guy was a pro, it had to be a Snype 100 or Snype 100 pro. That means nine shells, side loaded, no changeable mag. Good, Conrad had an advantage. If only he could remember how many shots were fired.

Four! one nipped his knee, another just missed his nose, the third hit the top of the car and the fourth took out the window. Just five left then.

"Hey, guys!" Conrad called out. "Make him shoot!"

"WHAT!" Barry yelled in disbelief. "Are you crazy?"

"No! Well...yes, but...Just do it!" A second later, and a bullet was heard bouncing off the road. Five; four left to go. Another shot was heard and James yelped with it. Three left.

"Shit that was close!" He said in a near panic. "Aaron, your turn."

Conrad slowly pushes the door open, to get a better look. As he does, a bullet blasts through the door and nips his chin. Conrad steps back, and wipes the blood from his chin. This guy is going to die! Two shots left. He stoops down and peers through the hole in the door. He could just see the car, and thought he could make out the shapes of his three friends, hiding behind it. One of them suddenly jumps up and starts running. It was Aaron. Where he was running to, Conrad couldn't see. But, just before Aaron is beyond his view, Conrad sees the bullet slam into Aarons thigh, and watches in horror as he trips and falls. No time to spare, he had to move before the sniper puts the final bullet into his friend. Conrad bursts through the door, guns blazing.

One bullet left.

'Pitow'

Conrad's robotic eye picked up the air distortion, and locked onto the bullet, before Conrad even heard the shot. As he had hoped, the sniper had turned his attention on Conrad, and fired. He threw his weight to his left in a vain attempt to dodge the bullet. Luckily, the bullet hit his right shoulder, and ricocheted of the metal of his robotic arm, to thud into the wall to his far right. Conrad had lost a lot of his shoulder when his arm was shot off, and it all had to be replaced. For the first time, Conrad was actually thankful for his new arm.

'Pitow'

Wait a minute, how did that happen? The bullet that bounced of his shoulder was number nine. So why is there a tenth bullet whizzing through the air? To late to think, he had to act. The computer chip in the back of Conrad's head, locked onto the bullet, and before he realised what he was doing, Conrad lifted his right arm and shot. Thanks to his replacement eye, Conrad could see his own bullet collide with the snipers, and then land on the floor. He didn't have time to be in awe, he had to find out if he could make his arm and eye work together like that again. He looked up and made his eye lock on to the sniper, which he could only just see with the aid of his electronic eye, and felt his arm lift automatically to aim where he was looking. Conrad pulled the trigger. The sniper moved, but the bullet made contact. Conrad, without a moments hesitation, ran into the building the sniper was in, kicking the door down on his way. His legs were also repaired with robotics, but the flesh could be saved, and was used to cover the robotic muscles and metal bones. Conrad didn't know this so was surprised when the door slid half way down the corridor after he kicked it off its hinges. He ran up the stairs, taking three steps at a time. Conrad looked down the corridor that confronted him upon reaching the top of the staircase. Third door on the right looked to be the right room. Conrad slammed into the door and sent it flying across the room. The sniper was laying on the floor, nursing a wound in his chest. By the looks of the wounds position, the bullet had punctured his lung. He was spitting up blood and was having difficulty breathing. Conrad walked up to the sniper and aimed. The sniper looked up, then smiled.

"You are the spitting image of the Manké General." He coughed up a bit more blood. "But a damn sight harder to kill. I thought I had you back then, but it was your mate. By the way, how did you do that with the bullet?"

"Like this." Conrad said, and fired.

Back outside, Barry was trying to stop the bleeding in Aarons leg. Conrad approached them, and squatted beside Aaron.

"How you doing old buddy?"

"Just a flesh wound." Aaron told him. Conrad took a look for himself. It was far from a flesh wound, but not fatal.

"If he had shot your leg clean off, you would still tell me it was a flesh wound." Conrad then became all serious, and put a hand on Aarons shoulder. "But...erm...maybe I shouldn't tell you."

"Tell me what?" Aaron said getting a little worried. "What's wrong."

"Well...I'm afraid..."

"What? What!"

"I'm afraid you're going to live."

"I'm going to live!? I'm going to... wait, *live*?" Aarons eyebrows drop into a scowl. "Very funny, very bloody funny! Ha ha, bugger off." As Conrad moves off to check the car, Barry looks at Aaron and asks, "Did you see him smile?" Aaron looks a little puzzled at first, but answers anyway.

"No. Come to mention it, I haven't seen him smile for ages."

"No, neither have I." James added.

"Something bad is going on in his head. I think, when we return to M-Tron, we should think about having him committed. Or at least take him to a psychologist. I think he's seen one to many battles."

"You think its gotten that bad?" James asks. Barry ran his hand through his hair, as he thought about the answer.

"Ask me that again when we're back on the boat. Then we can see if he really does have some great plan or not." They agreed.

Conrad couldn't hear their conversation, and wasn't interested either. What he was interested in though, was Aarons hair. It wasn't any secret that their hair was getting long. All of them could tie their hair back, including Barry, who was usually bald. They all needed a hair cut, and a shave come to mention it. Barry was getting a mean looking beard, which added to his unusual appearance. But it wasn't the length of Aarons hair that had him interested either, it was what he had done with it. Aaron had tied his hair back. Not in the usual way, but high up near the top of his head, so the pony tail stuck up in the air a little, just like Conrad used to do. No wonder the sniper thought Aaron was Conrad. But if that was what he thought, then why didn't he kill him? Why did he just shoot Aaron in the leg? Conrad's quick mind came up with the answer before he could take a breath. The answer was; the sniper wanted Conrad alive. Why?

Now this question may take a little longer, but Conrad was going to find out. For now, there was an election to rig.

Chapter nine

General Kil Spree was getting agitated. This General Chou Wong was a bit of an idiot. He had been running around barking orders at various soldiers, trying to find the four Utopians that had entered Norway. Spree had, on a number of occasions, offered information and ideas, but Wong had ignored or dismissed every one of them.

It had been five weeks since Jason Moon had given the order to kill them, and capture the Manké clone. Chou Wong wasn't doing a very good job of it. Kil Spree had gotten board with Wong trying to run the show, but instead of kicking up trouble, he had sent a few of his own men out to find them. Two days ago, one of them had contacted him to say he had found them. The soldier knew the orders, and would carry them out. But Spree had assumed the soldier would have had some news by now, but no. He had to assume his soldier was dead. Shame, the man was a damn good sniper. And he had his car! Never mind, he now knew the rough location of the four Utopians, and would see them dead within the month. And there was only two and a half weeks left of this month. Mind you, Spree would like to meet this clone of the Manké General. 'I wonder what the Manké clone would think if he came face to face with General Kil Spree?' he thought to himself. Spree smiled at the thought. It was settled then, he would go and meet the Manké clone himself. Assuming that his soldiers could capture him. The Manké clone was very resourceful and tricky. Mind you, he didn't have to worry about Chou Wong's men getting in the way. They would most likely be in the wrong continent if they followed Wong's orders.

Spree wasn't agitated anymore.

In fact, he was quite happy.

Captain Simon Spengler was on patrol. No need to fear, Spengler was here. The corridors were empty, and that was how Spengler was going to keep them. The corridors had been empty all day, so his job wasn't going to be that hard. His orders were, if anybody started nosing around the building, he was to kill them on the spot. Simon had a fright yesterday when a rough looking man suddenly appeared beside him. He was about to pull his gun and kill the intruder, when the man showed him a pass and told Simon that he was here to install the computer. Simon had been told that someone would turn up for this very reason. This man was authorized to enter the building. Other then that little mix up, Simons job had been fairly easy. Okay, so it had been down right boring, but lets face it, Simon wasn't the best soldier in the army. Far from it in fact, so to get a responsible job like this was a privilege for him. He had been at it for six weeks, since the election officials had been turning up to set up the room for the final election. Most of them had been using the service entrance on the other side of the building, which Sergeant Goon was patrolling. Only the computer network engineer had entered through the main corridor, scaring the wits out of Simon. He should have used the service entrance like the others, and Simon had given him a lecture about it. Besides, what was a network engineer doing taking his tools around in a back pack? And why would someone with a job that pays hundreds of thousands of credits an hour, look so scruffy? His hair was long and tatty, his beard was unkept, and his clothing looked like it hadn't been washed in a few weeks. Actually, considering the musty odour, he hadn't washed himself for a while either. Simon assumed he had been very busy, so hadn't had time for cleanliness. Simon was also starting to whiff a bit. He had been guarding the main corridor for weeks, with only enough time to sleep while another soldier took the night shift. At least he had had enough time to have a quick wash.

The man said he would be back, and asked if he could use the main entrance so he could use the bathroom facilities. So obviously, he knew he was in dire need of a bath. Simon said he could. He was going to be here about nine o'clock. Strange, the others are all gone by eight. Simon assumed the man needed them to finish so he could get on with his work.

There was movement in the corridor.

Simon crept down the corridor, back to the wall, gun at the ready. It was only eight thirty two, to early for it to be the computer man. All the other officials had gone home, and they don't come this way. Simon reached the end of the corridor, and took a tentative peek down the side corridor to the right. All clear. He turned around and peered down the other side corridor to the left. All clear. Strange, he was sure he saw something. Maybe it was the computer guy, and he had gone into the bathroom down the left hand corridor. Simon went to the door and opened it, calling out; "Hello! Is that you Tim?" The guy had said his name was Tim. Or was it Jim? Damn, he was bad at remembering names. There was no reply. Simon went in. It was empty. It must have been his imagination. He probably just needed some sleep. Three and a half more hours and he could get some.

***

Half past eight. Only twelve and a half hours left, and he would be proclaimed world President. When this happens, he will rule the world. But he will make the world a safe place to live. Life will be good. He will no longer be a pawn in this war. The war will, finally, be over. No-one will take this victory away from him. He was already in power, just nobody knew it. He will have revenge, with victory. Revenge was sweet, but victory was sweeter. Twelve and a half hours will mark the start to the end of the war. After that, nothing could stop him. He had only one thing left to do, find Him. He held up his knife. The knife was nine inches long, it had a slightly curved tip designed to cause maximum damage when thrusted into someone, the blade ran the whole length of one side of the blade and only two inches down from the tip on the other side. The knife had a split handle made of metal, it was made using three long and narrow pieces of steal, one piece was slightly curved to fit the palm of the hand and another was designed to fit the fingers. These two pieces were connected using two short and very narrow pieces of steal to the third long piece of steal. This gave the grip a look as if it were floating separately from the main body of the knife. The handle gave the knife a simple, but effective presence. A close look would reveal the painstaking detail and master work of the whole knife. But what was really amazing, was the hole in the blade of the knife. Most killing knifes were designed with a groove or slot down the centre of the blade, this was so the blade didn't get stuck when thrusted into a person. The slot in the blade of this knife was in the shape of a dragon. Even though the cut-out section only gave a silhouette of the dragon, there was no mistaking the shape of it. Soon the cut-out shape of the dragon would be filled with His blood.

Soon the blade will be tasting His death.

***

The time was five to nine, and Simon was still on duty. He hadn't seen any more ghosts in the corridor, as that was what he assumed it was earlier. He didn't actually believe in ghosts, he believed they were a manifestation of the mind. So it didn't bother him. The corridor was empty again. The computer guy would be here soon. Which would mean he would have someone to talk with. He got bored and a little lonely standing around all day. He had a chair to sit on, and plenty of food and water, but he wasn't supposed to be sitting on the job, so he had to hide the chair whenever he thought someone might come and check on his progress. No-one ever did come, so the chair stayed out. But he kept himself on his feet as often as possible, just in case one of his superiors did decide to pay him a visit. He decided to sit now. He started thinking about the clone of the Manké General. As an M-Tron outcast, he knew all about the propaganda that surrounded the son of the most formidable leader ever known. Simon had once been a casualty of war, as they call them, and was privileged to come face to face with the General himself. At the time, Simon had been a hostage in the death grip of a Black Tron soldier. He was only sixteen then, and the Manké General was a Lieutenant. Simon remembered seeing the man on telly, he had a kind face and smiled a lot. He seemed almost shy, and compassionate. In the arm of a man with a large gun to his temple, Simon could remember hoping that this shy, timid and friendly man would come and rescue him. Then when he appeared, salvation appeared with him. Simon knew General Manké would talk the Black Tron soldier into giving himself up and letting Simon go. But as the General got closer, Simon saw the look in his eyes. The kind, shy and friendly man was gone. General Conrad Jacques Manké was in a rage. The same rage his so called son had inherited. Then he did something Simon would never had thought he would do. He lifted his own gun and blew the Black Trons head off, then walked by like nothing had happened. Simon was left, standing there, with bits of flesh and brains, mixed with a large splattering or blood, on his face. Being in that situation would leave a mental scar on most children. What Lieutenant Manké did would have left a serious mental scar on any kid for life. But it was the look in the General's eyes that gave Simon nightmares. Simon was now fifty two. He still had the nightmares.

He shook the thought from his mind. He was a Black Tron now.

Something moved in the corridor. 'Not again' he thought, but then realised that it must have been the computer guy. Simon got up and walked the length of the corridor for the second time that day.

He saw a shadow moving down the right hand side corridor.

"Not that way Tim." He called out. "The bathroom's the other way." There was no answer. "Sorry, I meant Jim. I'm bloody useless with names. I'd forget mine if it weren't sown into my under pants." He laughed at his own joke. Still there was no sound. He turned the corner, nothing was there. Maybe there was a ghost. 'No, don't be so stupid' he thought to himself. He took a quick sweep of the rooms down that corridor. They were mainly small boardrooms for the IC leaders to hold meetings in. One room was a toilet, and the last was a kitchen. They were all empty. As he turned back into the main corridor, a large black cat, standing on top of a wooden bureau, suddenly hissed at him. Simon yelped and jumped back. As he did so, he tripped and fell. He had just enough time to think about the blow he would receive from the floor. But it never happened. As he fell, a pair of arms suddenly wrapped themselves around him, stopping his decent. This frightened him more then the cat had.

He looked up and saw the scruffy face of the computer guy.

"You alright man?" He asked. Simon stood up with

the help of Tim, or Jim, or was it Akim?

"Yeah, thanks mate. That cat spooked me." Simon said.

"Looked more like it scared the crap out of you." Tim, Jim, Akim, or whatever his name was, informed him.

"No, the honour of scaring the crap out of me goes to you."

"Oh, sorry man. Didn't want you to crack your head open on the floor though." The guy told him.

"Yeah. I thought I was a goner there, thanks...err..."

"Jim." The guy told him.

"Yeah, Jim. Sorry, I'm terrible with names." Simon confessed.

"That's alright Simon. Look, I hope you don't mind, but I brought a colleague with me." Jim said.

"What, the cat? I've met him."

"No, not the cat, him." Jim said, pointing behind Simon. Simon turned and came face to face with a man. His hair was very long, and he had a scruffy beard like Jim had. Although his face was mostly covered with facial hair, Simon recognized the eyes.

They were the eyes that had him waking up in the middle of the night, shaking, and drenched in sweat.

The eyes that haunted his dreams, or at least one of them was.

The left eye was metal.

This was worse than his nightmare.

"Good night." the eyes said.

Then all went black.

Chapter ten

James opened the main doors, letting Aaron and Barry into the building. Conrad returned from tying up and hiding Captain Spengler. They ran down the corridor and entered the lift at the end. They needed to get to the main hall, but there were no signs. What floor they needed they didn't know, so they had to check each floor.

They found the hall on the third floor. It was huge. There were one hundred and twelve chairs, but there was room for ten times that amount, they were facing a small platform with a large computer to one side of it. This was the vote counter. The software on the hard drive was unchangeable. There were a few small changes that the software would allow for, but you couldn't change anything else. You could, for example, change the names of the people up for election, and you can change the country of which you where voting a ruler for. You could add a new country to the list, or remove one. Each IC leader had a code that allowed the changes to be made which affected their own country. If one Country were to assume control of another, the original ruler of the conquered country would have to enter his own code before the computer would allow the amalgamation. Since Black Tron would rule all Independent Countries, every IC leader had to enter their own code before the computer would accept the addition of Black Tron.

As the highest ranking officer left alive, Conrad had access to the M-Tron codes.

They started taking C4 out of their packs. They still had a lot of work ahead of them.

***

Private Kusrat Ladin was coming onto duty. He had to take over from that idiot Captain. As he entered the building he saw the chair at the other side of the corridor. It was empty. He must be in the loo. Kusrat went to the chair and shook his head in disgust. Okay, fair enough, the guy couldn't be expected to stand all day long, but to leave it on display like that was stupid. He put it in the cupboard that was a little along the corridor. Then he stood in the corridor and waited for Simon to return.

Half an hour later, and Simon was still missing. Kusrat decided to see if he was alright. He went to the main bathroom. It was empty. He must be in the other toilet. As he passed the main corridor he took a quick peek down it to see if Simon had returned. He hadn't. But Sooty was wandering towards him. The large, black cat had made an appearance a few nights ago. Kusrat thought it a kindness to feed it something. Now the bloody thing wouldn't leave him alone.

"Choney bashee Sooty." He said. Choney Bashee was Kurdish for; Hello, how are you. Kusrat was Iraqi by birth and so spoke his native language when he was alone, or around other Iraqis or Kurdish. "Wara, wara Sooty" Come, Come Sooty. "Wara sidi." Come sit. The cat walked past him. Kusrat shrugged, "Bid gem Sooty." Fuck you Sooty.

Sooty walked into the small toilet. The door was ajar. Why hadn't Kusrat noticed that before? Had Simon left the door open by purpose? He followed Sooty through the door.

"Choney Simon. Are you okay?" He called as he went through the door. Simon was tied up and laying on the floor. Simon looked up at him and started trying to say something.

"MMMM! MMMMM!"

"Hold on Simon, I'll cut you loose." Kusrat bent down to cut the ropes.

"MMMMM!! MMMMMMM!!!" Simon mumbled

behind the gag.

"Who the fuck did this!" Kusrat exclaimed. A voice behind him said; "I did." Kusrat spun his head round, and was in time to see a large katana bearing down on him. His head hit the floor, shortly followed by his body. Simon wet himself.

"You want to live?" Jim said as he stepped out from behind the door. Simon started nodding franticly.

"Stay here and keep quiet then." He said, then left. 'Yeah,' thought Simon 'like I can do anything else.'

As James walked back down the corridor, he looked at the sword and said; "This is a good sword. No wonder Conrad takes it around with him."

As James entered the main hall, Conrad called out for him.

"We need some more C4 over there. You're supposed to clean a katana after you kill someone. Sharp, ain't it?"

"Yeah, sharp as a razor."

"What about Simon?" Conrad asked.

"I let him live." James said.

"Big mistake. One that better not come back and bite you on the arse." James gave the sword back and returned to his work. Conrad went to the computer and entered the M-Tron access code into it. Barry had finished his task, and so went to watch Conrad.

"Okay, I don't get it. If you're doing what I think you're doing, then doesn't that mean, whoever wins this election, will also get control of M-Tron?"

"Yep." Was all Conrad said.

"But...Why...I mean...Jeez, I hope you know what you're doing."

***

The IC leaders were gathering. They had their votes ready. All they had to do now was to sit down in the great hall, listen to some adjudicator ramble on about the rules of the election, and then push a button. They didn't even have to get off their seats to do so. Each chair had a box with a set of numbered buttons on it. All they had to do was push the button with the number corresponding to the person they wish to be ruler. It was as simple as that.

The Columbian President was chatting with the Japanese President. 'Probably trying to get in her knickers', thought the Russian President. The Chinese President was trying to look all important, like usual, thought the German President. When China declined unity to M-Tron, the people were outraged. They formed large protests in the streets. But when the Chinese government didn't heed to their pleas, the protests turned to rioting. In the end, a small section of mainland China was left in control of the Chinese government, while the rest of China elected themselves a new president. The M-Tron president.

The Kurdish leaders were huddled together. And the Austrian President, New Australian President and many other IC Presidents were trying to make conversation with the Black Tron representative. Australia actually joined the M-Tron union, but because they were surrounded by Independent Countries, when the Black Tron union started gathering the IC armies, Australia was forced to flee their land and find refuge in the main lands of M-Tron. Australia still has a Presidency, but, because they couldn't reclaim their land, had to form a new state in the USMA (United States of M-Tron America). Because the Vote Counter computer needed the right code to give power over a land, the man who named himself President of Australia, had to rename the land; New Australia.

The Black Tron representative was a strange man. He kept to himself, and tried avoiding the constant questioning from the IC leaders. Mainly, they kept asking where Jason Moon was. In answer to their questions, he would answer; 'He is indisposed' but when they weren't listening he would mutter; 'piss off and leave me alone'. Yosi Kanomi was a hardened soldier, so having to be nice to upper-classed IC leaders was a little straining on his patience. But he was ordered to keep proceedings. And, of cause, drop a few hints as to why they should vote for Jason Moon.

Whoever wins this election would be the Black Tron leader. Black Tron would have total control over all the IC armies, but not the lands themselves. But with the armies, Jason could, forcefully, take control of the lands one by one. And no-one could stop him. Jason knew he would be elected, so he didn't come to the election. Besides, Black Tron wasn't a country, only a union of combined armies. With this united force, Jason won the war. Everything that was associated with the military, would be handed to Black Tron for good. And Jason Moon would soon be the official Commander of Black Tron. The excitement was too much to bare, so Jason had gone on a pub crawl. Good job he wasn't going to the elections then, as he was found, paralytic, in his local bar. He would have the mother of all hangovers when he finally woke.

The doors opened, and the Black Tron representative ushered the IC leaders in, and showed them to their seats. The chairs were arranged in groups. Each IC leader had an array of officials with them, and they were all seated together. In front of each group of seats was a small table with two microphones placed on them, with a small flag of the groups associated country.

The IC leaders took their pre-reserved seats and waited for the adjudicator to start the proceedings.

The adjudicator was the Black Tron representative. He stepped up on the stage and cleared his throat.

"Ladies and Gentlemen, governors and honoured leaders of the Independent Countries; welcome. My name is Commander Yosi Kanomi .

"In a few moments we will be starting the Vote Counter, which we all know is a tamper proof computer system that controls the rules of conduct during an official election vote.

"First I would like to apologize for the absence of the Black Tron Commander, Jason Moon. He sends his apology and asked me to stand in his place as the adjudicator of proceedings. He also gave me a message he would like relayed to you." Yosi cleared his throat again, then proceeded to relay the message.

"He says, 'My good friends and loyal comrades, my deepest apologies for not being here with you on this historic day, but I regret I must stay to take care of a few loose ends that must be taken care of. I hope, in my absence, my good friend and colleague here, will be a suitable replacement.

"Remember, this election will change the way the Independent Countries run forever. So vote with your heads, as well as your hearts, and you won't go wrong.

"I look forward to meeting the new Black Tron leader, unless that man turns out to be me. If it does, I would like to ensure you that I would keep Black Tron running exactly as it is. I would make no changes. I believe Black Tron works fine the way it is, and our recent victory over the Utopian depression is proof of that. But all I ask, is that you all vote wisely. Obviously, if I am not elected, I would be just as happy to help with the running of my beloved Black Tron.

"Be well my friends, and good luck to you all.'

"This is all he told me, and I'm glad I remembered it so well." The IC leaders were oblivious to the slight hint of humour. Yosi never was very good at jokes.

"Beside your chairs is a small remote with fifty

buttons on it, marked, one to fifty." The IC leaders started picking the small white boxes up. "On the TV screen behind me is the list of corresponding numbers, name of the electioneer and the country they are associated with. You will note, Jason Moons name has the Black Tron logo beside it already. This is because he is, and always will be, Black Tron by heart. He will be very sad to see it go, although he would never admit this, so please vote for someone you can trust to keep Black Trons interests at heart, and make an old man happy." Yosi had been told that the IC leaders were already mostly swaying towards Jason's vote, but if he wanted to sway them more, he could. Yosi thought that if his speech didn't tip the balance, nothing would. Mind you, Yosi didn't have the gift of the gab like Jason had, or, as Yosi's father used to say, the ability to baffle people with bullshit. "At the bottom of the screen here, is a counter, when it reaches zero you can all vote by pressing the right numbered button." Yosi pressed a button of his own, and the timer started to count down.

10,

9,

"Hey! What's that filthy name doing on the screen?" The Japanese President yelled out.

8,

In the bottom, right hand corner of the screen, in position fifty, was the M-Tron flag and the name; Conrad Manké.

7,

"Err...I don't know." Yosi said astounded.

6,

"But don't worry, no-one will vote for him." Yosi didn't know if that was comforting news, or not. What was that name doing on the list?

5,

CLICK!

4,

"Don't anybody move! Your seats are rigged to explode if you do." The IC leaders stayed firm.

3,

Yosi turned to face the voice behind him. The first thing he came face to face with was the muzzle of a silver Glock handgun. Behind that was the evil eye of the Manké General.

2,

"Stand up and you go boom! Push any button other then fifty and you go boom! Don't push any button, and I push this button and you all go boom together!" Conrad yelled.

1,

Yosi looked at Conrad's other hand. It did indeed have a small remote detonator in it.

0,

The screen flashed a 'VOTE NOW' message, and the IC leaders started pushing buttons.

No-one blew up.

Conrad looked at the screen. Since there were only forty nine people voting, the Vote Counter flashed the results up on the screen almost immediately. The vote was unanimous.

Conrad was the world President.

The computer printed out a copy of the new code needed for future elections. Conrad tore the sheet of paper off the printer and memorized the code. Yosi took the opportunity to pull his own gun.

CLICK! Came the sound of a gun, that wasn't his, being cocked.

"That would be a big mistake buddy." A very deep and powerful voice said behind him. Yosi peered round, and for the second time that day came face to face with a gun. This time, it was a plasma gun. The dark skinned man holding it was the biggest man Yosi had ever seen. His knees went limp. Barry smiled at the familiar affect of his own overpowering presence. Yosi dropped his gun.

Conrad was now burning the code the computer had printed out. He turned back to the IC leaders, and threw the remaining piece of paper on the floor, where it continued to be consumed be the large flame spreading across it. As Conrad stepped forward to address the IC leaders, he lifted his gun and loosed a bullet into Yosi's temple.

"Ladies and Gentlemen, welcome." He said, mocking Yosi's posh voice. "All of you who are not an IC leader, are free to leave. Your chairs are free of explosives. But before you go, I would like to tell you something. I have left your countries with the option to part yourselves from the grip of Black Tron using your own codes. You can reclaim your armies whenever you so wish."

"You think we won't send our armies to hunt you down, you fucking clone!" A man shouted out.

"No. I don't think you'll honour the law stating that you can't kill me either. I just want you to know that you can leave Black Tron. Now all of you who are not IC leaders, can go." Several people got up, slowly, and, finding their seats free of explosives, ran out of the building as fast as they could. Conrad looked at the IC leaders again. He lifted his fist into the air and yelled, "M-TRON! M-TRON FOREVER!"

***

As the four friends where leaving the buildings faculties, Barry turned to Conrad and asked, "So what was that all about? Are you going to tell us your plan or what?" Conrad looked at him, and pondered.

"You'll see when we get home. If we get home, we're still in enemy territory remember." He said.

"What, don't you trust us or something?" Barry

asked.

"I don't trust anyone remember?" Barry stopped walking.

"You used to trust me." He said through gritted teeth, but Conrad had kept walking and, so, didn't hear.

Conrad went to one of the limousines left by the IC leaders, and opened the door. James jumped in and told Conrad; "I'll drive." Barry was about to enter the vehicle when the building suddenly exploded in a blinding flash. Barry ducked as if he was about to get hit by something. Aaron threw himself into the car and laid down, even James threw himself to one side in panic.

Bits of brick, wood, metal and some small pieces of flesh and blood, rained down on them, a few pieces bouncing off the roof of the limo.

Conrad didn't move.

"What the fuck!? Conrad, I thought you said they wouldn't blow up if they got of their chairs?" Conrad had lied about the chairs exploding if the IC leaders got up. They couldn't find the right devices to do this. Barry thought it would be funny to leave the IC leaders, still sitting in their chairs, to sweat about it. They were still sitting in their seats when the building exploded.

James stuck his head out of the limo's window. "Yeah, what happened?" Conrad lifted his left arm. The remote detonator was still in his hand. Conrad removed his thumb from the switch. The switch clicked back into place.

"Oops. Thumb slipped." Conrad said, without a single thread of emotion, then got into the limo.

"Home James."

Chapter eleven

Jason was still hung-over as he tried to make it to his office. The people in the street kept bumping him, as he tried to make his way. Why is it, when you want to go up a street, every other bugger wants to go down it? Even on a good day, it would take longer to get from the car park to the office, then it would take him to drive through the two countries from his house to the car park. And the car park was only half a block down.

A woman bumped him, hard. She turned round to apologize, but when she saw who it was she froze. This was very unusual, no-one knew Jason, except very high officials of the IC and their Presidents. Jason didn't know this woman, and was surprised to see that she recognized him.

"I...I'm...sorry," she stuttered, a hint of German accent betraying her nationality, "But you look just like a man I once knew." She smiled, "But that can't be, he died some years back." Jason forced a sincere look on his face.

"I'm sorry to hear it. Nothing bad I hope." He said, sounding as sincere as he looked. He had always been good at faking sincerity, and even with a throbbing head, he still had it.

"Heart attack. Died before he could reach the hospital." She frowned. "You sound like him too. Your not a relative of his are you? his name was-"

"No! No my dear, I have no relatives. I'm sorry, but I must go, gutten t'ag." And with that, he was gone.

A little farther up the street, a large Chinaman approached him, and walked with him. Jason thought nothing of it. This was someone he did know. The china man spoke.

"That was a little close. What does 'gutten t'ag' mean?"

"Good day. It means 'good day'. What was the results of the election yesterday?" The china man stopped dead in his tracks.

"You mean you haven't heard yet?" Jason stopped. He looked back at the man, with expectation.

"Please tell me it went to plan. The way you spoke leads me to think it didn't. So who did the little fuckers vote?" The china man wondered if Jason was upset. It was hard to tell. His voice was almost monotone. His voice was always monotone. And his eyebrows never move. It made it hard to tell what sort of a mood he was in. The china man hoped he was in a good mood.

"It was Him. He added his name to the list and forced the IC leaders to vote for Him." Even though Jason's eyebrows never moved, the china man could visualize the scowl on his face. Jason's monotone voice dropped an octave as he spoke through gritted teeth.

"Who is He? And it better not be who I hope it isn't." The china man swallowed.

"I think we had better get off the streets first, sir."

Jason agreed.

Jason's office wasn't very big. There was about enough room for the oversized desk and large, black leather chair, and some filling cabinets. A drinks cabinet was integrated into the wall, saving some space, but the trophy cabinet, on the right side of the room, made getting to the drinks cabinet a little tricky. It was this awkward task that Jason hated the most about his tiny office, but relentlessly, he squeezed his way between the large, glass trophy cabinet and his huge, pine desk.

Jason opened the drinks cabinet and poured himself a very large brandy. Then, with brandy in hand, he completed the journey around the desk, and settled himself in his leather chair.

The china man looked like he was having

difficulties deciding what to do. Should he assume the open drinks cabinet a sign to help himself to a drink, or, wait until offered. When Jason hears what he has to tell him, the offer might be retracted.

"Well?" Jason said in his monotone voice. The china man didn't move. "You could at least take a seat." The china man sat. "Who's the new Black Tron leader?" Jason asked without hesitation.

"You might want to drink that first, sir." He answered.

"Tell me." Jason said.

"Well...it's a little hard to explain-"

"Tell me!" Jason cut in.

"You see...there was a little-"

"TELL ME!" Jason's voice may be monotone, but he could sure yell when he wanted to. His face would change slightly also.

"I'm sorry sir, but it's the clone of the Manké General." The china man spurted out. Jason's face regained its normal look, as he lent forward in his chair.

"What about the clone? What's He got to do with it?" He asked.

"Well, sir...He is the new Black Tron President."

"WHAAAT!!!?" Jason's face turned black, as he pulled a handgun out of a draw in his desk, and shot the china man in the head.

"CONRAD! I'LL KILL YOU, YOU SON OF A WHORE!"

***

Four day's later and Conrad, Barry, Aaron and James were back at the old fishing boat. The date was now; Wednesday 22/4/3823.

The four men had a problem. Some Black Tron soldiers were waiting by the boat. As far as Conrad could tell, there were twenty soldiers laying in wait for them. Although he still hated the robotic improvements

110

done to him, at this moment in time, Conrad found the infra-red vision a god-send. Changing vision modes though was still a little tricky, but he was getting the hang of it. With his normal eye, he could see eight men, which the three other M-Trons could also. Conrad turned to the others, which he regretted, as he got a mixed view of infra-red and normal sight. He put his hand over his left eye to try and block the digitally enhanced view, but got a bright flush of red instead. He needed more practice at the changing vision thing. He tried his right hand instead, and was pleased to find this helped a bit. Although his vision was tainted with a dark shadow now, he found he could focus on his friends better.

Barry was looking puzzled.

"What's up B Man?" Conrad asked. Barry pointed at his hand covering his eye.

"What's wrong with your eye?" Barry asked back.

"I switched the infra-red on, and now I can't turn the bloody thing off again." Conrad told him. Barry looked even more puzzled.

"Why not? You turned it on, so you can turn it off, surely."

"Sorry mate, but you forgot to give me the bloody manual. I have to turn it off using my mind. It's a little like using your legs for the first time, your brain needs some time to work it out. That's why you can't walk when your first born." Conrad said.

"You did it in the hospital." Barry told him.

"By accident. It scared the shit out of me. Then it took me six hours to turn it off again. Give me a minute, I'll get it. But for now, we need to get to that boat. It looks like we can get to it from the left there." Conrad pointed to a small footpath to the left of the woods they were hiding in.

"What do you mean 'it looks like'?" Aaron asked.

"I can only see half the trail, there might be some soldiers down it."

"Can't you see using your infra-red?"

"Not through a bloody hill I can't! You've used infra-red before, my eye ain't no different you know. You can see the trail goes behind the brow of that hill."

"Okay man, keep your hair on." Aaron told him. "Besides, if you're not sure about that trail, why don't we go another way?"

"'Cos as far as I can tell, that trail is our best bet. Why don't you go down and scout it for us?"

"Why don't you?" Aaron retaliated.

"Because I can't get this bloody eye to change bloody vision!" Conrad shot back.

"I'll scout it. You girls can argue about it later." James said, and promptly shot of towards the footpath.

***

The limo had been dumped in the woods behind them. It had ran out of petrol, but they weren't far from the docks, so they decided to walk the last bit. Conrad looked at his watch. Half past three, it read. He knew it would, and wondered why he had still looked at it. The time was actually around mid-day. What really puzzled him though, was why the hell hadn't he taken the thing off his wrist. Conrad shook his head at his own stupidity, and looked back down the hill. Where was James? He should have been back by now. Conrad suddenly got one of his gut feelings. It had been a while since he had had one, and was surprised to get a feeling so strong. Especially a bad one. Something was wrong. Conrad jumped up and ran to the footpath. Now he had, finally, turned the infra-red off, he could make out the path better. He ran down the small trail, keeping his profile as low as possible, and stepping side to side to avoid the branches sticking out here and there. Just as he reached the section that had been hidden from his view, he saw him.

James had been tied to a tree, and was bleeding from a cut on his head and body. Conrad slowly moved down the path. James looked up and saw Conrad, but he moved his eyes past him in a slow sweeping arch. 'Clever boy' Conrad thought, 'Someone must be there with him, so he moved his eyes like that to make his observers think he hadn't looked at anything'. Conrad swiftly moved himself behind a tree. Conrad looked at the ground. Dry sticks! They were everywhere. Conrad couldn't sneak up on the enemy with those on the ground. No matter how hard he tried, he would step on one every now and then, and give his location away. He looked at the trees. They were close together and had strong branches. Conrad had a plan.

***

James looked at his captor. His uniform was like standard camouflaged gear, but the black patches were bigger then normal. Standard for a Black Tron. He could see the patch on the soldiers arm. It had a green, capital 'B' with a large bottom in a black octagon with a black out-line around it. Where the bottom of the 'B' became larger, it broke out of the main octagon and touched the out-line, which was also in the shape of an octagon. It was this lime green 'B' that denoted a Black Tron soldier.

The Black Trons own soldiers were better trained then the soldiers of the Independent Countries. These soldiers fought for no-one else. Although the IC armies fought for Black Tron, and were part of the same unity, they were not true Black Trons. Although Black Tron was not a country, but an organization, the Black Tron military was still an official army. They were, for all purposes intended, an independent army.

And James hated them.

James didn't know what the soldier was up to, but he, obviously, didn't want James to die. Conrad wasn't far though, and James hoped his wandering eye trick worked. If he had seen James look up the path, he would have assumed that James had looked at someone. So he didn't give the game away, he made out as if he had thought someone was there, but wasn't. He also hoped Conrad realised this, and disappeared into the trees like that because of it. Although, with the way Conrad was losing his mind, he wondered if he would rescue him, or get the both of them killed.

The soldier stood up. James wished he hadn't. While he was sitting down, James was sure he would be safe. Now that he was standing, James could vision the end of his life approaching. The soldier turned round and unzipped his trousers. Oh good, he was just having a pee. James would have a little longer to live. Where was Conrad? James thought he would have seen him dart between the trees by now. Mind you, Conrad was the founder of Delta force. It was because of him the fourth special force was created. There had only been Alpha, Bravo and Charlie force to start with. They had been the most specialized soldiers in the world. But when Conrad became a soldier, he broke all the rules, and Delta had been formed to accommodate the new breed of soldier. Conrad wouldn't conform with the normal practice of soldiery, even compared to the special forces, but proved there was a better way. Despite how good the soldiers of Alpha, Bravo and Charlie were, very few soldiers could get to grips to Conrad's strange practices. To become Delta was the hardest thing a soldier could do. In fact, it was so hard, some incredibly good soldiers actually died trying to become good enough for Conrad's elite force. Delta soldiers were identified by their black uniforms. Conrad had forbidden his soldiers from wearing anything shiny. Even when on parade, they had to wear black markings of their rank. James had spent weeks calling a Sergeant 'Corporal' because he couldn't tell if he had two, or three stripes on his arm. After a week of latrine duties, he never made the mistake again. If a Delta officer and a regular officer of the same rank met, the Delta officer would automatically be the highest ranking officer. Delta force mainly operated at night, hence the all black uniforms and lack of shiny objects, and operated in total silence. With Delta, the name of the game was 'stealth'. They could disappear anywhere. Even in broad daylight they could vanish before your very eyes, despite the uniforms. Most called them the silent death.

The soldier finished with his business and sat down again. James was getting impatient. The soldier looked at him.

"Comfortable?" He said with a low gravely voice. "Don't worry, the clone of the Manké General will soon be here. Then when I have him...you can die." He smiled a wicked smile.

"Fuck you, you scum!" James spat back. The soldier smiled some more.

"It doesn't matter. Even if I let you go, Wong's men will kill you."

"Who the fuck is Wong?" James asked. The soldier looked interested now.

"Oh. You don't know General Chou Wong? Well, he is the General for the Japanese army, but he serves Black Tron. Those are his men down there." His smile was still there.

"Strange question, I know, but, aren't you worried someone will hear you talking?" James inquired. The soldiers smile widened.

"No. You see, you, are not the bait. I am. If I suddenly die, you do. If Conrad appears here with me, you die and he becomes my masters slave. I am the bait. You are only the lure." The soldiers smile reaches a climax.

"It's a trap." James whispered. This was a statement, not a question.

Just then both James and the soldier spot something flying out of the trees, which lands in the soldiers hands. He turned the bloody mess over and looks into the eyes of a dead soldier. James' captor suddenly goes white and his smile fades into sheer horror. Another head lands next to his feet. Now the soldier looked terrified.

"How?" He looks up at James. "How? How can he do that?" He backed up until he was beside the tree opposite James. A metal hand shoots out and grabs the soldier. His eyes start bulging as the hand squeezed his throat. Conrad steps out from behind the tree.

"Never go for the target, neutralize the greatest threat first, then no-one can stop you. Delta's sixth rule." Conrad crushed the mans larynx and dropped him on the floor like a piece of rag. He quickly cuts James' bonds and motions him to be quiet. James understood. There was still enemy around. They quickly start moving up the path the way they had come in, but Conrad suddenly grabs James and stops him. James gave him a puzzled look, and Conrad points to the floor. He leans up to James and, in a whisper so quiet James had to strain to hear him, said, "Twigs. They make snapping sounds every time you stand on one. Use your toes and try to aim for clear areas or where there's lots of leaves. Keep low." James nods and was about to start moving again, when something at the edge of his vision catches his eye. He jumped back,

116

throwing his feet into the air and kicked Conrad clean in the chest. Conrad stumbles back, but managed to keep his balance. He was about to give James a beating when he noticed a large hole in a tree that wasn't there before. Then he sees the red dot flick onto his chest. Conrad doesn't move. In a split second, his robotic hand flicks up and catches the bullet, inches from his body. Conrad shouts out to the marksman,

"If you want to kill me, turn the bloody laser-sight off. It lets me know where the bullets going to hit. Talking of which, do you want it back?" A different bullet whistles past his ear.

"Fuck me!! You didn't have to take my advice that quickly!" He yelled out as he dived for a tree. Conrad pulls out his trusty twin Glocks and flicks the safety's off. James locates his PEEP which had been knocked from his hand when the Black Tron soldier captured him. He rolls over onto his back and fires a few bolts of plasma into the trees ahead, where the shots were coming from. The small balls of plasma disappear into the trees in an instant leaving gaping holes in the trees.

"Hey Jim. Ever wonder why I stick to the old style guns?" Conrad calls over.

"Not really, but now you mention it..."

"Faster rate of fire. Delta's fourth rule; the faster it shoots, the more it hits." With that Conrad steps out from behind the tree and empties his mags. "See what I mean?" He calls out after he was behind the tree again. "In the time it took you to fire six shots, I shot thirty eight."

"So what? You still didn't hit anything." James calls back. Conrad released the empty magazines from his hand guns and takes two more out of his inside jacket pocket, which he quickly shoves into the guns.

"You see much there?" James understands the question. Conrad wanted to know if he could see the

117

shooter better from where he was then where Conrad was.

"I've got a window." He calls back, meaning he could see a little of the shooter. Conrad cocks one of the guns and throws it to James.

"Time to scare the birds." He said. This meant he wanted James to shoot the marksman. James knew he didn't have a good shot, but he would force the shooter to move. And Conrad would be waiting to finish the job.

James takes aim and starts pumping the trigger. The shooter would start moving, and James knew he wouldn't actually hit him, but he had to keep the guy moving. As the shooter dives for another tree, Conrad, with his gun cocked and already aiming between the trees, opens fire.

"You get 'im?" James calls over.

"Yep, but not good enough. The bastards still alive and able. We're going to have to flush him out." James throws the Glock back to Conrad as he ran past him.

"Ever wonder why I like PEEP's?" James called back.

"Not really, but now you mention it...hmm, déja vu."

"Shoot someone in the leg with a bullet, and it makes a hole. Shoot someone in the leg with a PEEP, and you take the buggers leg clean off. So I'll stick with the PEEP." Conrad quickly ran to the next tree. "Hey Conrad. How did you get behind the other guy without making any noise?" James asks. Conrad looks up at the trees and tucks his guns in his trousers.

"Like this." He answered, then jumps up and grabs a branch. Conrad pulls himself up and then jumps from one tree to the other.

"Jeez. That man is like a monkey." James mutters to himself. James quickly runs to the tree the shooter was

118

hiding behind. He looks up, but Conrad had disappeared. He pointed the PEEP at the tree and points down trying to guess where the shooter would be. He pulls the trigger, but holds it. PEEP's don't fire until you release the trigger. Holding the trigger down charges the PEEP, creating a denser bolt of plasma. A small, green, LED light appears on the side of the gun, followed by another. The green lights switch on in a row, until there is five of them. The next LED light to switch on in the row was red. Now the red light was on, the gun would no longer charge. James releases the trigger. The bolt of plasma rips through the tree, and the shooters chest, leaving a huge hole. The shooters head sinks down into the hole that was once his chest, and then the shooter falls over onto his side.

"YES! Got the bastard!" James turns round to find Conrad, calling as he does. "You can get out of the trees now, I got him." As James completed his turn, he comes face to face with a large Chinese man. The man quickly takes the PEEP out of James' hand.

"Hello." He says. "You must be Private James Rogers. Nice to meet you. My name is General Kil Spree." James goes white. This is a name he *had* heard before.

"You going to kill me?" James asks.

"No. That would be pointless. Besides, General Chou Wong's men down there would get bored if I killed you all. No, I just want the clone." James is confused.

"Who's the clone?" He asks. Kil Spree looked disappointed.

"You mean to say, you have never heard of the clone of the Manké General?" James gets the meaning.

"Oh, you mean Conrad. Why don't you just call him Conrad? It would save a lot of confusion."

"We never say his name. We try to avoid the name

Manké if we can. But that man you are fighting with is a clone. Because he is a clone, he doesn't have a soul. If he has no soul, he can't have a name. So we call him, the clone."

"Do fish have souls?" James quickly asks.

"No. We eat fish, so they don't have souls."

"Really? Well I used to have a fish. I named him George. Does that mean that that was wrong?" James pointed out.

"No. A fish is a pet. You don't follow a pets orders, do you."

"What about a police dog? They have names, and if a police dog growls at a criminal, he usually assumes that as an order to drop the stolen goods, get on the floor and put his hands behind his head. Is that wrong?" James cleverly points out.

"Oh, do shut up. Your getting on my tit. If you would like me to kill you now, and spoil Wong's men's fun, then by all means, continue."

"Okay. What about-" Kil Spree punches James in the face, knocking him out, and cutting his sentence short.

"That's quite enough of that." He looks up into the trees. "Oh, Conrad. Conrad. Here boy. Good dog, come on now boy. Come to papa." He calls out in a mocking voice. He nods to a man standing to one side and motions him to get into the trees. The man jumps up and gracefully pulls himself into the tree.

General Kil Spree spots something coming out of the trees, and moving very fast. He twists his body and, bringing his arms up, slaps his hands together, palm to palm, capturing the small object. When he opens his hands, there, laying in the palm of his left hand was a small, platinum star with sharpened points. A shuriken.

"Hmm. This is going to be interesting. I knew it would be hard to kill you clone, I'm glad to see you

120

won't disappoint me."

Chapter twelve

Barry was getting restless. James had been gone for too long, and now Conrad was missing. Aaron suspected trouble and, reluctantly, so did Barry. The sound of a snapping twig catches Barry's attention. The sound came from behind them, so he assumed it was James and Conrad returning. Barry turns to greet them.

"It's about bloody time. Can we get down that path or-" A large man bearing the Black Tron logo on his arm, and a plasma gun in his hand, smiled back at him. "Ah, wrong person." Barry taps Aaron on the back. Aaron turns round.

"That's not James is it." He said. "And he's too big to be Conrad." The man motions them to get up. They obey. The man smiles again and says, "Well, well. What do we have here? A couple of Utopian spies." He nods his head towards the boat in the distance. "Your ship I presume? We thought you'd be back for it." Barry thought about knocking the gun from the mans hand, using a technique Conrad taught him, but knew this highly trained soldier could pull the trigger quicker then he could do so.

"Oh, no. That's not our ship." He said. "And we're not spies. We were Utopians once, but were deported a few years back. We're deserters."

"Sure. The great Barry Man deserting his friend, the clone of the Manké General. I believe you. Not."

"Why don't you people call him 'the Manké clone'? It would be a lot quicker to say."

"Why don't you tell me where he is." Barry thought about it.

"No." He said flatly. Aaron looks at him.

"No? What do you mean no?" The large man smiles again.

"Does that mean you'll tell me where he is?" He said to Aaron.

"Hell no mother fucker! You want to know where he is? Then get down on your knees and blow me you squinty eyed German bastard, before I put a cap in your arse!" Aaron told him. "Now that's what you should have said B Man." This last bit he said to Barry. The Black Trons smile had vanished. He brought the PEEP round on Aaron. Barry quickly took this opportunity to strike, and lunged at the gun, knocking it to one side. The Black Tron got off one shot before Barry had his hand around the mans throat. The bolt of plasma just missed Aarons face. Aaron yelped and dove to one side. The soldier dropped his gun, as Barry held him in the air with one hand.

"Now," said Barry, "you tell me how many men are down that path, or I'll crush your throat!" Barry gave a small squeeze to let the man know he was serious. The mans eyes bulged.

"Okay! Okay!" He forced out with difficulty. Barry released his grip slightly. "There are three men down there. General Kil Spree is one of them. Now let go." Barry didn't. "You said you'll let me go if I told you." Barry squeezed with all his might, crushing the mans larynx, and killing him.

"I lied." Barry said as he dropped the dead man on the floor. "Fucking Kil Spree! That mans almost as infamous as Conrad's dad is famous." Aaron stood up, his hand covering the left side of his face. "What's wrong Aaron?" Barry asked.

"Oh nothing much. Just got a little too close to that FUCKING PLASMA BOLT!" He screamed at Barry. He removed his hand from his face. The left side of his face looked badly sunburnt.

"Ooh, that looks nasty." Barry said, trying to stifle a laugh. Aaron noticed.

"It's not funny, man! He almost got me!" Aaron virtually pleaded. Barry couldn't stop himself, and burst out laughing.

"You look like a fifty fifty bar!" He burst out in between fits of laughter.

"What the fucks a fifty fifty bar?" Aaron asked.

"It's a chocolate bar that's half dark chocolate and half white." Barry said trying to subdue his laughter. "Come on. Lets go get James and Conrad." Aaron picked up Conrad's shotgun.

"I don't know why he brought this thing with him. I've had it most the way." He pulled the pump action loading handle, loading the gun with a shell. "But I'm gonna put a large hole in someone with it." He said. "And if Conrad doesn't get his act together, it's gonna be 'im." Barry smiled, and the two men headed towards the path.

***

General Kil Spree was waiting. If his man didn't kill Conrad, he would. But if Conrad did what he hoped he would, then he would come out of the trees and try and kill Kil Spree. And Kil Spree would be waiting. He strained his ears, trying to hear the sound of death, or of Conrad creeping up behind him. He heard nothing but silence.

The cold muzzle of a silver Glock F17 touched his ear. Kil Spree was quietly surprised. How did he do that without making any sound? He turned. It was Conrad. Kil Spree quickly grabs for the gun and moves his head to one side. He knew Conrad wouldn't hesitate with pulling the trigger. He would only wait long enough so Kil Spree knew he was going to die.

The bullet whizzed past his ear. Kil Spree wasn't going to die this day. Not by the hands of the most hated man in all the Independent Countries.

Conrad was a little surprised himself. How did this

124

man move so quickly? That bullet should have left a hole in his head. Instead, it whizzed, harmlessly, past his ear hole. And he had a surprisingly strong grip on his gun. Conrad pulled as hard as he could, but couldn't get his gun out of the mans grip. The Chinese man smiled at him.

"Conrad. It's been a long time my old friend. But then, we were never friends were we?" He said. Conrad knew the face as General Kil Spree, but the voice was familiar. He had heard that voice before, but not so deep. "I like what you've done to your self. That eye looks mean as hell."

"Who the fuck are you?" Conrad asked. Kil Spree looked hurt.

"You mean you don't remember your old school buddy? I remember you. And Barry, and Aaron. Oh yes, nearly forgot, Martin Sadler." Martin! How did he know Martin? He was killed by three kids at school. Conrad had killed the three kids. No, wait! One had survived. But this man before him couldn't be...

"Chen? Lou Chen?" Conrad asked.

"I changed my name to Kil Spree many years ago, but that name is still who I am. Yes Conrad, you remember. I wanted to kill you, but I met someone. Someone I want you to meet. But I have to take you to him. So either you come quietly, or..." Conrad knew what the 'or...' meant.

Conrad pulled with his robotic arm and then pushed forward with his elbow, hitting Kil Spree in the side of the face. But he didn't let go of the gun. With blood dripping down the side of his face, Spree stepped forward and head butted Conrad. For a couple of seconds, Conrad saw tiny points of bright, flashing light. He shook his head to clear the image.

"Ha!" Kil Spree said. "This is going to be interesting. I knew you were good Conrad, but I didn't

125

know how good." Spree let go of the gun, but before Conrad could point it in the right direction, Spree had hit him, twice, in the chest. Conrad fell on his back. 'That was fast.' Conrad thought, 'Too fast.'. Then he remembered. Chen had been illegally modified. He had been taken by the military and put into a military school. Chen had been kicked out of that school when he was eleven, and brought to the Manké Militant School for boys. The same school Conrad and his friends were at. If Conrad's memory was correct, Chen's eyesight was a close match to Conrad's metal eye. This helped with his speed. Chen was almost as fast as Conrad, and almost as strong as Barry. This was not going to be easy. Conrad used his back to flip himself up onto his feet. Chen, or Kil Spree as he was now known, was on him already. Conrad twisted his body to avoid the straight punch Spree had launched at him, then slammed his metal fist into the mans chest. Spree coughed as he backed up a little, and held his hand to his chest. Conrad stepped in and threw his left fist at his face. Spree quickly blocks this and slams the palm of his hand into Conrad's chest, followed, very quickly, by the palm of his other hand.

Conrad's anger was building.

Conrad could use his eyesight to the edge of his vision. This is known as peripheral vision, and Conrad uses it almost constantly, except when sighting a target with a gun, then he uses 'hunter' vision. Hunter vision is when you ignore what's around you, and focus only at what's in front of you. Conrad taught himself to use peripheral vision when fighting, so he could see as many of his enemy as possible, so they couldn't jump in and surprise him while he's fighting someone else. Conrad learnt this when he was very young, and had stuck by this technique all his life.

But right now, as his anger was building, he could

feel himself trying to focus on his enemy and ignore his peripheral vision. But Conrad knew there was another man around somewhere, and forced himself not to do this.

Spree came at him with a high kick to the face. 'Stupid man.' Conrad thought, 'Feet are too slow.'. Conrad blocked the kick with both hands, holding his leg in the air, and kicked Spree in the groin. Spree doubled up.

"Delta's fifth rule; Hands are faster then feet, so use your hands to attack, and your feet to move." Spree was up before Conrad could grab him. He backed off a few paces and started rubbing his groin.

"Ooh, I'll get you for that! Kick a man in his gonads would you?"

"Sorry. I was aiming for your head. Better luck next time, ay?" Conrad said, then stepped towards Spree. Spree retaliated by pulling a large knife from a sheath on his belt. Conrad slowly reached down for the huge knife on his leg, keeping his eyes on Spree. Compared to Conrad's knife, Spree's was a toothpick. "You shouldn't use knifes. Especially when the other guys is bigger then yours." Spree smiled.

"What? The knife? Or were you talking about something else?" Conrad resumed his approach. Spree lunged at him. Conrad twisted his knife around, so it was upside down in his hand. As Spree lunged at him, Conrad twisted his body and brought his knife up slashing at Spree's wrist. Spree was quicker though, pulling his hand away to the side, so Conrad's knife cut air. Spree stepped back again.

"You tricky bastard! You nearly had my hand off." Spree stepped to the side and cocked his head. "I've studied your fighting technique though. The way you never step back, only forward. You twist when attacked, counter attacking to force your opponent to move away. Very clever. You move as little as possible, and you keep your eyes steady, but you look at everything at the same time." Spree tilted his head to the other side. "When we were young, I was inexperienced at fighting. But I was a good fighter all the same. Since we last fought, I've been thinking about how you beat me. I taught myself your technique. I learnt how to counter your attacks."

"Really? You don't seem to be doing a good job of it." Conrad taunted.

"You think? Last time I fought you, I nearly died, and you walked away without a scratch." He jumped forward and thrusted the knife at Conrad. Conrad twisted away from the blade and brought his blade up towards Spree's chest. Spree twisted his own body, moving his knife away from Conrad, and moving his left shoulder toward him. This was a tricky manoeuvre, but as he did, he brought his left fist up and punched Conrad in the nose. It was Conrad's turn to retreat. Conrad wiped the blood from his face. "But you won't get off so lightly this time!" Spree growled at him.

Conrad was getting really angry. He dropped his knife and held his hands out in a Tai Chi style stance, hoping to control his anger. Conrad knew, if he didn't keep his anger under control, his fighting would be unbalanced and uncontrolled. He had to focus on what he was doing, or he might as well give up.

Spree lunged at him again, taking no notice of the fact that Conrad had no weapon. Conrad grabbed the mans wrist in his right hand and twisted it. He put his thumb behind Spree's hand and pushed, forcing Spree's hand to bend over at a ninety degree angle. At this angle, Spree couldn't keep his grip on his knife, and the knife fell out of his hand. Conrad's left fist was already making contact with Spree's face before the knife hit the ground. Spree hit he ground seconds after his knife did.

The second man, that Spree had sent into the trees after Conrad, entered the small clearing where his commander was fighting Conrad.

Conrad didn't notice him. His anger was now out of control. Conrad was standing above Spree, hitting him. Punch after punch, Conrad wouldn't stop, even when someone's arms circled his body and threw him to one side. Conrad just rolled over and bounced back onto his feet. The soldier came for Conrad. Conrad's psychosis was being fuelled by his increasing anger. Conrad was like a rabid dog. His eye were wide open and blood shot. His teeth were bared, and his breath was coming out with the sound of growling. Conrad didn't stand still. As soon as he was up on his feet, he had started running towards the soldier. The soldier didn't know what to do, so struck out as hard as he could. The blow caught Conrad across the head. Conrad didn't feel a thing. He just continued to ram the man in the chest with his head, until the man was up against a tree. Conrad pushed his head up, slamming the man under his chin, and then proceeded to beat the living shit out of him.

When James finally woke up, he saw Conrad bent over a dead man, still landing blow after blow. He spots Kil Spree standing to one side. Kil Spree throws something at Conrad. James shouts out. "Conrad! Look out!" Conrad turns round, but is too slow. The shuriken hits Conrad in the shoulder. Conrad barely notices. He pulls out his sword and runs for the man. Kil Spree turns and runs, calling out as he does.

"I'll kill you next time clone!"

Conrad stands still taking deep breaths. He looks down, then pulls the metal star out from his shoulder. James gingerly approaches him.

"You alright Conrad?" Conrad turns his wide eyed

gaze onto him. James backs up, frightened. "Okay. I'm sorry."

Barry stumbles into the small clearing, shortly followed by Aaron. Conrad takes a quick peek behind him to see who it was, then resumed with his calming exercise. Barry walked up to James and put his hand on his shoulder.

"You alright Jim?" He asks. James nods his answer. " You sure? You look a little spooked. And what the hell is Conrad doing?" James looked up into Barry's eyes.

"He's crazy. I mean one hundred percent wacko. He was beating the life out of a dead man. And did you see the look in his eyes?" He said, then shakes his head, "Eye. I meant eye." He said correcting himself. Barry nods.

"I've seen it before. Back when he had two eyes, even. And his father had the look." James looks up at him again.

"You've met General Manké? General Conrad Jacques Manké?" He asks in awe.

"Of coarse. I went to school with his son remember. He would come take Conrad away just before each summer term. It was kind of hard not knowing the General was there. He would have a large escort with him, and the principle would spend the day running around looking like a frightened rabbit." Barry smiled at the memory. Then his smile dropped as he remembered something else. "He used to get real mad sometimes. Never at us kids, with us it was all smiles and pleasantries, but...adults were a different matter. Usually, just one look from the General would make even the toughest looking men stop in their tracks." He looked at James and smiled again. "Conrad just perfected it, that's all."

"Yeah? Perfected, and then some. He's mad!"

130

"No. He's psychotic. And he needs help. But for now we need to get to that boat." An idea came to James.

"If one of us could get that chain gun Conrad brought with him, we could clear a path and get to the boat." He said.

"Nice one Jim. Now we just need to get to the boat to get the chain gun. So how do we get to the boat?" Aaron pointed out.

"Oh yeah. We left it on the boat, didn't we." James said downhearted.

"No shit Sherlock!" Aaron mocked.

"Leave it out Aaron. He's just a kid." Barry warned. Just then, Conrad walked past them.

"I'll get it." He said on his way past.

"You what?" Aaron asked.

"You lot get back to the path and follow it down. Stay out of sight. Then when it's time, head for the boat."

"Nice one Conrad. And when will we know it's time?" Aaron teased. Conrad shot him a glare.

"When all hell breaks loose." Conrad said, then vanished into the trees.

"Nice one." Aaron said again. "'When all hell breaks loose'. So, what the fuck happened to stealth? I thought we w-"

"Aaron! Shut the fuck up!" Barry said.

Chapter thirteen

Eyes opened wide, panic driving him on. His feet pounded the floor as his legs pumped with adrenaline, fuelled by fear. He swung, recklessly, around a corner, and ran down corridors of stone. He could see the monorail. All he needed to do was run over the bridge to the far platform and jump onto the waiting train, then he would be safe.

As he was about to descend the stairs on the other side of the bridge, he heard the departing whistle blow, sounding the trains departure. "NO!" he shouted as he half ran, half fell down the remainder of the stairs. "WAIT!" But he was too late.

Zach slumped down onto one of the nearby benches. He watched the tail end of the train disappear into darkness inside the tunnel of stone. He wasn't going to make it now. Zach already knew what his teachers were going to say to him, when he turned up an hour late. He pulled his rucksack off his shoulder and opened it. He rummaged around for his radio-phone and, upon finding it, pulled it out.

Radio-phones are mobile (or cell) phones that can only make and receive calls. Only five numbers could be stored onto the phone, with the use of a computer, and there were no numbers on the keypad. Radio-phones were the only type of phone allowed in schools, as the pupil owning it couldn't use it to play games, or phone their friends when they should be studying.

Zach only had two numbers stored on his phone, the emergency number to phone the police, fire brigade or ambulance (this number is fixed on all Radio-phones), and his mothers mobile number. It was his mothers number he sought after now. Zach pressed the down button and the screen lit up, showing the only two numbers available to him. He pushed the down button again to scroll down to his mothers number. Zach wished his mum would let him have at least one other number on his phone, so the directory didn't look quite so pitiful. Sighing, Zach pushed the 'make call' button, and put the small black phone to his ear. As he listened to the dial tone, he looked up to see what time the next train would arrive. Just as he thought, the next train was fifty three minutes away.

"Hello Zach. What's wrong?" Came the familiar, and accusing voice of his mother.

"Hi mum. I err..." He started.

"You missed the train again, didn't you." His mother guessed correctly. Zach bit his lip.

"Yeah." He confessed. He could hear his mum curse under her breath.

"This is the fourth time this week. Fine, I'll call David and ask him if he can pick you up. If he can't, then I'll just have to let the school know you're going to be late, again." She took a collective breath. "You're going to have to do something about your time Zach. You can't keep being late for school. Look, I'll call you back." She hung up. A couple of minutes later, and the familiar sound of an unchangeable ring tone filled the quiet platform. Zach looked at the pitiful display of controls on his phone. There was an up button, a down button, a green 'make call/answer call' button and a red 'end call' button. Zach pressed the green button.

"Hi mum." He said.

"You're lucky, David is coming to get you, so make your way to the monorail entrance now. David isn't happy about this, so don't wind him up. Where are you?" Zach was confused about that question. Why did she ask where he was, she should know that.

"I'm at the mono-rail. You know that." He said.

"Yes, but where about at the monorail?"

"I'm sitting on a bench on the far platform."

133

"Then GET OFF YOUR DAMN BUTT AND GET TO THE ENTRANCE LIKE I TOLD YOU TO DO!" She yelled down the phone at him. He should have seen that coming. When Zach's mother told you to do something, you did it.

Ten minutes later and David appeared out side the monorail entrance. Zach didn't like David. David didn't like Zach much either, but was in love with his mother. Problem was, Zach's mum was married. Zach had never met his dad, and, as far as he knew, never would. His father was a soldier, so that meant he was probably dead. Since the news that Black Tron had won the war and had made claim on M-Tron, no-one suspected there to be any M-Tron soldiers left. But Zach's mum wouldn't believe her husband to be dead.

David opened the door to the Buggy. Zach looked up at the small electric vehicle. The Buggy was the largest vehicle allowed in the city, and the largest vehicle he had ever seen, except the monorail. Zach's mum told him about bigger vehicles outside the city, and that someday he would see them.

"Don't just stand there, get in." David moaned. He would never help Zach to get in, despite how small Zach was, he would rather watch as Zach struggled to pull himself up into the high seat. Zach might be small, but he was bigger then all of his class mates, and stronger too. In fact, Zach was stronger then the kids in the class above him, and some above that even.

David smiled at him, when he was finally settled in the seat.

"What?" Zach asked.

"I just asked your mum to marry me." David answered.

"Mums already married. Nice try though." Zach said. David kept smiling as he drove off.

"She didn't tell you then." David said.

"Didn't tell me what?"

"She signed the certificate of death eight months ago." David turned his grin on Zach. "That means she hasn't been married for eight months now."

"So what? That doesn't mean she's going to marry you."

"You're right there, but, when I asked her to marry me, she said yes." Zach's eyes went wide. He couldn't believe what he was hearing.

"If mum signed those certificates, then why didn't she tell me?" He asked.

"She thought you might be angry. That you might, secretly, be hoping your father was still alive."

"I don't believe you."

"Whatever. But just so as you know, when I move in, things are going to change."

"No doubt."

"If you don't get your arse out of bed in the mornings, you're going to get the belt. Then you'll soon be jumping out of your bed before the alarm goes off." Zach glared at David.

"You even try it, and I'll break you!" He said through gritted teeth. David started laughing.

"Yeah right. A twenty two year old man being beaten by a nine year old boy. That would be the day."

***

"You're late!"

The head of his year was waiting for him. He was a stern looking man, short and slim, with a sharp nose that looked like he could cut glass with it. He was standing in the corridor with his hands on his hips, peering across the top of his thin spectacles and tapping his foot.

"Sorry sir, I missed the train." Zach told him.

"Four times in a row? I think there's more to it then just that." Zach didn't know what to say. He didn't mean to get up late. He didn't know why he had such trouble getting up, but he felt tired all the time. The head of year pointed in the direction of Zach's classroom. Zach made his way to class.

His teacher didn't say anything to him. She just kept going on with the lesson as if he wasn't there. The day went by slowly. At lunch, Zach met up with his friend Damien. They shared their lunches together.

"Zach? Are you all right?" Damien asked. Zach looked puzzled.

"Yeah, why?"

"You look like you're on mars or something." Zach raised an eyebrow.

"But we are on mars, didn't you know that?" Zach toyed. Damien smiled, then looked serious.

"No, really. You don't look well. Are you sick?" Now Zach really was puzzled.

"How can you tell? I'm black." Zach said. "No, it's David. He said mum signed dads death certificate. And he said he was going to marry mum." Now it was Damien's turn to look puzzled.

"Can he do that?"

"He said he asked. He said mum said yes."

"He's a poo-head!" Damien said.

"He's a doggy-do-head!"

***

Zach hated maths. There was something about maths that made his head hurt, and made him feel sleepy. Adding, subtraction, even multiplication and division made some sense to him. But algebra? What was the point?

Zach was trying to work out what the divisible of X was. He knew the answer came from the numerical representation of Y. But what the hell was Y? It was either 16 or 26, which, he didn't know. It didn't help that his ribs were slowly becoming painful. He must have laid awkwardly on his chest and left a bruise. Strange how it was hurting only now.

"If you turn to page six of your maths books, you will see your next task. Now, I'd like you all to take note of the question at the bottom of the page. I would like to see your brain storms on the same sheet as your final answer. Don't just work it out in your heads, think it on paper." The teacher told the class. Zach hadn't finished the last page, and now he had to think about a whole new set of probabilities. The pain in his chest was getting worse, and so was his school work. Zach was finding it hard to breath. He needed to find the solution to Z multiplied by Q assuming T was 15. Zach realised that it wasn't the difficulty of the sums that was making it hard to breath, it was his rapidly tightening chest.

Before he knew it, it was time for his next class. This time it was arts and crafts. Zach usually liked this lesson, but the pain in his chest was making it hard to concentrate. He was trying to draw a bowl of fruit, but his sight was getting blurry. All of a sudden, he realised that Z was 8, so the answer was 52. Oh well, too late now.

Just as that last thought left his mind, everything went black.

Chapter fourteen

He was so close. How he got this close he didn't know, but he had to get there. The boat was in sight. Conrad watched as some soldiers walked down the ramp from the boat. They had the chain gun. It had gotten dark, so Conrad had left his camouflage jacket behind and was using his black clothing to blend in with the shadows. He had put on some black gloves he had had in his pocket. He also had a balaclava but didn't put this on because his face was covered with hair, beard and dirt.

Three soldiers had left the boat, one of them carrying the heavy gun. Conrad surveyed the area. If he attacked now he would be seen by others. The soldiers seemed to be following the make-shift path from the docks to the building Conrad was hiding next to. He guessed they were using the building to store the weapons they had taken from the boat, and as a command centre for the small unit of troops surrounding the area. Conrad was pressed into a corner of the building, dark shadows wrapped around him. If the three soldiers got close enough to him he could kill them before anyone knew.

Sure enough, the soldiers walked right by him. Conrad took one last sweep of the area, to make sure no-one had moved into an area that let them see down this ally between the main building and a smaller building right next to it. The soldier holding the chain gun had taken the lead. Good. Conrad waited for the last soldier to walk past, then, keeping in the shadow, quickly but carefully sneaked behind the soldier taking the rear. Conrad pulled his large knife from its sheath on his leg. Like everything else he had, the knife had been painted black, to stop the polished metal from catching the light. Conrad held his breath as he came right up behind the first soldier. He put his left hand

138

over the soldiers mouth at the same time as slitting his throat, then as the soldiers body became limp, he pulled the man into the shadows. The next man he killed by stabbing the knife down into the top of the soldiers skull. The man dropped instantly, making no noise. Conrad had to be quick with the last man. If he let the gun drop onto the ground it would alert the nearby soldiers just around the edge of the building. Conrad quickly ran up behind the man and stuck the knife into the back of his throat up to the hilt. Quickly, he reached around and grabbed the gun from the soldiers grip. The soldier hit the floor.

Without bothering to hide the bodies, Conrad ran back the way he came, toward the boat. He stopped just before a large gap in the shadows and peered around the edge of the smaller building. There was a soldier patrolling the area. Conrad waited until the man turned his back on him, then ran as fast as he could to the boat. As he was running up the ramp he heard the first shot. Conrad turned once he had reached the top of the ramp and kicked it into the water. Then diving behind the metal walls of the boat to avoid being hit by a plasma burst, he started loading the gun. Unfortunately, big guns take a while to load. During which, a grenade landed on the deck in front of his very eyes. Conrad took one look, picked the grenade up and absent-mindedly tossed it over his shoulder. Where it landed beside two Black trons who were unlucky enough to reach the dock first.

Cocked and ready, Conrad lifted the gun onto the side of the boat and opened fire. The gun was also painted black, but the heat of the extremely rapid firing gun made the paint start flaking off. The soldiers all ran for cover. Conrad took his finger off the trigger. Just beside his right leg, Conrad noticed the PERL, ready to be taken from the boat. Conrad almost smiled at seeing his luck. A Plasma Enhanced Rocket Launcher, or PERL for short, could blast through walls before exploding. The almost liquid like plasma would be sent hurling through the air, so, if the main explosion didn't kill you, the sticky plasma would burn through the flesh and bone of anyone unfortunate enough to be hit by it.

Conrad set the gun to one side and charged up the PERL. Some soldiers were setting up an anti-tank cannon, Conrad's first target.

***

Barry sat up when he heard the sound of rapid fire. Aaron looked quizzically at him. Barry listened to the sound. It was the fastest firing weapon he had ever heard.

"I think Conrad got that chain gun." Just then, a large explosion had the three men jumping onto their feet and running through the trees down to the docks. James looked to Aaron and asked, "Does this mean all hell has broke loose?" Another explosion sounded through the air, followed by the sounds of men screaming in pain from plasma burns.

"If it hadn't, it has now." Aaron called over his shoulder.

***

Conrad checked the ammo in the PERL. Most PEPs would last for over a thousand shots before the plasma canister needed changing, but the PERLs massive plasma bursts could deplete its ammo in only ten shots. Conrad had two shots left. He decided to save them for the moment and so reached over for the chain gun. As he did so he noticed three plasma shots burst through the trees and hit three soldiers. Barry, Aaron and James most have joined him. He pulled the trigger on the chain gun and held on for dear life as the powerful weapon emptied its load. The ammo box on the side of the gun was thrown off as the last shell in the strip was

140

pulled through the gun. Throwing the spent gun to one side, Conrad pulled his handguns from their holsters on his back. Although his own rule stated that all weapons should be black, he had left the rich platinum exposed. Thankfully, the pistol grips were black and so were the holsters, so when he put them away, most of the shiny metal was hidden.

A soldier ran around the side of the helm. Damn! Conrad didn't think if there could be anyone still on the boat. Before the man could get a clear shot, Conrad put a bullet through his head. Conrad looked to his right, and then to his left, to check if anyone else was on the boat. Four more men appeared from the same direction as the first. Without even thinking about it, Conrad put a bullet through the first mans head. As he did, he heard more men running up behind him. Conrad knew he wouldn't win this fight. He got up and launched himself of the side of the boat, landing on the jetty, on his feet. As he ran to the end of the docks, he replaced the Glocks into their holsters and reached around for the PERL. He saw one of the soldiers lift the chain gun, flakes of paint falling from the barrels as he did. 'Stupid man, it's empty.' Conrad thought. One of the other soldiers lifted an ammo box onto the side of the gun. 'Bollocks!' As soon as he reached the end of the docks, Conrad turned and, putting the PERL on his shoulder, fired at the man with the chain gun. He knew, as soon as the burst of glowing plasma hit, that he was too close. Conrad turned and ran. He only managed two steps before the blast from the explosion lifted him from the ground and threw him through the air. Conrad landed face first this time. He stood and was about to attack the man standing in front of him when he realised it was Aaron.

"Aaron. You look like a fifty fifty bar. What happened to your face?" Before Aaron could answer,

Conrad noticed smoke coming from his right arm. He looked down to see plasma burning into his metal arm. He swiftly moved to a barrel full of water and shoved his arm into it. He had to swish his arm around to make the plasma come off. The plasma would sink to the bottom and burn through the bottom of the barrel. But at least it was off his arm. He looked to see what damage had been done. Except for a rough patch of black, his arm had very little damage.

Barry ran up to him as he was shaking the water off his arm.

"I think we got them all." He nodded his head, indicating toward the boat. "I think you sunk the boat as well." Conrad turned to see the boat. Sure enough, the boat was up on one end and was slowly sinking into the murky waters. Conrad looked around and spotted six Octopods.

"Never mind, we'll make better progress with them."

The long, narrow, white ships known as Octopods were the prime fighting ship for Black Tron. They had four large wings at ninety degree angles from each other, giving the ship an X shape, with a large pod on the front of each ship in the shape of a three-dimensional octagon. This twenty six sided pod could be jettisoned from the main body of the ship as an escape system, as this is where the pilot sits. Depending on the ships function, each wing tip was fitted with either plasma rods, or plasma cannons. Plasma rods, or sniper rods as they were known, could be used for long distance shooting, but were useless for close range firing (as they have a very slow rate of fire). These Octopods were used to take the enemy out from the side lines and were marked as OCT-S models. The ships with plasma cannons were used for the close up fighting and were marked as OCT-F models. There were three of each kind sitting at the docks. Conrad,

Aaron and Barry took the OCT-F versions, while James was left with one of the OCT-S type.

Conrad was surprised to find they manoeuvred very well. The Octopods had one large booster protruding from the rear of the main body of the ship, giving it high speeds, and four small thrusters on each wing tip behind the weapon mountings. These were used for manoeuvring. What surprised Conrad the most though, was how well they flew. The wings on the Octopods weren't designed to keep the ship in the air. For this reason, and a few others, the ship was very badly designed. But the downward thrusters did a very good job of rectifying this problem. Octopods used a lot of fuel because of this, one of the reasons that M-Tron ships made full use of modern wing technology. Conrad found that the Octopod had very responsive handling. Although he didn't yet know how well it would handle in a dog fight. The pod itself was made of reinforced glass so the pilot could see all around. Conrad didn't like that idea much, as it made him feel too vulnerable.

Suddenly, something hit his wing. Conrad looked through the rear of the pod and saw smoke coming from his top left wing. There wasn't anything on the scanners, so it had to be one of the other two OCT-S Octopods. The Octopods had better scanners then the small ships of M-Tron, but only the OCT-S type had the enhanced view. As James was in the OCT-S model, he could see their attackers.

"It's both of them Conrad. The two Octopods left in Norway."

"Okay guys, lets see what these things can do. Jim, take them out from here, and try to remember which of those dots on the screen is us." Conrad turned the Octopod around. The ship juddered, a sign of bad manoeuvrability. Now Conrad knew the limit of this ships ability, he suddenly wished he was piloting an ASAU.

James started shooting as soon as he had turned his ship. Conrad, Aaron and Barry had to get closer to the two enemy ships before they could start shooting.

"You know, we could always jump the sky." Barry pointed out. What Barry was referring to was, flying out to space to either: gain manoeuvrability or: outrun the enemy.

"Only three problems with that B Man." Conrad replied. "And they all come down to the fact that we're in Octopods, same as them. One: An Octopod can't outrun an Octopod. Two: An Octopod can't out manoeuvre an Octopod, and three: They can hear everything we're saying because, yep, you guessed it, they're in Octopods."

"Whatever you guys decide to do, decide quick. Or I'll have to take the both of them out myself." James scolded.

"Hello Jim." Came a familiar voice. "I hope you're ready to die, because I'm going to kill you."

"JAMES! I warned you about this! You should have killed him when I told you to!" Conrad bellowed through the radio. James suddenly figured out who the voice belonged to.

"Captain Simon Spengler I presume." He said.

"The clone is right, you should have killed me. Now I'm going to be rewarded with gold when I kill all four of you."

"Sorry pal, but you're on my scope. You're going down." James taunted.

"Don't get suckered in Jim! Keep your eyes on the targets, and let us know where to go." Conrad said as two large bolts of plasma shot past him in the direction of the enemy. "That was a bit close Jim! The first three dots are friendly, remember?"

"Don't worry Sir, I knew I'd miss you." James replied. A wicked laugh came through the radio.

"You missed me too Jim." Simon said. "We know how to handle these things better then you, remember?" Conrad pushed the speed button. He wasn't used to speeding up and slowing down with his fingers. M-Tron ships used a pedal to accelerate, operated by the right foot, and reverse by the left.

The two enemy Octopods blipped on his screen, finally. Conrad could now see that the Black Tron soldiers really could handle them better.

"Jim, hit the sky! I need you to be quicker!" Conrad knew that without air forces pushing on the four wings of the Octopod, Jim could turn in tighter circles, making him more manoeuvrable. Also, it would give him a clearer shot of the enemy. Barry nudged his ship past Conrad's and opened fire. From slightly further back, Aaron did the same. Conrad dropped his nose and started plummeting towards the ground. After about twelve feet, Conrad pulled his nose skyward again and opened fire himself. Conrad's computer display flashed to let him know he was firing on friendly units. The computer wouldn't let him lock on to the two enemy ships, but he knew it wouldn't. This gave him an advantage, because then the computer wouldn't try to assist him. Conrad hated having semi-automatic cannons, they tended to lock on to the wrong target. Computer controlled weapons would lock on to the nearest target, but this wasn't always where the danger lay. Conrad liked to have full control, so he could make up his own mind. And he was always right. He had his cannons on manual, but the computer still kept warning him of errors. The flashing display was getting on his nerves.

"They're not bloody friendly, you stupid computer!" He yelled at the screen. This was, of coarse, of no use.

The computer in an Octopod would always see another Octopod as a friendly unit, no matter who was piloting it.

"Are you shouting at your own ship Conrad?" Barry asked.

"Ignore me, keep your eyes on the enemy. I don't want to...shit! I lost you!" Conrad cursed.

"What do you mean, lost me?" Barry asked, sounding a little worried.

"I've got five white dots. Which ones do I shoot at?"

"Try the one shooting you, clone!" Simons voice taunted him. Conrad couldn't see where he was, but could see points of light moving towards him at a fast velocity.

"Watch the shooting stars man." Aaron told Conrad. Quickly, Conrad made the calculation, using the direction of the points of light and matching them with the dot they came from. He turned the ship to avoid being hit by the moving lights (which were bolts of plasma) and manually targeted the dot. Conrad shot.

"I'm hit! I'm hit! Spree, save me!" Simons voice came over the radio. Conrad almost smiled. He was always right.

As he flew up to meet the other ships, he momentarily spotted Simons Octopod hurtling towards the ground. The escape pod missing.

"If you can, shoot the pods. I don't want this next guy escaping!" Conrad told the others. A ship came up beside him. One glance let him know it was Aaron.

"Why's that man?" Aaron asked.

"General Kil Spree is in that pod. I want him to stay dead this time!"

"Conrad my friend. You said you could see five ships. You destroyed one. That leaves four. There were six ships to start with, so, where's the other ship?" Two explosions caught Conrad's eye. He used his zoom function on his metal eye to see what it was. He saw an Octopod on fire and out of control. Conrad zoomed in a little more. James was in the pod!

"You bastard! Barry! Give James some cover! NOW!" He yelled. Barry wasn't fast enough. Conrad watched in horror as two more bolts of large yellow plasma tore through the escape pod of James's ship. James managed to get off two shots before he died . Conrad, Barry and Aaron saw the bolts of plasma hit. Now they knew where the last enemy ship was. Conrad put the ship in full throttle and opened fire all the way towards the last enemy ship. Aaron and Barry hot on his tail. Spree's ship exploded.

"He won't come back from that one." Barry said. Conrad kept silent, and turning his ship around, headed home.

Chapter fifteen

White.

All he could see was white.

Snow? No. It wasn't snow. It was too smooth to be snow. So what was it? He knew he had seen this white thing before, but his mind didn't seem to want to work at this moment. As his eyes adjusted to the dim lighting, he started to see a grey line. A moment more and he could see more grey lines. As the grey lines appeared, he noticed that they made a large, grey grid in front of his eyes.

Tiles!

That's what it was: ceiling tiles.

That meant he was laying on his back.

Was he in bed?

He sat up to have a look. Big mistake. The pain hit him hard, and he flopped back down onto the softness of his bed. Soft? It was a bed then. Good, because he felt tired. He closed his eyes.

A thought struck him at that moment. Why was he in bed, and why was he in pain? He tried to think of the last thing that had happened to him. Nothing came to mind. He couldn't remember what had happened, where he had been or what he had done that day. Actually, he couldn't remember anything about the day before either. Nor the day before that. Or any day that week, month, year even. He couldn't remember what day it was, or what year it was. He tried to remember his home, his mother and father, anything that should have been easy to remember. But nothing came to mind. No memories. The easiest thing to remember is your own name. It wasn't there. He remembered nothing, not even his own name.

Panic tried to set in, but he was too tired. As he fell

back into a lonely and dreamless sleep, a single tear born of fear, rolled down his cheek.

***

Not a sound could be heard. The radios were silent. Only the sound of a slow wind, and the near silent hum of stabilizing jets broke the silence. But it was the silence from the radio that made the quiet unbearable. If only it hadn't of happened. If only they had paid more attention. But it did happen, and there was nothing they could do about it. Barry knew He would be angry, so he didn't want to disturb Him. Aaron, on the other hand, had been badgering Him for hours. Still, twelve hours had passed since it happened, and still He kept quiet. Who is He, you ask? Who else!

Conrad.

"Oi! Say something dog breath. Shout. Scream. Get angry. Throw a tantrum; anything, just make a sound for crying-out-loud. Hit something even."

"For fuck sake, Aaron! Give it a rest!" Barry boomed. He was feeling a little angry himself.

"Conrad hasn't made a sound for nearly twelve hours, man. He needs to let it out." Aaron informed him.

"I wish I could let you out." Barry retaliated.

"Look, this silence is getting on my nerves-"

"Same thing here. Only, you had to open your mouth, so now I'm wishing for the silence to return. So why don't you make this big man happy and SHUT THE FUCK UP!!"

"ARRRRRRHHH!!!! FUCK! WANK! CUNT! BASTARD! SHIT!" Came the sounds they had been waiting for. Conrad's constant cursing was backed by the sound of banging.

"Ah. Conrad must have gone for the tantrum idea." Aaron said.

The cursing and screaming from Conrad went on for

149

quite some time. Then, suddenly, after a nasty smashing sound, Conrad abruptly stopped. Barry got a little unnerved by this, so decided to find out what had happened.

"Conrad? You okay?" He asked.

"Oh shit. Crap. I...er...I think I broke something. Erm..I'm okay though, I think." Conrad answered. Barry was getting very worried.

"Conrad? What did you break?"

"What is there to break?" Aaron asked. "I mean, there ain't much in these things *to* break. You got a seat, two little computer terminals, a stick and a tiny bit of floor that holds it all to the nine tons of rocket behind you."

"Yeah, I think I broke the floor." Conrad admitted. "And one of the control terminals." Barry heard some more cursing, this time from Aaron, and a little quieter.

"Conrad. There happens to be a steal bar that runs from the middle of that little bit of floor, straight through into the main body of the ship. At the end of that bar is the release mechanism for the escape pod. Now, since your pod hasn't fallen off yet, I'm assuming you've broken the bar from the bottom of your seat." Aaron said, then took a deep breath.

"My seat seems fine, so I guess I'm alright. Besides, its not my fault they made it so flimsy." Aaron was gob smacked.

"Mate. Those bars are made from hardened steal. They're two feet wide and one foot deep. They can take up to six tons of pressure. They don't need to be any stronger then that."

"Then how in the hell did I manage to bend it, eh?" Conrad said testily.

"Easy. You've got robotic muscles in your legs." Barry said matter-of-factly.

"What!?" Conrad slowed his ship and levelled it

150

with Barry's, so he could look at him to show the surprise on his face. Barry looked over and knew Conrad wanted an explanation.

"Well, when your arm was shot off, and your eye removed, they had also done something to your legs. I don't quite know what, but your leg bones were shattered and the muscles damaged beyond repair. Edward Julius replaced your bones for metal, and your muscles for motors." Barry looked back over to Conrad. The scowl on Conrad's face said it all. A slow growl was heard over the radio.

"And you just forgot to mention this, eh? Slipped your mind, yes?" Barry spotted a piece of metal laying at the bottom of the glass pod on Conrad's Octopod.

"Did you break the floor off?" He asked trying to change the subject.

"Yes. But the support beam is still there. A little bent, but still there. Why?" Conrad asked back. Barry pointed to the underside of Conrad's pod.

"There's pieces of metal below you."

"There's bits of computer down there too. What I meant though was, why did you change the subject?" Barry felt trapped. Conrad could always do that to him.

"Which computer did you break?" He asked instead.

"Fuck the fucking computer! Why didn't you tell me about my legs? Do I have any more surprises? And why are you sweating?"

"No. I've told you everything. I didn't tell you at first because you were angry enough about the rest of it. And I'm sweating because we're coming up to some mountains and you haven't started climbing yet. How do you know I'm sweating?"

"My bloody eye is stuck on zoom! I know about the mountains, I saw them before you did. I can't climb, because I broke the controls that control height. I'm stuck at this level." Barry was shocked.

"Then why, in the name of god, haven't you hit the escape button yet?!" Barry burst out.

"I have." Was Conrad's reply.

"What? But…But…Wait, I'll think of something. We could-"

"B Man. You're panicking. Calm down." Conrad said calmly. Barry was awestruck. How could he be so calm?

"Conrad? You do know you're about to crash, don't you?" He asked.

"B Man. Don't worry. I said I can't change height, not direction. I'll just have to go around. I know these things aren't as fast as an ASAU, but it won't take long."

"Yeah. Stop panicking will'ya." Aaron chimed in. "It'll only take eighteen minuets. Then he'll be right on our tail again."

"Well, that's okay then. And when we get home he can jump out and parachute down." Barry retaliated.

"Don't be daft! We haven't used parachutes since the twenty eighth century. Besides…oh." Aaron suddenly understood what Barry was getting at. "He's right mate, how you gonna get down when we're home?"

"Easy. I can still control my speed. All I have to do is stop when we're above the volcano and…" Conrad suddenly had to think what to do after that. The ship will automatically turn the down thrusters on to hold the ship at the same level once he had stopped in midair, but to make the ship go down still required the up and down controls. The very controls he had broken. An ASAU had controls to lift and drop the nose while in flight, so you could raise and lower your flight level. There would also be separate controls to lift and lower the whole ship when hovering. The Octopod, however, performed both these two things with the same up and

152

down controls.

Conrad checked his control deck (the one he hadn't broken). He couldn't find anything to help his situation.

"You could park up next to the volcano, then jump out and climb down the sides." Aaron offered.

"Now who's being daft? The sides of that volcano are shear rock faces. They were artificially designed like that to accommodate that stupid strip of mono-rail, and keep it hidden." Barry said back.

"What did you say? Mono-rail?" Conrad asked.

"Oh! Didn't you know? You've got a section of mono-rail and a small station up there." Barry told him. Conrad suddenly made a loud cheering noise. "Did you just have an idea?" Barry asked.

"No! I had the idea ages ago. I just turned my zoom off."

"Right." Barry said slowly. "So what about this idea?"

"Well, I knew about the mono-rail, and I just figured, if I was the right height, I could pull up like a train." Conrad answered.

"Are you the right height?" Aaron asked impatiently. Conrad went silent for a while, then said, "Close enough." Conrad veered off to go around the mountains.

***

After a while, they were crossing the sea. Conrad suddenly went west.

"Conrad. The volcano is straight on south southeast." Barry informed him.

"I know, but the mono-rail is on the west side, so I have to approach it from the north or south." Barry kept quiet.

They flew west for a bit, then Conrad turned south to approach the mono-rail. Aaron checked the height difference.

153

"Conrad. The rail is too high. You won't make it."
He said. Conrad kept going.

"Plenty of room." He said.

"If you're going to do what I think you're going to
do, then you'd better slow down." Barry pointed out.
Conrad did. Barry and Aaron kept back as they
watched Conrad pulling into the station.

"You're still going too fast." Barry said. Conrad
ignored him. As he reached the rail, a loud crashing
sound could be heard over the radio. Barry couldn't
watch, but at the same time, he couldn't close his eyes,
or turn away from the scene unfolding before him. The
bottom of the hard glass dome at the front of the
Octopod shattered and fell to the ground, thousands of
feet below. Conrad kept going. There was an almighty
screeching sound from the radios. Conrad knew he
couldn't let the Pod stop now, or he would never reach
the platform, so he pushed the ship to go faster. The
boosters were blasting as much as they could, but the
friction from the rusty old rail was still slowing him
down. The bottom of the Octopod was being ripped
apart. Finally, at the crescendo of the screeching, the
Pod stopped. Conrad opened the huge Pod, watching as
more pieces of glass and debris fell to the ground
below. He could just reach the platform. Barry and
Aaron flew into the giant opening at the top of the
volcano and down to the landing area inside. Conrad
took the lift down and joined them.

Barry walked up to him and sighed. Aaron was right
behind him.

"Conrad. We have to talk mate." Barry started.

"Yeah. This has gone on long enough." Aaron
added. Conrad was confused.

"What has? What are you guys talking about?" He
asked. Barry sighed again.

"Conrad, you're crazy. You're psychotic. You're a

154

danger to us all. I know it isn't your fault James died, and I'm not trying to put the blame on you, but, it was because of your stupid quest he died. I trusted you, and where did it get us? One man down, and you're now the World President."

"What you getting at?" Conrad asked.

"If we keep following you, we'll end up dead too. So Aaron and I are going to try and make a life for ourselves, in Germany." Conrad couldn't believe what he was hearing.

"That's Black Tron territory! Are you mad?" He said. Barry sighed again.

"No Conrad. The whole world is Black Tron territory. They won the war remember. We can't make a difference here. We lost. It's time to move on. I know people in Germany who will help us. I just need to loose my accent, and no-one will be the wiser. You can pass yourself off as a Black Tron if you tried, you are from a French family. Come with us if you want, but no more fighting. We can't win the war, because it's already been won."

"Some of the most remembered war hero's spent most of there time believing they had lost the war. But they kept going in hope that their effort would somehow make a difference. Usually, it did." Conrad said quietly.

"What does that mean?" Aaron asked. It was Conrad's turn to sigh.

"Something my dad once told me. It means, there is always a way to win, even if you think you've lost already. Fine. If that's what you guys want, then so be it. But I will win the war." Barry snorted a laugh.

"No you won't. You'll get yourself killed. But, hey, what do we care? We've only known you for all of your life. Get it in your head man! There is no war! We lost! Finito!" Aaron growled at him.

"BOLLOCKS!! We can still win! There is more hope then you can ever believe! We have AICS and-" Barry's deep, booming voice cut Conrad's sentence short.

"AICS can't do shit! There is no hope! We have only one choice, and by god, we are going to make it. Goodbye Conrad." Barry left, fuming. Conrad scowled at Aaron.

"What about you? You going to be his shadow?" Aaron scowled back.

"It's a damn sight safer then being yours!" He said, then walked off to find Barry.

Chapter sixteen

Conrad was in the computer room. Barry and Aaron were packing their things, getting ready to leave. Barry couldn't go without saying something to Conrad. He didn't want to leave in bad terms. The three of them had been friends for so long, it didn't seem right. Barry remembered the first fight he had had with Conrad. Conrad had been so fast, yet, because of his anger, he didn't concentrate on what Barry was doing. Barry had won the fight by a knockout. The very next day, Conrad ran up to him and invited him to a secret party. The party had to be secret because no-one was allowed to have parties at the military school. They had been firm friends ever since.

Barry turned to go to Conrad, but Conrad was already there. Barry opened his mouth to say something, but Conrad beat him to it.

"I know I'm mad Barry." He said. "I can feel it inside me all the time. It's a constant battle to control myself. I know I'm crazy, but I *know* I am, and that's the first road to recovery. But, as crazy as I am, I'm not stupid."

"I never said you were." Barry told him.

"I know, but you think it. I didn't go all that way to become the World President, and I didn't want anyone to die. I went for a reason. There is a way to win this war." Barry threw up his hands.

"I don't believe it! You just told me you weren't stupid, then you go and say something like that! For god's sake Conrad, there is no way to win this war! We are going, and that's final!"

"Okay B Man. Sorry, Barry. I know you don't like that nickname. Just tell me one thing." Conrad said. Barry let out a loud sigh.

"Okay. What?"

"What do you want me to tell your wife when I see her?" Barry was speechless. He had never told Conrad about his wife. He had wanted to, but Conrad didn't like his soldiers to have family. This wasn't because he was selfish, but rather, because it broke his heart to tell the soldiers family about the soldiers death. So when Barry got married, he done so in secret. But how did he now know?

"What you talking about?" Aaron asked from the other side of the room. "Barry ain't married. Are you?"

"Yes, he is." Conrad said. "Tatiana Man. Married to Barry Man on the fifth of august, thirty eight, thirteen. Seven day's before the nukes hit, and everyone hid in the underground bunker." Barry stared at him.

"How did you know?" He asked. Conrad held up a piece of paper with a number on it. It was the M-Tron codes from the election.

"But…How? Those codes were for New M-Tron." Conrad shook his head.

"No. As the highest ranking officer alive, I had access to the real codes. I entered them into the election computer. The codes I had only allowed me to enter M-Tron into the election, or hand M-Tron over to the victors. These codes tell me everything. I know you guys don't want to help me win this war, but you can at least come with me to the underground bunkers and see your families again." Aaron nodded his agreement.

"Okay Conrad. One last trip together."

***

"Genetic defect? What the hell does that mean?" She cried out at him. The doctor took a deep breath.

"Whatever is causing the blackouts is genetically related. Whatever is causing the problem isn't some bug, or virus, but has been inside of him since the day he was born. It grew with him, and now, it's killing him." She sat on the chair behind her and went over what the doctor had just told her.

"Can you do anything for him?" She asked tearfully. The doctor shook his head.

"Only make him comfortable. We have no idea what is causing the abnormality. It's like nothing we have seen before."

"How long does he have?" She asked. This was the hardest question she had ever asked. She didn't want to know the answer, but needed to prepare herself for the day. The doctor sighed.

"One week, one month maybe, but no longer then that." She broke down in tears. The doctor put a comforting hand on her shoulder, but nothing could take the pain away from her now.

She dried her eyes, then, putting on a brave face, she went into his room.

Zach was laying on the bed, staring at the ceiling. He didn't notice at first when she called his name, but turned to face her the second time.

"Hi mum." He said. She took his hand and smiled at him.

"How is my little soldier doing?" She asked him. Zach smiled at her.

"Dieing." He said simply.

"Don't say that. You never know, they could find a cure tomorrow for all you know." Zach shook his head.

"It's a genetic defect mum. The only way they can cure me is by mapping my whole DNA sequence and searching for the part that's wrong, or finding someone with the defect who isn't effected by it. Finding someone who has naturally overcome the defect is a billion to one chance, and mapping my DNA would take so long that I'll be dead by the time they invent a cure." Zach told her.

"Why did you have to be such a smart arse? You're nine years old for god sakes, why did it have to happen

159

now?" She said bursting into tears again.

"Why did you sign dad's death certificate?" He asked. She looked up at him with a puzzled expression.

"I didn't. Who told you I did?"

"David." He replied. She frowned.

"That bloody liar! What's he go and say a thing like that for?" She said.

"He told me you were going to marry him." She burst out laughing.

"You silly bugger! I'm married to your father, remember?" Zach nodded.

"That's what I thought." He said.

"That's what you were suppose to think." Came a voice from the doorway. Zach and his mother turned to look. It was David.

"What you go and tell him that for?" She asked him. David smiled at her.

"Because that's exactly what you *are* going to do. That no good father of his is long dead and buried. It's time you came to grips with it and moved on. Then we can get married, send him away somewhere, and live a long and happy life together." She scowled at him.

"David? What's gotten into you? I'm not going to marry you. Ever." David grinned a wicked grin.

"Yes you are, or I'll be signing your death certificate." Zach gripped the metal railing to his bed and squeezed.

"You do and I'll kill you!" He growled at him. David turned his grin on Zach.

"You'll do what now? A nine year old boy thinks he can have me does-" He cut his sentence short when he noticed the metal railing that Zach was crushing in his hand. It was bent and buckled. David looked into Zach's eyes.

"How'd you do that?" He asked. Zach grinned back at him.

160

"Give me your throat, and I'll show you!" Zach snapped back at him. David hesitated, then grabbed Zach's top and lifted him from his bed.

"How about I show you instead?" David growled at him.

"Put him down! NOW!" She screamed at David. David didn't listen. Zach quickly put a hand around David's throat and squeezed. David started choking, and dropped Zach. Zach didn't let go. He squeezed a little harder and David's neck snapped. David fell to the floor, dead.

***

Conrad was up on the mono-rail platform, looking at the Octopod. It was a mess. Over seven feet of rail was stuck in the belly of the ship. Most of the glass dome was shattered, and the lowest two wings had been bent when they had hit the sides of the mountain. Conrad was down on his knees, checking the ship over, when Barry stepped up behind him.

"It's dead Conrad. She isn't going to fly again." He said. Conrad sighed.

"I know. But we have to get to America. Those Pod's have only got room for one in each. How do we get all three of us to the USA?" Barry pondered a moment.

"What about the ASAU's?" He asked. Conrad gave him a funny look. "We didn't loose all of them, did we?" Conrad shook his head in puzzlement.

"What are you going on about? What ASAU's?" He asked.

"The last battle we had. The one where we lost all of our men. Did you send in all the ASAU's or just some of them?" Conrad smiled.

"Good lad. Now that's what I call thinking. Yes. There may be a couple left. Is that car still outside?" Barry nodded. "Good. We can use that to go have a look see. I'm not walking again. We've done enough of that for a while. Come on, let's go." Conrad jumped into the lift and pressed the down button. Barry quickly jumped in, before the doors closed.

"We off?" Aaron asked as they ran past him.

"Yep. Off to find some ships. You coming?" Conrad asked. Aaron nodded and followed them down the corridor. Once outside, Conrad and Barry looked around for the car.

"What you looking for?" Aaron asked as they ran around in circles.

"The car. Where's the bloody car?" Barry asked. Aaron looked sheepish.

"Oh." He said. Conrad stopped searching and looked Aaron in the eyes.

"Oh, what?" He asked. Aaron hung his head.

"I got rid of it." He said. Barry's jaw dropped. Conrad frowned.

"You did what?" He asked calmly.

"I got rid of it." Aaron repeated.

"WHAT THE HELL DID YOU DO THAT FOR?!" Conrad screamed at him. Aaron backed up a few steps.

"So no-one would think anyone was here. It would seem a bit odd, don't you think, a volcano with a car parked outside. So I dumped it in the pond over there." Conrad slapped himself on the head, repeatedly, and muttered 'idiot' to himself, over and over again. Barry shrugged.

"Looks like we're walking after all. Good job it ain't far. Only twenty miles or so." Aaron looked Barry in the eye.

"It's not my fault. I was trying to be cautious." Conrad stopped muttering to himself, and held out a hand.

"Okay, okay. You did the right thing. How were you to know we might need it."

"You can always take the Pod." Aaron offered.

"No. It's had it. I ripped it up too bad." Conrad told him. Aaron shook his head.

"No, not that one. The Pod itself. It can get you there quickly enough." Conrad shook his head.

"No, I told you, I damaged it too much. It wont fly."

"What about the one behind the make shift hospital? The doctor told us that two Octopods were shot down around here. One crashed head first into the roof, the other crashed somewhere else, but the Pod ejected and landed behind the hospital." Conrad stared into Aaron's eyes. Then all of a sudden, he grabbed Aaron around the head and planted a wet kiss on his forehead.

"Aaron. You're a genius." He said. Aaron wiped his head clean.

"Thanks, I think." He said.

They started walking down the road towards the make shift hospital.

"I can't believe we're walking again." Barry grumbled.

"At least it's only a few miles this time, and not twenty odd miles." They took a few more steps, then Conrad stopped and stared at them both.

"What's up Conrad?" Aaron asked. Conrad frowned at them.

"Why are you guys coming with me?" He asked them. They looked at each other.

"Where else do we go?" Aaron asked. Conrad's frown became deeper.

"Back to the volcano base. Where *your* Octopods are. I'm the only one who needs to walk." Barry laughed at himself and Aaron blushed.

"Oh yeah. Good point." Aaron said. He and Barry turned round and went back to the base.

Conrad hadn't got far when the high pitch sound of stabilizing jets made him look back. Barry and Aaron were waving out of their Pod's and laughing.

"Yeah, laugh it up boys. You won't find this shit funny for long." He mumbled to himself. The deeper sound of the Pod's boosters firing sounded their departure. Conrad knew they would be drinking tea and playing cards when he arrived, just to piss him off. He shook his head and kept walking.

***

The old church and now make shift hospital came into sight. Conrad was pleased that he didn't feel the least bit tiered after the long walk. It must have been the robotic motors in his legs that made the walk so easy. Conrad wasn't sure about the robotics in his body. In a way, they were handy, if he could get the hang of using the different features. But it was like he had lost a part of himself, a part he can no longer get back.

As he rounded the church, and temporary hospital, Conrad heard the sound of a game of poker. Just as he had thought, they were drinking tea and playing cards. Conrad stormed round the corner and opened his mouth to shout at them, but he was pulled back behind the wall and a meaty hand clamped around his mouth. Conrad was about to start fighting when he noticed it was Barry. Barry put a finger to his lips in warning. Aaron waved at him from around the corner, the one that lead to the front of the building. Barry and Conrad joined him round the front of the building.

"I thought they were you guys." Conrad said in a near whisper. Barry nodded.

"I thought you did, that's why I grabbed you. You're the only one with weapons." Aaron frowned at him and waved his baseball bat.

"I got a weapon." He said. Conrad rolled his eyes.

"Not going to do much with that now, are you." Conrad told him. Aaron pointed at the front door of the building. A Black Tron soldier was laying on the ground with his head caved in. Conrad looked in surprise.

"It's a weapon." Aaron said simply.

"Where are the Pods?" Conrad asked, changing the subject.

"Down the road a bit. They see us fly over and started waving to us. I think they're waiting for an evac." Conrad pondered for a moment.

"So they're expecting company." He said. "Better not disappoint them."

"Wait. What were they doing here in the first place?" Aaron asked. "It don't seem right for six Black Tron soldiers to be hanging about an old church for no reason." Conrad shook his head.

"We were using it as a hospital, remember. Well, not us personally, but M-Tron I mean. It's possible they went in to kill all the people in there. Has anyone had a look?" Both Aaron and Barry shook their heads to this. Then Conrad remembered. He had seen around the corner. Only for an instant, but long enough to imprint an image in his mind.

"Hold on guys, give me a minuet and I'll see if I can remember what I saw round there before Barry yanked me back." He said. Aaron looked at Barry.

"Since when could he do that?" He asked. Barry looked sceptically at him.

"He's always been able to do that. Didn't you know? He has a photographic memory." Aaron rolled his eyes.

"I meant, since when could he think. Last time he tried that he thought a ship on fire was a shooting star." Barry chuckled as Aaron grinned.

Conrad brought the memory of walking around the corner in his mind.

As he rounded the church, and temporary hospital, Conrad heard the sound of a game of poker. Just as he had thought, they were drinking tea and playing cards. Conrad stormed round the corner and opened his mouth to shout at them, but he was pulled back behind the wall and a meaty hand clamped around his mouth.

Conrad paused the image. Then he played it backwards until he was looking around the corner, then paused the image again. It was like looking at a picture. Nothing was moving. Conrad used his great memory to smooth the picture. Every tiny detail came into focus. He could see the six men, just as Aaron had said there were. With his mind's eye, he looked the scene over. All six men were carrying standard plasma rifles. Maybe it was just a search and destroy mission after all. Then he spotted a box with a small dish-like object protruding from it. Conrad focused on the box. It was a little blurry, so he tried to recall different items into his mind and tried to match them to what he was looking at. Then it came to him. What he was looking at was a DNA scanner.

To Barry and Aaron, it seemed like Conrad had only just that instant closed his eyes, when Conrad suddenly said, "DNA scanner."

"What the hell are they doing with one of them? That's not standard Black Tron equipment. Even for Black Trons own personal army." Barry stated. Conrad shushed him.

Conrad was using his minds eye to search the scene for something else. What, he wasn't sure, but there had to be something. A small piece of white came to his attention. It was a piece of paper. Conrad looked closely at it. It had writing on it, but he couldn't quite make it out. He brought it into focus as much as his mind would allow, but only two words were readable. **Edward Julius**.

Conrad opened his eyes, wide, and mouthed a curse. Barry lip-read the word and understood it's meaning.

"What did you see?" He asked. Conrad stared at him for a while, then said, "Edward Julius. They were looking for Edward Julius." Barry frowned.

"Well, that's all right. What are they going to do with a Doctor of robotics?" Conrad grabbed him.

"A lot!" He growled. "Edward Julius could tell them the codes to every piece of moving technology M-Tron have. A ship on their radars could be anything. All they see is a blip without an identification. That's the only way they can see the enemy. Could you imagine what actions we could take if we knew exactly what type of Pod was coming towards us? If it was a Sniper Pod, we could go in for the kill without worrying about being killed to quickly, or if it was a Fighter Pod, we could avoid being in it's path so it couldn't shoot at us. I've seen good pilots get shot out of the sky because they didn't know what type of ship they were up against. What if it was a Battle Pod? Or a Double Pod? They look the same on a radar screen, but one can shoot you out of the sky, while the other can blow up AUC's. But with the right codes they will know exactly what they are up against. Not only that, they could also build our technology. Could you imagine coming face to face with a bloody Black Tron built AUC? Our technology with their quick build weapons? They could build a ship that no-one could destroy. They would have the monopoly on weapons. Could you imagine what they could come up with? I mean, could anyone imagine him actually building robotic parts to attach to a human being?" Conrad said, waving his robotic arm around for emphasis. "No, but he did it." Aaron shook his head.

"So what do we do then?" He asked. Conrad looked at him.

"We must find him first. Then rescue him, or kill him." Aaron and Barry looked at each other in surprise as Conrad walked away. He walked to the edge of the building and stopped. Something came to his mind. Something he missed when he played the sequence in his mind of looking around the corner of the building. He called back the image. *The soldiers were sitting there, playing card games and drinking tea.* Why were they just sitting there? Why weren't they looking for Edward Julius? If they had found him, then why were they still here? Conrad surveyed the image in his mind. In the background was a box, no, a cage. A man was in the cage. Edward Julius! They had found him, and they were waiting for transport so they could take him away. Conrad turned to the others.

"They've got him." He said.

"Got who?" Barry asked, turning to him.

"Edward Julius. He's in a cage round the corner. We got to kill him." Aaron snorted a short laugh.

"What happened to rescuing him?" He asked. Conrad walked back to the two men.

"How do we do that? He's surrounded by six Black Tron soldiers wearing full body armour, and armed with better weapons then us."

"We could surprise them with the Pods. Then as they're standing there, waving their arms around, we could use the Pods guns to blast them into bits." Aaron offered. Conrad nodded.

"Good idea. But Edward is in a cage. A police style holding cage with beams of laser keeping the prisoner in. Like our police force use, except theirs will kill the prisoner if the key holder is killed." Aaron snapped his fingers.

"Then we don't kill the key holder." Conrad rolled his eyes.

"Which one is the key holder?" He asked rhetorically.

"Well, when we come in with the Pods, we can hold them there while you search them. We can tell them to

168

drop their weapons or we'll shoot them." Barry rolled his eyes and said what Conrad was thinking.

"They're Black Tron soldiers, not IC soldiers. Even if they know they're going to die, they'll still shoot Conrad dead when he goes in to search them. Either way, Julius is dead. If they know we are around they'll try to kill us, then we'll be forced to kill them. Key holder dies, Julius dies." Conrad started pacing up and down the short pathway.

"I didn't see the Pods escape pod." He said. "We'll have to wait for their evac vehicle, then steal it. Don't go in front of the evac vehicle or it'll shoot you. There isn't a lot of cover round there, so as soon as you run out, keep moving. I'll take care of Doctor Julius."

"You don't need to shoot Julius." Aaron said. "Killing the key holder will do the job for us." Conrad shook his head.

"No. I've seen how those things work. When the key holder dies, it sets off the execution device. It's quite a simple device. It injects a chemical into the prisoners back which eats through living tissue. After twenty minuets it will have eaten through your spinal column and your spinal cord, leaving you paralysed. After just one hour it will have eaten through your intestines. From the moment it starts to eat your intestines, you will be in the most pain you can ever imagine. After twelve hours, all that will be left of you will be a puddle of liquefied flesh and bone. You'll be dead in just six hours though, when it eats through your heart. Although, it'll eat through your lungs first, so it'll be a race between you dieing from having your lungs full of blood, or the chemical eating your heart. I've seen two men die from that stuff. I know I'm crazy, but I'm not crazy enough to want to see a third person die from it."

"So what's the plan?" Barry asked.

"Wait for the evac ship. Run around the corner and kill every man you see, then steal the ship. The ship will come from the east, so we need to be on the west side of the building." Conrad told them. Barry shook his head.

"No good. As soon as we come out shooting, the evac ship will dart. We need to get the ship to land." Barry looked over at the dead soldier Aaron had killed. "And I think I know how." He said with a smile. "What's the ident number for the Pod I was flying?"

"Alpha, Charlie, seventy four." Conrad said without thinking. Aaron gaped at him.

"How did you know that? I know your mind is quick, but I didn't think it was that quick." He said. Conrad smiled.

"My mind thinks of lots of things at the same time. Some of it useful, some not so. My mind seems to be a little erratic lately. *I* don't even know where some of my thoughts come from."

"It's a symptom of psychosis. I must admit though, it seems to come in handy for you." Barry said. Conrad nodded.

"So what's this idea of yours?" Conrad asked. Barry smiled and revealed his plan.

Chapter seventeen

"We have him sir."

Jason smiled. This was what he had been waiting for. He was sitting at his desk doing paper work. It seemed like he was always doing paper work. He was the potential President of the world and he had mounds of paper work to do. Is this what it means to be in charge? It was bad enough that he has to take the world by force now, now that Conrad had buggered things up for him. Never mind, he still had his army. Now he had the clone.

"Bring the Clone to me." He told the soldier.

"Sorry sir, wrong guy." The soldier told him. Jason frowned. If it wasn't Conrad then who was it?

"I want Conrad. Why are you talking to me if it isn't the Clone?" He asked the man.

"You asked us to find Doctor Edward Julius, sir. We have him." The soldier replied. Jason looked up from his work.

"Edward Julius. Good man. Bring him to me, then find the Clone."

"Yes sir. Julius should be with us in a couple of hours, and I have word that the Clone has been spotted. We should have him by tomorrow." Jason stood up.

"Tomorrow? If I see him in my office tomorrow, I'll promote you to General." Jason wasn't smiling, but the soldier knew he was happy.

"Thank you sir, but I'm already a General." Jason looked into the mans eyes.

"After your cock-up the other day? You had four targets and you killed the unimportant one and let the others live. And, to add insult to injury, the one you killed almost killed you. If that isn't a major cock-up, then I don't know what is. You're an ex-M-Tron soldier. Alpha team for goodness sakes. If anyone can do the job, it should be you. So what happened? You failed, that's what happened. You should be thanking me for not killing you." The soldier bowed and turned to leave. "Hold on." Jason called to the man. "One last thing. If Conrad isn't in this office by tomorrow, I will kill you. You're the best soldier I have. Act like it! Make me proud Spree." Spree smiled.

"Yes sir."

***

The soldiers were making another round of teas, and setting up a fire to cook on. A man ran around the corner of the old building and pointed a plasma rifle at them. One of the soldiers jumped up and pointed his own rifle back at him. The other soldiers quickly followed suit. The first soldier lowered his gun and looked at the soldiers uniform. It was a Black Tron uniform. The man who had ran around the corner lowered his gun a little.

"Identify yourselves!" He called. The first soldier lowered his gun farther and called back.

"Black Tron army! Reconnaissance group! Feed back!" Feed back was an order to return the identification.

"Black Tron army! Pod pilot, fighter class! Alpha, Charlie, seventy four!" The other soldiers lowered their weapons.

"What you doing out here soldier?" The first man asked. Barry, disguised as a Black Tron soldier, walked up to the man.

"You bastards left me here to die! I've been trying to get home ever since my Pod was shot down. Please tell me you're waiting for an evac." The soldier smiled and nodded towards the food being put on the fire for cooking.

"Yes we are. Come join us soldier. We're about to have some food. Please, have some tea." Barry thanked

172

the man.

"May I ask why you made us give our identification?" Another soldier asked. Barry took the cup of Chinese tea offered to him before answering.

"Too many Utopians trying to pass themselves off as Black Tron soldiers. Look out for that one." The two soldiers looked at each other in puzzlement.

"Haven't you heard?" The first soldier asked. "We won the war ages ago." Barry lowered his cup of tea and stared at the soldier in surprise.

"What? How? Then why was I left here for so long then?"

"We didn't know there were still soldiers left here from the war." Barry scowled at the man.

"So I've been spending the last, god knows how many months, hiding, from dead men? Bid gem!" He said. The soldier lifted his eyebrows.

"You speak Kurdish?" The soldier asked. Barry looked at him with a puzzled expression.

"Of coarse. I'm a pilot. If I get shot down, it helps to be able to speak to the locals. These Pods don't go far without juice." The soldier nodded his head.

"My name is Danius." The first soldier said, offering his hand. Barry took the hand and shook it.

"I'm Second Lieutenant Barlow. You can call me 'sir'." Danius physically blanched. None of the other men had a rank any higher then Sergeant, and that was Danius.

"I'm so sorry sir. I didn't realise." He saluted. Barry smiled at the man.

"It's okay. I'm just happy to be going home. Back to good old New Australia." One of the other men pricked his ears at this and stepped closer to the conversation.

"New Australia? Where about?" He asked.

"Mikathara." Was the reply.

"Wow! I didn't think anybody lived that far from

the cities anymore. I'm from Sydney myself." Barry almost corrected the guy but thought better of it. If he was a true Australian he would have a broad accent. Instead, he barely had a Russian accent. It was strange to hear all the different accents and see people from different nationalities. The IC may lay claim to selected countries, but the people could come from anywhere. It wasn't uncommon to hear a Black Tron soldier speaking with an accent from a country deep in the heart of M-Tron.

"So when is this transporter going to turn up?" Barry said, changing the subject.

"It was about an hour away the last time we checked. That was forty minuets ago." Danius said.

"Good, good. Well, until then, I think I'll just..." Barry pretended to spot the holding cage for the first time. "Is that..? That's Doctor Edward Julius! What in gods name are you doing with him?"

"Sorry Sir. That's classified information. Orders come from the top. Although, to be honest, even we only know half the reason." Barry was a little disappointed by this. He was rather hoping to get some intel on the situation. But then the soldier continued with, "And when I say 'from the top', I mean Mr Jason Moon himself. Apparently for some guy called Jacques. No one has ever met, seen, or even heard of him. We don't even know what he does for us. The only person who knows anything about him is Mr Moon, and he's keeping it to himself."

Barry let this piece of info sink into his head. He had never heard of a man named Jacques before. No one of any importance that is. So he kept it for Conrad. Maybe he knew something. For now, he would sit back and listen, while drinking Chinese green tea.

And wait for the ship to arrive.

***

Edmund was an important man. Since they lost communications with the world above, he has been the leader; the man-in-charge. Even his closest colleagues call him 'Mr President'. The media also picked up on the unofficial title and had been calling him 'The President of the underworld'. Edmund wasn't too sure about that one. It made him sound like the head of some mafia gang. He had many important things to do. The running of the under ground cities was a full time job. Not only were there the normal things like; preventing crime, conserving life and peoples health, education, resource (people needed food and fuel to burn) and many other things. But there were also new problems. The biggest of which is air. Water wasn't a problem, there was a large, natural spring and an underground stream that flowed through and kept the spring alive with fresh clean water. This also helped to bring in a little oxygen and kept the giant caves fresh. However, with so many people, vehicular activity and a huge mechanical and industrial economy, air was being used a lot faster then the spring could supply. So air ducts were drilled into the mountainsides to let air in. This, of coarse, created the biggest problem of them all. The whole reason they were under there in the first place.

Nuclear fallout.

And so, all water and air coming into the caves had to pass through huge purifying systems, and it was Edmunds job to make sure his men were keeping them in good working order. If even the smallest amount of radiation got in it would kill hundreds of people. The caves could protect them from the war raging outside, but it created another problem. If anything happened on a large scale down here, you couldn't escape. You can't evacuate the cities. You can't move people to a safe area. You couldn't go anywhere, because there was nowhere to run to.

Ultimately, they were trapped.

So when Edmund had to do tedious, mundane and pointlessly boring tasks, it really grated on his nerves. Take now for example. Right now he was on his way to meet some unimportant adolescent who was taking up his time because he was in hospital. Lots of people were in hospital. Being under ground meant that fungal infections and fungal based ailments were becoming a common occurrence. So what made this kid any different?

Well, too late to go back now. He had arrived.

As with all the underground buildings, the hospital was a monolithic structure made by hollowing out the surrounding rock to form individual rooms and areas. In fact, the entire underground was made in this fashion. The rock had been cut, chiselled and polished. Everywhere you looked, polished stone would reflect your image. Edmund kind of liked the look, but it wasn't like that for aesthetic purposes. The smooth surfaces were easy to keep clean and reflected light, helping to keep the cities illuminated.

Edmund entered and was greeted by the usual mob of media and paparazzi. One of the reporters was asking about some incident that happened a few days ago. Typical! He was there to see some kid and they were asking questions that were completely unrelated. Why should he care about some man who was strangled to death three days ago? The murderer had been caught. Actually, she confessed right away and gave herself up. She was probably working the west wall right now, with all the other convicts. Besides, he was here to see the kid. Not that he cared much about him either. But he couldn't let the mob know that.

The dean of the hospital approached, announced himself and warmly shook Edmund by the hand. Then, finally away from the media, he was led to the kid's room. A few reporters were waiting for him, but these were the more upper class televisual type. The dean made a quick speech then opened the door to the kids room. They all walked in. A small but stocky looking boy was laying in the bed. He was black, but illness had made him pale. His eyes were slightly bloodshot and his fingernails were yellow.

"Mr President." The dean started. "I would like to introduce patient zero. The first ever person in M-Tron history to have an incurable genetic defect. Well, the first to be born with one that is."

"Fascinating. What is the boy's name?" Edmund asked.

"Zachariah Man." Edmund frowned. Now, why was that last name familiar? He thought to himself.

Chapter eighteen

It was a Double Pod. This was good. A Double Pod was essentially two Octopods connected together with a multi-purpose bay between them. This bay could be used to house either a tank, two terrain buggies or a host of infantry. Conrad liked them when they had infantry. Because the bays were not sealed, the Double Pod (or transport vehicle as the IC named them) couldn't fly above 12,000 feet or the soldiers would run out of air and suffocate. They also couldn't reach top speed which made them an easy target. The IC had been using them for years and Black Tron still swear by them. They used to call them 'The Rolling Death' because of their slow speed in to battle. Of coarse, once relinquished of their load, they could return home with their turbo boosters in less then half the time.

However, Conrad's fondest memory of 'The Rolling Death' was just after M-Tron built the Armed Unit Carrier (AUC). The first time an AUC got in to a fire fight was only four months after their launch. It had been on its own and managed to get surrounded by six Double Pods. Remarkably, the AUC had barely been scratched. The Pods however had been totally annihilated, including nine of the escape vessels that gave the ships their name. Pods. The pods were made from reinforced, double strengthened Plexiglas. Unfortunately, due to the process to make this stuff, they could only produce flat sheets. So the pods were built in a three dimensional octagon shape. Hence, Octopod.

As the huge ship lowered before his eyes, he readied himself for what was to come. Aaron was waiting round the right of the building. Conrad had done his usual disappearing act. The ship landed and the cargo bay opened wide, like a huge beast yawning. Then, strangely, both the pods opened. Barry thought this was bad military training. Then he remembered. The soldiers thought the war was over. No need to be cautious. The Black Tron soldiers started to board. As they did, they would stow their weapons in a specially built unit at the side of the cargo bay. Barry pretended to be organising the boarding. This was so he would still have his weapon after the others had relinquished theirs. Four of the soldiers had been busy attaching the cage to the back of the cargo bay. Then they too proceeded to board. As the last soldier stowed his gun, Barry raised his and smiled. Danius was about to speak, a look of confusion on his face, when they all heard the gun fire. Aaron had shot the gunner who had been sitting in the left hand pod. The pilot sitting in the right hand pod had reached for his sidearm, but Conrad had appeared from nowhere and killed the man. Aaron ran to the cargo bay and helped Barry to cover the Black Tron soldiers. Danius's hand twitched. A second after and they heard a scream of pain from the rear of the ship. Danius had been the key holder and had activated the execution device in the cage. The scream stopped suddenly. The silence was deafening. A few moments later and Conrad appeared, cleaning his sword. He had a solemn look on his face. Barry knew what he had done. Conrad had killed Doctor Edward Julius. He hadn't wanted to, but the chemical that had been injected in to the Doctor would have killed him slowly and painfully. There was nothing that could have been done. Conrad had spared his suffering.

Aaron and Barry herded the soldiers back off the ship and had them kneel on the ground with their hands on their heads; fingers interlocked and ankles crossed. Conrad was still cleaning his sword, despite it already being clean.

"Did you identify the key holder?" He asked no one

in particular.

"Sergeant Danius here." Barry answered whilst nodding towards the man in question. Aaron helped the man to his feet with a swift kick in the side. He pushed him forward a couple of paces.

"I should have known." Danius muttered. "My father always said the Clone can not be killed. And here you stand before me." At hearing this, the other soldiers suddenly recognised Conrad and started whimpering. All except one. The soldier who had said he was from Sydney, Australia.

"How do we know for sure he is the Clone?" He asked. "A great leader would not allow his beard to grow so. Or his hair so unkempt." Conrad shot the man a glare. He turned away instantly. Some of the other soldiers started wondering if he was the Clone.

"What do you want with the Doctor?" Conrad asked the Sergeant.

"I'll never tell." He answered.

"Some guy called Jacques ordered them to fetch him. Moon signed the order." Barry revealed.

"Jacques?" Conrad asked, a hint of recognition in his voice.

"Yeah." Barry confirmed. "D' you know him?" Conrad didn't answer.

"Who is Jacques?" He asked the Sergeant instead.

"You won't get a thing from me." Quick as a flash, Conrad swung his sword. In one swift motion he had cut the man in quarters.

"Who's next in command?" He asked. Aaron located the Corporal. It was the so-called New Australian. As soon as the man was on his feet, Conrad stood toe to toe with him.

"It's hard to shave and get a haircut when you're constantly on the run." Conrad said. Then he just stood there, glaring at the man. Twenty eight seconds later

180

and the man cracked up.

"Please! Don't kill me!" He sobbed. "We don't know who Jacques is. No one does. All we know is, every now and then, we have to do things for Jacques. I don't even think we're supposed to know about him, but someone overheard President Moon talking about him. Now we all know the name, but not the person. Please! I'm telling the truth!"

"What do you want with the Doctor?" Conrad asked.

"President Moon is doing something in secret. We don't know what, but he and this Jacques person are collecting all these mechanics and engineers. In fact, anyone who has advanced knowledge in robotics and microchip technology." Conrad started pacing. Barry recognised this as his way of thinking.

"Robotics. Suits like our HC suits?" Barry offered.

"And computers." Aaron piped. "Maybe they got the same idea as your father, like Ace."

"AICS." Conrad corrected. "A, I, C, S."

"Sounds like ace to me, but with an accent." Aaron muttered.

"Or a fucking army." Barry said, ignoring the previous exchange.

"That's what I was thinking." Conrad said back. "An army of robots. But men are better. Even Moon knows that. No matter the technology, you still need a humans way of thinking. Machines are too logical and do things by numbers and percentages. Sometimes you need a bit of creative thinking."

"Like AICS." Aaron offered, pronouncing the abbreviation correctly.

"They can't do that." Conrad replied. "You've seen how big she is. You would need a robot one hundred feet tall to fit that in its body. Unless you had a central brain that didn't go anywhere, that could control all the robots simultaneously. No. That's ridiculous. Even AICS can't do that."

"Robot army it is then." Aaron retorted. Barry shook his head.

"No. We already ruled it out."

"No we didn't." Conrad said. Aaron and Barry looked at him, waiting for an explanation. "We ruled out everything else, but not robots. It's not very practical, and I can't see why they would do it, but we didn't rule it out. An army? Maybe. Workers would make more sense, but still an odd thing to do. Besides, why keep it a secret if they were building work droids."

"And why advanced micro-chips." Aaron asked rhetorically.

"But robots were used in war once before." Barry argued. "They thought they would be brilliant. They thought they had perfected AI technology, but the automatons were crap. America nearly lost that war because of that." Conrad was nodding. He remembered doing a history lesson on it. The cold war had re-sparked in the late twenty second century. The word 'robot', although still widely used, was an outdated word. They had called their metal soldiers 'automatons' instead. The Russian automatons were weak, but could take a lot of damage before they would stop working. The American counterparts were much stronger and very powerful. It took a lot to damage them. Unfortunately, due to their tight tolerances, it only took the slightest damage to render them almost useless. But both sides had problems with keeping in contact with their machines. Every now and then they would stray from their programmed route and start firing on random targets. Sometimes those targets were on their side. Some had randomly decided that a harmless tree was an enemy. Some had even walked (or rode, if they were the tracked version) right past their intended target and it had taken the operators hours to get the thing back on track. No mater how much technology was put in those things, as soon as you took away the human and left them to get on with the job, they would go wrong. All the tech and AI programming in the world, and ultimately, they were crap!

"Still." Said Conrad. "It's the only answer that has any plausibility. Anyway, what do we care? The war is over right." This last statement had Barry and Aaron staring at each other in surprise. Conrad put his sword away and retrieved his Glock from its holster. He shot the New Australian and turned to the other prisoners.

"Anyone got something useful for me?" He asked them. The soldiers looked panic stricken as they searched their memories for some info that might save their lives.

"Jason Moon has the only full sized army left in the Independent Countries. The rest are only a mix of soldiers made up from what's left of the IC armies." One man burst out. Conrad shot him.

"Something I don't know would be good."

"There's something strange about Jason Moon." Another called out.

"I know that. He wants to take over the world. Did you not hear what I said?" Conrad pointed his gun at the man.

"No! Something else!" The soldier pleaded. Conrad took his finger off the trigger, but kept the gun in the soldiers direction.

"What then?" He said.

"According to our database, Jason Moon is eighty six years old, but he doesn't look a day over forty." Conrad's finger twitched. "We thought it was plastic surgery as his expressions don't change. But I heard from a senior officer that he was shot once and his face went funny. He couldn't explain how it went funny, but it wasn't natural. It only lasted a fraction of a second, and after... it was though nothing had happened. No blood. No mark. No nothing." Conrad lowered his gun to his side. He was thinking.

"You got an idea?" Barry asked. Conrad shook his head.

"No B Man. Just a theory. Let me think on it for a bit. But for the mean time, lets get ready to leave. Aaron, can you locate the tracking device on this ship?" Aaron nodded.

"But if I remove it, we won't be able to see the enemy."

"I know." Conrad answered. "But I don't want them to know where we are going." Aaron saluted. "Barry. Tie these mongrels up and man the gunners chair." Barry did as was asked.

Once the soldiers were tied and the ships location device removed, Conrad gathered the two men and spoke to them out of ear shot.

"We need some breathing apparatus and helms. Any ideas?"

"We can look in the hospital here. They may have some from other wounded soldiers." Aaron offered. "Why?"

"We are going to enter a heavy rad zone." Conrad answered. Rad was short for radiated. All the soldiers had taken medication that would allow them to enter radiated zones, but only light radiation. The medication had made the men very sick, but they were glad to have had it. They all knew what even a small dose of radiation could do to a man. Sometimes they had wandered in to medium level radiated zones. As long as they didn't stay too long, the medication would protect them. But heavy rad zones were avoided at all costs. Their military issued clothing could protect their skin from burns, but they would still breath it in. Oxygen

184

tanks and a helmet was needed to traverse these areas. And even so, only at your own risk.

Conrad's clothing was adequate enough for the job, and so was Aaron's. Barry however was wearing a short sleeved t-shirt. All the soldiers carried gloves in their pockets, but this wouldn't protect Barry's arms. Luckily, Aaron had thought about this and had returned with three helmets, three twin O2 tanks, and a rad protective shirt for Barry. Even though they were wearing some civilian style clothing, everything they wore hade a special lining in them to protect from radiation burns. They may not like military issue clothing, but they weren't stupid.

Once boarded, Conrad started the engine and they took off. The soldiers were being looked after by what staff had survived from the attack on the hospital. Well, if they ignored them beating the shit out of the soldiers, they were being looked after. Barry was in the gunners pod. He was keeping a close eye on the sky. Without the locating device, he had to use his own sight to spot the enemy. Thankfully, they were flying deeper in to M-Tron territory.

Chapter nineteen

"I think, perhaps…" Hmm. Should he use the word 'perhaps'? It was a difficult speech, and he had only just started. The media had kicked up a fuss about that woman who had strangled her boyfriend to death. They were all too happy to see her locked behind bars. But now that they know her nine year old son was dying from an unknown genetic disease, they all felt sorry for her. They want him to free her, saying it was a crime of passion, or some such nonsense. Edmund was sick with the whole thing. He had often toyed with the idea of just giving up his position and handing it to someone else. It wasn't as though he was in it for the money. This was M-Tron. They haven't used money for almost a thousand years now. Status was gained through your name or your deeds, not from the size of your bank account.

Edmund sighed.

He had to make a speech to stay in favour with the people. Even if that meant annoying the committee members. And he knew this would. But it was the people who gave him his status, and the people who could take it away from him. Not the committee.

"Ladies and gentlemen." He paused. Then he scribbled something down on his paper and started again.

"Members of the committee. I think…" Again with the scribbling.

"Ladies and gentlemen of the committee. I think…" The time has come for… The people have spoken… What does he say!?! Edmund scrunched his fists and gave a quiet cry of despair. This was getting him nowhere.

He was about to start writing again when a flushed

faced man barged in to his office. Edmund assumed the man had run a long way to reach him.

"Yes?" Edmund asked quizzically. "What's the meaning of this?" The man stepped forward.

"I've come from the watch room. We checked and double checked, but there's no mistake." The man paused to catch his breath.

"What the hell are you talking about? Spit it out man!"

"We are tracking a ship on the scanner. It isn't giving out a signal, so we didn't know whether it was friendly or not. We kept an eye on it as it seemed to be heading directly for us." Edmund was getting inpatient.

"What is it?! For the love of M-Tron! Speak up man!"

"It had no signal, was giving out no identification, and wasn't answering his radio. So we had to use the scope for a better look." Edmund slammed his fist on the table. The puffed man jumped.

"If you don't…"

"It's an IC transport vehicle." Edmund sat, his eyes open wide.

"What flag is it wearing?" Then to the mans puzzled expression, "What markings are painted on it?! Who's bloody ship is it?! Russian? Iraqi? Kurdistan? Japan? BLOODY WHO?!" The man seemed reluctant to speak.

"Black Tron." He said simply.

Edmund's face paled.

***

He hated surgery. Ever since that damn Utopian soldier shot him out of the sky, he had been having surgery. It grated on him. The chemicals they used to harden his body and strengthen his muscles would eventually kill him. Or send him mad. He wasn't sure which would come first.

After seeing Jason Moon the night before, he was secretly wondering if perhaps his master had gone mad. He was obsessed with finding the Manké clone. He knew why. Only nine people knew Jason's secret. Of which, only he was left. Only a short time ago there had been three. Chou Lou had been one, but Jason had had him killed after he failed to capture the clone. Actually, to be fair, Lou had captured him. But for some inexplicable reason had let him go after he nearly killed him. Spree wasn't sure if Jason had killed him for letting the clone go, or for nearly killing him.

The other man was General Gapul, an Indian man who often ran errands for Jason and Jacques. Jason had shot him down in a fit of rage. Spree could almost understand. He would have been angry too if his dreams of world domination were snatched from him like that. But Jason had been furious when he learnt that the clone had allowed the IC members to take back their lands. But when Jason learnt that he could take his precious Black Tron back, he suddenly fell quiet and has spent the rest of the week sitting in his office, rocking back and forth. He had been mumbling to himself, and refused to acknowledge anyone. All the IC leaders had reclaimed their lands, but when Spree had told him that some of the IC leaders hadn't rejoined Black Tron, Jason had started whimpering.

Spree was almost back to his fighting self again and was waiting for another shot of liquid steroids. He was looking at his scars and admiring how quickly they had been vanishing, when the man himself had entered the room. Spree was speechless. Why would Jason come to see him?

Jason seemed to be happy. Although it was hard to tell with his lack of proper expressions. He sat on the bed uncomfortably close to Spree.

"I see your wounds have healed nicely. You look

much better then you had the last few times we met." Jason said in his old mannerism. Spree was unsure what to say.

"Yes sir. Thank you sir."

"Oh, you don't have to 'sir' me. We are old buddies you and I. You are the only man alive that knows my little secret."

"Yes sir. I mean, Mr Moon, Jason, sir." Jason leaned closer.

"We are friends aren't we?" He asked. Spree didn't know how to answer.

"Of coarse sir, Jason, sir." He finally managed.

"I know Jacques can depend on you, can't he."

"Yes sir."

"So tell me, my friend. Why would you kill every leader of the Independent Countries, steal their lands, and then just… hand it back?" Spree thought about this.

"Amnesty, sir."

"Explain this." Was Jason's immediate reply.

"As President over all the lands, he would have amnesty. Many would adhere to that and will refuse to attack him."

"But if he gives back the lands, he loses his amnesty."

"True, but if he had done so in good faith, he may have made some new allies."

"Allies? Do you think he was trying to make allies of us by giving us our land back?"

"No sir." Jason tilts his head to one side.

"Call me Jason, Spree."

"Sorry sir. Jason. In my opinion, I think he did it to piss you off." Jason's head snapped back to an upright position.

"Do go on." He said.

"Conrad was being methodical. He has gained control of his own country. This gives him power and control he previously lacked. Killing the leaders of the IC countries caused chaos and fear in those lands. Those who stepped up to take their leaders place were thrown awry by being given the choice to take back their lands. They are still in turmoil because of it. The lands are divided, their people unsure as to what to do. And because all this is a result of Conrad's doing, his name has spread more fear and has made the problem multiply. He has done this for you."

"For me?" Jason asked.

"You are the leader he wants the most. The one who got away. You are the Kahn. He isn't interested in the IC. He wants to bring down the Kahn and annihilate Black Tron."

"You know old friend. I think you may be right. This has caused me many problems. It has tied my hands.

"But I think this is only the beginning. Conrad has an ace up his sleeve and he's itching to use it. He has a plan.

"I want the entire Black Tron army deployed! He must be found by all means!"

"Yes Jason." Jason stands and takes a couple of steps towards the exit. He then turned to face Spree again.

"And Spree."

"Jason?"

"What happened to tomorrow?"

"Sir?"

"After your… unfortunate accident, you told me you would have Conrad in my office by tomorrow. Tomorrow has come and gone." Spree got the point.

"I'm sorry sir. I have no excuse."

"My name is J-Jason remember."

"Yes Jason."

"If you happen to get Conrad in your sights again, -"

"Bring him to you. I remember." Jason was shaking his head.

"That man has stolen three Octopods and a transport vehicle. He has destroyed three other pods, and he stole my victory. All that without an army. That man has pissed me off for the last time. So if you happen to get him in your sights again…

"Kill the mother fucker!"

***

"They have landed outside the main entrance sir." A soldier informed him.

"Can they get in?" Edmund asked.

"Not likely sir. These doors are made from the same skin as an AUC. It would take an atomic explosion just to dent these doors." Answered a Lieutenant.

"So they can't get in?"

"We're perfectly safe sir."

"Good. I don't want a fight on our hands. They aren't ready yet." A worried looking soldier stepped forward and saluted.

"What is it private?" The soldier asked.

"The outer door has just opened sir. They're in the air-lock."

"That's impossible!" Edmund snapped. "They need the right pass code and an M-Tron clearance!"

"Air-lock sealed and de-contamination in progress sir." Another soldier called out.

"But that's impossible!" Edmund repeated.

"De-con complete sir. We have visitors." The lieutenant went in to battle mode.

"Guns to the ready! Cover the door! Protect Mr McKay! Do not fire until I give the order! Are we clear?" Seven soldiers all replied at the same time.

"Sir, yes sir!" The inner doors to the air-lock slowly slid open. Three men stepped forward.

"Identify yourselves!" The lieutenant ordered. The

191

three men slowly removed their helmets. The first to do so stepped forward and announced himself.

"I am Sergeant Aaron Hammond of Bravo force. M-Tron special forces." As he finished speaking, the big man had removed his helmet and had stepped beside the first man.

"I am Sergeant Barry Man of Delta force. M-Tron special stealth force." The soldiers had hesitated at the first mans words. The second mans words had them lowering their weapons. The third man had removed his helmet and had stepped beside his comrades.

"Do I really need to tell you who I am?" Conrad asked. "Or can you work it out for yourself?" The lieutenant gasped.

"It can't be. You're dead." He said.

"I take it I do then. Fair enough. I'm the man formally known as Sergeant Major Conrad Manké, but if you had taken the trouble of checking your database, you would know I've had a slight promotion." The soldiers had all lowered their weapons and were staring in awe at the three soldiers.

"What promotion?" Asked Edmund, squeezing past the soldiers guarding him. "What is your rank now?" Conrad smiled.

"In military terms, I am now a Commanding General. But you can call me Mr President."

Edmund fainted.

Chapter twenty

Edmund was sitting in his office. He had a headache and was trying to digest what he had been told. Conrad had given him a full report of what had happened. Edmund was reeling from it all. He had the son of the most famous General ever to have lived sitting in his office. A man who was as famous as his father. And he was also the M-Tron President.

"Edmund McKay." Conrad said. "Wasn't your uncle Kevin McKay originally given your job?"

"Hmm? Oh yes." Edmund said, snapping himself back to reality. "But the pressure got to him and he handed the task to me." Conrad was looking around the room. He then stopped and seemed to be staring at something.

"Mr President." Conrad said.

"Oh! Sorry Mr President. Of coarse, you're quite right. I'm forgetting my manners." Conrad eyed him from the corner of his eye.

"I meant you." He said. Edmund looked confused.

"Me? What do you mean, Mr President?" Conrad pointed to a newspaper article that had been framed and hung on Edmund's office wall. "Oh! That! Well... I can't control the media I fear, Mr President."

"The soldiers call you Mr McKay, and your staff call you Edmund. I thought your actual title was that of Curator. Not President of the underworld." Conrad said. Edmund was feeling a little hot under the collar. He hoped he hadn't offended the President. He didn't expect to have the real M-Tron President sitting in his office.

"Well, yes Mr President. It's just, that title usually means a keeper of a museum. The media thought it sounded like we were referring to the people as old artefacts." Edmund gave a nervous laugh at what he

193

thought was a funny anecdote. Conrad didn't laugh.

"A Curator is a keeper or *custodian* of a museum or other *collection*."

"Exactly Mr President. They chose the wrong title." Conrad was looking him in the eyes and shaking his head.

"No. The title is correct. You are the custodian of the M-Tron collective. Hence; Curator."

"Oh. I hadn't thought of it like that. You're right Mr President. It was the right title after all."

"One other thing." Edmund was feeling hotter.

"Yes Mr President?"

"Stop calling me Mr President. I'm only borrowing the title until the people choose a new candidate. Until then, just call me Conrad. Or Sergeant Major if you must."

"Yes, um, Conrad."

"I also want you to second something for me. As Curator you are automatically the Presidents right-hand man."

"Of coarse Mr- er, Conrad."

***

Conrad was walking down a street. Well, the people referred to them as streets, but they were in fact huge tunnels. Barry and Aaron had already been shown their apartments and had now gone to find a local bar for some well earned food and drink. Conrad was on his way to find them. He wanted to give them some good news and also join them for some decent food. Well, I say 'decent' food, but raising livestock in a cave isn't an easy thing to do. So most of the food was either, reconstituted meat heavily mixed with soya and drenched in beef stock, or was all soya and been curd. Apparently, the beer was excellent though.

Conrad was just passing a fruit and veg stall. Unfortunately, due to lack of sunlight, the fruit and veg was small and hard, but they still tasted the same. Actually, Conrad marvelled at their ability to grow vegetation at all. Yet they had this in abundance. Mushrooms were also widely found, including other fungi and mould related substances. This, Conrad wasn't surprised at.

He spotted the bar and turned to head in that direction. As he did, he noticed a crowd of people at the very edge of his vision. He stopped and turned to them. They were looking at him with awe and fear. He ran his fingers over his freshly shaven chin. It felt good to be washed and clean again. That bath and shower were a long time in coming. His hair had been cut back to its usual length. He had shaved but left a tuft of hair under his bottom lip. If he had to look like his dad, he thought he should at least update the image slightly.

One of the people stepped forward.

"Is it true? Are you really him?" The young woman asked.

"That would depend on who *He* is." The woman stepped closer.

"Conrad Manké? The saviour of M-Tron?" Conrad almost grimaced. He hated that title. It was his fathers fault. Conrad had thought it an idiotic idea when he was a child, and thought no better of it now.

"Well, I don't know about the saviour part, but I am Conrad Manké, son of the late General Conrad Jacques Manké." The people started talking all at once. A tiny image appeared in his eye. He had seen it before. He assumed it was a digital representation of his robotic arm. A flashing red dot on the back of the images hand, he assumed, meant that his hand was in contact with something. Or in this case, something was touching his hand. He looked down and saw a tiny child. She was indeed touching the back of his hand as the image suggested.

"Hello." Conrad said. The little girl looked up and smiled.

"What happened to your hand?" She asked. Conrad pulled up his sleeve to show her the rest of his arm.

"A very bad man took my arm off. A very nice man gave me this metal one so I could still fight in the war."

"Oh." said the little girl. "Did he hurt your eye as well?"

"Yeah. Well, I think it was him. I'm not sure, as I was kind of asleep at the time." The little girls bottom lip dropped and she immediately wrapped her arms around his legs. She buried her head in to his thigh and said, "Please not be hurt. I make you better. I love you Conrad, 'cos you make all the bad men go away. Daddy said we can see the sun when you come back." Conrad felt a lump in his throat.

"You can't go see the sun yet." He told the child. A man behind him suddenly shouted in anger.

"What do you mean?! You were supposed to free us! We've been trapped in these caves for over eight years!"

"Nine years!" Another shouted. "But he's right! We want out! And you're supposed to get us out! "

"We've had no communications from the outside world!" Came yet another. "Why can't we leave yet? Why!?" Conrad lifted the little girl and held her in his arms. He turned to face the crowd, who were rapidly turning in to a mob.

"I have returned to collect some things." He called out for all to hear. "The war is not over yet. I have one more battle to commence. But only one. We are in the strongest position ever. We can not lose now. It has taken all this time to be ready for what is to come. Listen to me now! My father once made a speech about how he was a child when the war started. How the war continued with his children, and how it will continue

196

with yours. He told us how our children were our future. Now, I have no children of my own, but I still share his passion." He looked in to the girls eyes. "Look at this child. So young. So innocent. Do you want her to grow up in a world of war?"

"NO!" The crowd cried.

"AND NEITHER DO I!" He yelled back. "I have returned, not to free *you*!" He said, pointing to the adults. "But to free *her*!" This time he indicated the child. "And those like her! You are already children of this war! But she doesn't have to be! And I will make sure of it! I am here to free your children, so they do not grow in fear! So they can have a life! I have returned to take what I need to END this war ONCE AND FOR ALL!" The peopled cheered at that bit. Not loudly, but a cheer all the same. "I have already destroyed the IC armies." Again, a cheer. "I have killed their leaders." The cheer was more felt this time. "I have created CHAOS in their lands." The cheer was much stronger. "The only thing that stands in my way now, is Black Tron itself. But after what I have done to them, I guarantee, Black Tron are quaking in their boots at the thought of another attack from me!" The cheer was almost a roar. "Of coarse, they think we are only a few men. Wait until they see what YOU have been building for them! When they see us marching over that hill, they will CURSE the day I was born, and I will leave NO BLACK TRON ALIVE!!" The roar was deafening. Conrad could have sworn it sounded like there were more people then he could see. Maybe it was the acoustics in the cave. But when he turned, he saw thousands more people had gathered behind him. They were cheering and clapping. They were calling out things like, 'We never doubted you', 'M-Tron forever', 'Long live Conrad Manké' and 'Bless the General'. Conrad located the child's mother and handed her over. Actually, it was the girl who spotted her mother and had called out to her, saying, 'Look-e mummy. I founded lovely Conrad. He my friend now'. The mother had taken her daughter and planted a kiss on Conrad's cheek. Conrad was once more glad at having a shave.

He found Barry and Aaron in the bar and went to join them. A huge, bald headed man stood and saluted.

"Sergeant Barry Man, finally back to his old self, and ready to get pissed sir." He said. Conrad shook his friends hand and smiled. Aaron made a mock salute and pointed out his own personal grooming.

"I'm sexy again too. And already rat-arsed." Conrad placed a wooden box next to Aarons drink. "What's that?" Aaron asked.

"You know I said I'd make you a captain?" Aaron's face dropped.

"You haven't?" He said.

"No." Conrad answered him. "I haven't." Aaron looked relieved. He opened the box at the same time as taking a swig from his pint. Then all of a sudden he coughed, half choked and spat the golden liquid back out, almost getting Conrad.

"You bastard! That's worse!" Barry was frowning.

"What is it?" He asked. Aaron held up a hand full of black, diamond shaped pins. These are known as 'pips' in the military, and are usually silver. Barry counted them and halved the number (The pips go on both shoulders and you identify rank by how many are on one shoulder, not both).

"Bloody hell!" Barry exclaimed. "If I'm counting right, you just made him a Sergeant Major."

"Your counting is as good as mine then. That's what I made it." Conrad offered Aaron his hand.

"Well done Sergeant Major Hammond. The MSA is yours." Aaron dropped the pips back in to the box.

"Mine? But the MSA was always yours. You commanded them. You created Delta from them. I can't take it from you."

"You haven't got a choice. I've made my decision. The MSA is yours. A 'thank you' wouldn't go amiss right now." Aaron stared at the pips a moment longer. Then he stood and saluted Conrad. He took his hand and shook it.

"Thank you Commander. Thank you my friend. I won't let you down, I promise." Aaron seemed touched by this.

"I know you won't. You never have." Then Conrad turned to Barry. "I've got a box for you too." Barry took the box as it was offered to him. He opened it and found six silver crown shaped pips and a set of brown shoulder tassels. Barry didn't need to count the crowns (crown shaped pips are always referred to as crowns), The brown material was all he needed to know what rank he had been given. The tassels only came in three colours. Yellow, for a Commander General, issued by the President. If the President held an officers rank in the army, he could take the rank of Commander General himself, and would wear red tassels. And finally, brown. Brown meant; General.

General?

Barry sat down.

"I think I need a drink." He said flatly.

"You got one." Aaron told him, pointing to his beer.

"I think I need something stronger." Barry said and showed him the brown material. Aaron looked at it for a moment. Then he turned, caught the attention of a waitress and ordered two pints of vodka. Conrad almost smiled. Especially when the waitress approached and questioned the word 'pint'. Conrad ordered a measure of whisky and the waitress went to fetch their drinks.

"Have you guys eaten?" He asked them. They were

still staring at their new ranks. Slowly, they nodded in unison.

"Well, I'm starving. What's the most meatiest food they do? And when I say meatiest, I mean, what do they serve that has the greater mix of real meat in it?" The men point at their plates. There was a little bit of salad on them.

"Please tell me you had something else on those plates besides salad. Aaron looked up and smiled.

"Yeah. Been curd. Seems meat is becoming a scarce commodity. You want meat, you need to go to a top notch restaurant."

"And even that's mostly soya." Barry added.

"Never mind. Plenty of rats around. Could always kill a few and have a proper burger." Aaron said, his smile getting wider.

"Funny. Look. Don't get too drunk. I have something I need to…" Conrad was staring towards the entrance with his mouth open. Aaron looked behind himself to see what had made Conrad stop talking. All he could see was people. A couple of guys getting lairy, a couple making out and a woman crying and searching for something. He turned back to Conrad.

"What is it?" He asked. Conrad didn't answer. Instead, he turned to Barry.

"Hey, B Man. Sorry. General B Man." Barry looked up. "That's a pretty cool promotion you just got. You should tell your wife. I bet she'd be over the moon to hear her man is now a General." Barry scowled at him.

"Sure. I'll tell her. If I could ever find her. I don't know if you've noticed, but it's a bloody big place this."

"True. Two miles wide. One mile deep. Three levels high. How are you going to find your wife in all this? There's three and a half billion people here. That's about one point three billion people on each level. All moving about, changing places, running around in their little cars and-"

"Thank you manky boy!" Barry growled at him. "I already know how hard it'll be to find her. Why don't you tell me something I don't know!" Manky boy was an unpleasant nickname the others had called Conrad at school. Conrad let it slide.

"Hmm... Something you don't know. Tatiana Man is five foot four with long mousey brown hair. She has blue eyes and chocolate skin. She is slim built and is currently wearing a red dress with a black cardigan thing. Oh, and black shoes." Barry slammed his fist on the table.

"I said, something I don't... How do you know what she is wearing?"

"She's standing about four and a half feet at your seven o'clock." Conrad answered immediately. Seven o'clock was over Barry's left shoulder, behind him. He turned around and started scanning the room.

Their eyes met.

He stood.

She ran and threw herself at him. He caught her easily and wrapped his arms around her.

"Oh, the crying woman." Aaron stated.

"I knew you were still alive. I knew it. No one would believe me, but I knew it." She said.

"I thought I would never see you again." Barry almost cried back. "I thought about you all the time." She pushed herself back a little and looked in to his eyes.

"Oh Barry. There's something you need to know. We have a son."

"What?!" Barry cried out. "When? How? Oh my god!" He pulled her close again and hugged her with renewed vigour. "I have a son! That's the most wonderful news I have ever heard. Conrad, Aaron, I have a son. I'm a father."

"Way to go B Man!" Aaron cheered. Tatiana pushed herself back again.

"No, listen. It's bad news."

"What could be bad about having a son? Conrad won't tell me off you know. Besides, he's known for... Actually, how long have you known for?" But before Conrad could answer, Tatiana cried,

"He's dying!"

Chapter twenty one

They were running through the tunnels. Three men, one woman. Hearts pounding. This was why he hated his men to have family. He was a great leader, but he hated giving bad news. He was a hard, ruthless man. He was a leader in every sense of the word. But even with his current madness, one thing about him would never change. He loved his men like brothers. It hurt him greatly to see them in pain.

They were met by Curator Edmund at the entrance to the hospital.

"I came as soon as I could. I'm such an idiot! I should have made the connection. Follow me. He's been moved to ECU." They followed Edmund through the winding maze of the hospital. The Emergency Care Unit was awash with activity. Guards had been placed at the door to stop the media's constant presence. The ECU was built mostly for radiation burn victims, and hadn't been used for a while. The boy was their only patient in this wing, and he had the doctors milling around like a horde of ants.

Edmund explained that the media had become an annoyance ever since they discovered Zach's predicament. Barry strode over to his son like a charging bull. The doctors quickly, and quite rightly, got out of his way. He took his sons hand and looked down upon him. Zach opened his eyes slowly and looked up at his father for the first time ever.

"Dad?" Came Zach's weak voice.

"Hello son. It's nice to finally meet you." A tear formed in the big man's eye.

"I knew you would come." Zach said. Conrad stepped up on the other side of the bed. Zach looked over at him and gasped.

"Hello Zach. I take it you know who I am."

"You're Conrad Manké." Zach replied. "What happened to your eye? You look in worse shape than me." Barry laughed.

"Well you're definitely my son. On your deathbed and still making jokes." Zach smiled weakly at this.

"Come now B Man. Deathbed? You make it sound like he's dying." Conrad said.

"I am." Was Zach's reply. Conrad shook his head.

"Not on my watch you're not." Conrad rounded on the closest doctor and pinned him with a look. "Report. I want to know everything you do about this boy's condition." The doctor started rummaging through his paperwork.

"It's some kind of genetic defect. I'm afraid there is little we know about it. His systems seem to be over loading, then shutting down. It's as though his body is trying to work harder and faster then it's supposed to. Unfortunately, his organs aren't made for that, so they just keep burning themselves out and switching off. We keep trying to fix the symptoms. Every time we fix one thing, another organ fails. Then after a while, the first organ fails again. We are running around in circles constantly restarting organs. His organs are getting weaker and weaker. This causes them to shut down faster. It won't be long before we won't be able to restart them.

"The biggest problem though, is we don't know what is causing this." Conrad cocked his head to one side in thought. He turned back to Zach.

"Squeeze my hand." He told him, and offered his left hand. Zach took it and squeezed. "Harder." Conrad ordered. Zach did as told.

"What's that going to prove?" Aaron asked.

"Give him your hand." Conrad told Aaron. Aaron complied, and Zach squeezed his hand.

"Whoa!" Aaron exclaimed. "That's an impressive

204

grip for an ill boy."

"Exactly." Conrad said. "If he was well, he would have crushed the bones in your hand."

"But I don't get it. How could that be?" Aaron asked.

"I bet he gets it from his father. And his father got it from genetic manipulation." Conrad turned back to the doctor. "I need a computer." He told him. The doctor motioned for them to follow. Tatiana stayed with her son.

With a computer in front of him, Conrad uses his Presidential code to access the militaries secret files. No one knew what he was looking for, but he seemed to be getting annoyed at not being able to find it. Barry was getting impatient, and decided to interrupt him.

"What are you looking for Conrad?" He asked.

"I'm looking for your file. What did they call the project that created you?"

"Me? What do you want that file for?" Barry asked.

"Because whatever is happening to your son, is a result of having you for a father. Whatever they did to create you, is affecting your son."

"How do you figure that one?" Aaron asked.

"Easy. Zach's condition is genetic. Genetic conditions are contracted through your parents. Hereditarily. When a woman becomes pregnant, the fetus is injected with GM to stop the baby being born with defects. The only way Zach could have a genetic defect, and the GM added at birth would miss it, would be if the defect was man made. If the defect is man made, then so is one of the parents. And that would be you, Barry." Conrad frantically tapped at the keyboard. "What was the name of that damn project?!"

"Hercules." Barry said flatly.

"Hercules! Of coarse it was." Conrad typed it in. A list of names ran up the screen. Conrad selected the only name to be marked 'Active'. That, of coarse, was Barry Man. The doctor had become very interested in the screen and seemed to be getting closer by the second.

"What was the project?" He asked.

"Super soldiers. The oldest project in the book, and even now we try to make it work." Conrad looked up at the doctor. "Take this seat doctor, and read through this file. I bet you find something to help Zach here." The doctor took the seat and started reading through the documents.

"Do you really think those files will help my son?" Barry asked.

"I hope so, because they won't find an answer anywhere else."

Chapter twenty two

Barry was sitting beside his son. Zach had not long returned from surgery. The doctor had indeed found some useful information from Barry's files. Barry hadn't thought that his genetically modified genome could affect his offspring. It was a lucky thing that Conrad had. After thirty one years, Barry was still amazed at Conrad's ability to think of things that others would overlook. Tatiana was sleeping. Her head pressed against Barry's muscular chest. Her face was still wet from tears of relief. The doctors had said that it would take some time before Zach's organs fully repaired themselves. They wanted to keep an eye on him still, as they weren't fully convinced they had solved the problem. But Zach's body had started to repair itself, and his organs were working at a more manageable pace. Also, there was no sign of them failing again. They had him hooked to so many machines, there was hardly any room for the doctors to move around him. The machines were still there as a precaution, but Zach's body was working, mostly, without aid. This was very good news. Barry wondered why he hadn't suffered the same effects. It was Aaron who had reminded him that, those who created him, would have given him drugs to stabilize his bodies sudden erratic surges.

Aaron had stayed for a while, but had left when Edmund had given him the location of his own family. Aarons parents had been thrilled to see him. His three sisters were even more exited to see their brother for the first time ever. The reunion had been a long and very tearful one. The eldest of the three sisters was married and had a son of her own. The next eldest was in a steady relationship. The youngest had only that year started collage. Conrad hadn't wanted to interfere, so had given Aaron a weeks R & R and left them at it. He stayed only long enough to meet them all and give his best wishes. After, he had returned to the hospital to see if Zach's operation had been successful. Once he had the information he had sought, he had given Barry the same weeks R & R and hadn't been seen since.

Zach opened his eyes and looked at his father.

"Who are you?" He said sleepily. Barry smiled.

"Morphine making you forget son?" He asked. Zach suddenly worked it out.

"Dad? I knew you'd come." Then he looked puzzled for a moment. "I've already said that, haven't I?"

"Four times son. First time yesterday, and thrice today. Nice to know you're remembering though." Barry's smile was so broad and sincere, that Zach couldn't help but smile back. He looked at his mum.

"I haven't seen her looking that peaceful for quite a while."

"I know." Barry said. "But she's always been this beautiful to me."

Chapter twenty three

A week later, and still Conrad had not been seen. Barry and Aaron had met up. They were ready to give Conrad the news. They had meant to part ways with their leader almost two weeks ago now. But after all that had happened, they were no longer sure if they should. A part of them wanted to stay with their families. Another part was still a soldier though. They wanted to find out, once and for all, what Conrad had planned. He had rallied the people and had them praising his name in the streets. But they were all old men, women of all ages, children and people of stature; scientists and the like. The only real soldiers were only forty strong and most of them were past it. More like the Home Guard. But Conrad had told them to take notice of the peoples ages. They did but, hadn't understood.

An hour had passed with no sign of their fearless leader. Barry got fed up and decided to go look for him. Whilst searching, he had met with one of the underground soldiers. Upon asking, the soldier revealed Conrad's location. Apparently, he had spent the entire week in the barracks. He had been going through their stock list. It would seem the underground military complex had a rather healthy supply of arms. They even had ships. Barry thought that, if he had to go and do more fighting, then the use of a few ASAU's would be wonderful.

He saw Conrad entering a large structure, and followed him in. Conrad didn't seem quite himself. Barry assumed something was bothering him. The room was dark, but the sheer blackness gave Barry the impression that the room was immensely vast. Conrad perched himself on the edge of a table that was sitting beside the entrance. Barry stood in front of him, putting his back to the huge room.

"Turn the lights on." Conrad asked in a weary voice. Barry looked up and found the switch just over Conrad's right shoulder. He flicked the switch and heard the sound of many fluorescent tubes warming up.

"You seem a little down my old friend. What's up?" Barry asked.

"How's Zack?" Conrad asked instead.

"Fine. He came home two days ago. He has to have regular checkups, but at least they know what to look for now. Thank you for saving his life. Tatiana was hoping to give you her thanks also. We owe you a lot."

"You owe me nothing. The doctors saved his life. I just showed them what they needed to do so." Barry put a meaty hand on Conrad's shoulder.

"And if you hadn't, my son would be dead. You saved his life, and I could never repay you for that. You've given me the greatest gift I could ever have asked for. Thank you. You really are a saviour." Conrad gave a short laugh.

"One life saved. Millions dead. Some saviour." Barry took back his hand.

"They were the enemy. It was our job to kill them. Like it or-"

"No!" Conrad cut in. "I meant M-Tron lives. Millions of M-Trons are dead because of me." Barry was frowning.

"Utter nonsense! Billions died from the nukes. You didn't launch them. These people here are alive and thriving. Because of you and your father. The only other M-Trons to have died are our own soldiers. But they knew what to expect. Black Tron beat us."

"No." Conrad said a little quieter. "I let them win." Now Barry was getting confused.

"How can you say that? You did everything to save them. You, you…" Barry stopped as he noticed Conrad shaking his head.

210

"AICS was originally built to be a tactics and strategy computer. I was modified for the same purpose. We both came to the same conclusion as my father. I had a chance to help keep those soldiers I sent to war, alive. But I didn't use that opportunity because we wouldn't win if I had. I let my entire army die, so we could win. Barry... You once scolded me for keeping secrets. You thought it was because I was going mad. But I've been keeping a big secret from you, ever since we were kids.

"I can't keep it any longer.

"My father, AICS and myself had come up with a way to win the war. But to do so, we had to lose. I tried to tell you that day in my office, but I couldn't face your anger. I told you I had a bad feeling. But it wasn't a sense of what I didn't know. It was what I did know. I knew we would lose, because I had already calculated it." Barry was in so much shock, he was physically reeling.

"What? But? How?" Was all he could manage. A tear rolled down Conrad's face.

"I had calculated every win and every loss. AICS perfected the plan. My father approved it. But I set it in motion. Me! I killed our brothers! ME!" He was almost sobbing. His left eye could no longer produce tears, but his good eye was flowing with them. "It's like sacrificing your pieces on a chess board. You move them over to one side of the board and watch them die, so you can complete a check-mate on the other side of the board. Only I made the board look empty. They had all the pieces. I have none. Except, I cheat! I had a load of pieces hidden. Except, this isn't a chess board. Hidden pieces don't sit there doing nothing. My pieces build!"

"What are you going on about Conrad? What are you saying?" Barry was almost pale from what he had heard.

"Look behind you Barry! What do you see?" By now, the lights had warmed and had flooded the huge room with light. Barry turned.

The room was much bigger then he had first thought. It was almost the same size as the underground caverns. Conrad had said the caves were two miles wide and one mile deep. But that was only what the people had been told. Only the soldiers and Edmund knew about this part. And now, so did Conrad and Barry. Barry didn't know if it were possible to see the far wall, but even if it were, you couldn't. The room was full of ships. ASAU's, ASAC's, Mini-tanks, QMMHU's, HC suits and much, much more! But what had Barry transfixed, were the AUC's. Slowly, as if in a dream, Barry walked amongst the ships. Brushing a hand on a ship here, running his fingers along the nose of an AUC there. And then, smack-bang in the centre, he saw it. A complete AUC-C with all the extras. This was the ship that earned the AUC its nickname.

The Flying Fortress!

"Oh. My. God!" Barry said, incredibly slowly. "This is a command module. It's got a cargo bay and M4 transport bay attached. That's a bloody Scout on top! Why would they build this?" Barry turned to Conrad. "Who's it for? We can't fly all these."

"How old are the people in this city?" Conrad asked quizzically. Barry frowned.

"What?" He asked.

"How old? I told you to take notice."

"The men are old. So are most of the women. The younger women are all mothers. Oh, and a whole lotta infants."

"Of all the children that were brought down here ten years ago, you would have thought some of them would have made it to their teens by now."

212

"That's true. Now you come to mention it, there should be thousands in their teens and even early twenties. Where are they?" Conrad finally gave a smile.

"Who do you think these ships are for? Hidden pieces remember." Suddenly, the penny dropped. Barry understood.

"They've been training soldiers down here. How many are there?"

"About fifty thousand."

***

Aaron was playing with his food. He had ordered some sort of burger. It didn't look too bad, and tasted alright. But it wasn't a proper burger. Mostly though, he was bored. Barry had left to find Conrad six hours ago. His sisters had come to keep him company. Well, the youngest two had. But they had things to be doing and had left over an hour ago. Tatiana had kept him company for a short while, but she only came out to get some food for Zach, and had had to return to him. It was nice to know Zach was better. And eating like a horse apparently.

Aaron's boredom was broken by an excited Barry. He came in and almost shouted at him. Aaron calmed him down.

"What is it?" He asked.

"You're gonna need a drink for this news!" Barry told him.

"Conrad went nuts and has finally been committed?"

"No. What? No."

"Conrad found a woman and has been shacked up with her for the past week? Good on him."

"No. What?!? Aaron! Really?"

"Okay. Conrad finally realised that, although we are very thankful for our promotion, we don't have an army?"

213

"No. Well, no. But you're in the right area. Trust me. You'll need a drink. I know I do." Aaron called a waitress over and ordered a couple of beers. After a couple of sips, Barry told Aaron the news.

"Conrad wants you to report to the barracks at o eight hundred hours tomorrow."

"Eight o'clock? What the hell for?" Aaron asked.

"Well, you know that nonexistent army he keeps going on about?" Aaron took another mouthful of beer.

"Not really. I haven't met them yet. What with them not existing and all. Why? You met them?" Aaron started laughing at his own joke.

"Spent the last two hours talking to them actually." Barry took a swig of his own pint. Aaron had the glass to his lips, but was laughing too much to drink it.

"Ha ha! Really? And Conrad wants me to meet them does he? Oh, Barry! I'm gonna get a stitch in a minute!" Barry started laughing with his friend.

"Wait! You haven't heard the funny bit yet. You know he gave you black, Delta force pips?"

"Yeah?"

"Well, he's only giving you a month to train a thousand soldiers to Delta standards!" Aaron roared with laughter.

"And where the hell is he going to find a thousand men." He said through a fit of laughter.

"You know how the people here are either really old or really young?" Barry laughed back.

"Yeah. I had noticed." Aaron giggled.

"That's because those of recruitment age have been trained and are in the barracks." Barry said, still laughing. Aarons laughter died down a little.

"What?"

"Yeah! They have an army fifty thousand strong!" And then in a serious voice, Barry finished with, "And Conrad's giving you a thousand men for Delta. Not

214

laughing now are ya'." And indeed, Aaron was not laughing. In fact, he looked quite alarmed.

"Are you serious? An army? Fifty thousand?" Barry nodded. "And he wants me to do WHAT?!" Barry took another swig of his pint.

"Why do you think he gave you those black pips? He's known about this for fifteen years. We have one month to get the men ready for war. Then we are going on a mass bombing raid on Black Tron territory, and Delta is heading the attack." Aaron felt feint, and promptly said so.

"Why didn't Conrad tell us?" He asked.

"He was worried the Black Trons might find out. He couldn't afford to risk it."

"But... I don't get it. Why didn't he use them to back our forces? Why did he let all our men die, and hold this army back?" Aaron was getting angry now.

"He wanted to. But statistics showed that we would still lose the war if he had. We had to devastate the enemy as best we could, then let them think they had won."

"But why let *all* our men die? From the original army, you, me and him are the only ones left. He could have saved **thousands** of lives if he had brought them out **sooner**!" Aaron had gotten so angry, he had thumped the table with his fist.

"If he had, we would still have lost the war. He needed the enemy to think they had completely destroyed us all. That way, we get the element of surprise, and they will still be partying. He needed this to be a total surprise for them. If they are even slightly ready for us, we would lose before we even got started."

"Well it's definitely a surprise. I'm surprised! Fifty thousand men!" Then quieter, "Fifty thousand."

"We got one month."

"Where's Conrad now? Still prepping them?"

"No." Barry put his glass down and looked solemn. "He's left." Aaron almost spat his drink out.

"Left?! Why? Where's he going?"

"He thinks the Black Trons are ready for another attack. They know he's still alive. So I'm inclined to agree with him. He's heading back to enemy territory."

"What?! Why?"

"As long as Conrad lives, Black Tron will be ready for war. So he's going to get himself killed."

"Killed?" Aaron said quietly.

"As far as the Black Trons are concerned, Conrad alive is a war waiting to happen. Conrad dead... War is once and for all, truly over for them.

"Then we, get our advantage."

Chapter twenty four

Cruising speed was great. Conrad felt so good to be in an M-Tron built ship. The Octopods were good, but they just didn't handle right. Conrad, like most other soldiers, had been trained in the ASAU. The Air and Space Attack Unit was the backbone of the M-Tron army. They were fast, agile and powerful. As with the Octopods, they also came in two versions. Also, like the Octopods, they were identical to each other. The only difference was their weapons. As mentioned earlier, the Octopods came in either the OCT-F or OCT-S version. It was the same with the ASAU. Except they were identified as either the CR or LR version. CR stood for Close Range. Like the OCT-F, these were the fighter class ships. LR, as you've probably guessed, are the Long Range class. Although the ASAU's could take more damage then the Octopods, they only had three weapons. The three cannons (if CR class) were mounted under the ASAU's great delta wing. They were positioned for accuracy and balance; one under the nose of the ship and two spaced evenly near the rear. This meant the ASAU was almost as manoeuvrable in air as it was in space (the Octopods were awful in air). The LR version was less powerful then the OCT-S as it only had two Sniper Rods (the OCT-S, if you remember, had four) mounted at the rear, in the same place as the CR's two rear mounted cannons. But where the OCT-S was vulnerable in close combat, due to the Rod's incredibly slow rate of fire, the LR had an ace up its sleeve. The Rods took time to fire, and needed a good distance to be accurate. So when in close combat, unlike it's OCT-S counterpart, the LR also had a single cannon mounted under its nose.

Of coarse, like all good M-Tron engineers, they

couldn't help but tinker with their ships. The ASAU was no exception. And so, a slightly bigger, and much faster version of the ASAU was built. This came in only the CR version. It had two turbo boosters mounted at the rear, where the ASAU had one. It was a little stronger then its predecessor, and a little more accurate. They ended up being used as a Squadron Commander ship. In proper battle formation, you would often see one of these ships leading a small group of ASAU's. For this reason, they named it the ASAC. Air and Space Attack Commander.

Whilst walking amongst the ships back at the underground city, Conrad had discovered an all black version. The only splash of colour was the large, dark green tinted screen. This huge, angular sheet of Plexiglas was tinted thus to make it seem all black when in space, whilst giving the pilot a clear window of the battle, above, forward and a little to each side. Scanners and a few micro, mounted cameras made up the rest of the view. The inside of this ASAC was also all black, except for the two vents that allow air to be circulated around the cockpit. They were chrome plated. Conrad knew instantly that this ship was built for the Delta force Commander. Technically, they had built it for him, but he had given his old job to Aaron. So he felt a little guilty for taking it. But he was sure Aaron would forgive him. The ship did, after all, have Conrad's name etched into the metal inside the cockpit.

Conrad wasn't in a hurry, so had tried to have a conversation with the onboard SIS computer. The SIS, or Strategic Intelligence System, was a new feature to the M-Tron fleet. The computer units had been built in to every ship, but hadn't been programmed. This had required the use of AICS. AICS had interfaced herself with the underground computer system weeks ago. But she didn't want the anti-virus program to think she was breaking in. So Conrad had to give her permission to access the computers. Of coarse, if AICS had wanted to, she could have fooled the anti-virus program and broken through every firewall on the computer in a second. But she didn't want to be mistaken as a threat, so had waited for Conrad to… open the door? Terrible analogy, I know.

AICS had gone straight to work, programming the SIS computers with a part of her mind. They were filled with strategic and tactical data. Including maps, ship identification charts, and even survival tips. The SIS was fully voice operated, and even kept watch as the battle unfolded, giving helpful advice from time to time. Unfortunately, Conrad discovered, she wasn't very good at idle conversation. He had started by asking if there was anything good on TV. She had replied by reminding Conrad that there was no televisual receiving device present on board. Conrad had then asked if she could find some pre-recorded shows on the internet. He knew there was an internet connection on board. SIS had replied by quoting rule 313 of the military guidelines: Onboard internet devices were to be used sparingly in case of enemy detection or hacking, and should also be used for military use only. She further added that the SIS computer was not to be used as a multi-media or entertainment device and such usage would be in direct violation of the previously mentioned rule 313.

Conrad told her to fuck off.

She replied, 'Does not compute'.

***

Aaron was standing in front of The Flying Fortress. Not 'a' Flying Fortress; 'The' Flying Fortress. He was even drooling.

"Want a tissue Aaron?" Barry asked. Aaron didn't seem to hear. "Earth to Sergeant Major Hammond.

Come in Delta force Commander." Barry mocked. Aaron lifted his hand and raised his middle finger.

"It's alright for you. You get to ride this thing." He said.

"It ain't that exciting. I'm only sitting in the command chair."

"I know. It's just you've got your ship. Conrad nicked mine!" Barry started laughing.

"You could always fly this one if you want." Aaron spun round.

"What?! And have the entire Black Tron fleet shooting at me? You do know, when the Black Trons see this thing, they will do anything to bring it down?" Barry nodded.

"I know. It was only a suggestion." Aaron seemed thoughtful for a moment.

"Actually, that would be fun. Okay, I'll fly it." Barry shook his head and handed Aaron a large, black... actually, he didn't know what it was. He gave Barry a quizzical look.

"It's a personal SIS computer." Barry answered the look.

"What the hell is a sis? Is that like one of those big, pus-y blisters?" Barry had to think about that one.

"No. I think you mean a cyst. That, however, is a SIS. An S, I, S, computer. Strap it on like a wristwatch." Aaron does as told.

"Comfy. What's it for?" He asks.

"Think of it like a strap-on PDA. Only, you can talk to this one. You might recognise the voice."

"Oh god! It's not Conrad is it?" Barry smiled. Aaron pressed the top. It flipped open. A three-piece keyboard unfolded from its centre, while the lid piece lit up and became a large screen. The face of AICS appeared and she spoke.

"Hello Sergeant Hammond. How may I be of

service?" Aaron slammed the lid down.

"Typical! Not only do I have AICS strapped around my wrist, she got my bloody rank wrong!" Barry laughed.

"Don't worry. It isn't AICS. And I can sort the rank thing out. But that's not what's really bothering you, is it?" Aaron lowered his head.

"No. I'm still thinking about Conrad. Why'd he have to do that?"

"You're not going on about the ship again, are you?" Barry asked. Aaron gave him a look.

"No. I mean, going off to get himself killed. And you not letting me go after him." Barry shook his head.

"I've explained this to you already. Look, it was his choice. I didn't like it either. I still don't."

"So let's go after him. Bring him back."

"No. We can't."

"AND WHY THE FUCK NOT!?!" Aaron exploded in rage. Barry grabbed him and lifted him slightly off the ground.

"Because he ordered us not to." He growled through gritted teeth. "Now get a grip Sergeant Major. You have men to train. Do I make myself clear?" Aaron made a quick salute.

"Yes General." He said.

Chapter twenty five

Cup.

Pea.

Eleven feet.

He aims.

He shoots.

"How the fuck did I miss that?" Wong asked. Spree patted the man on the back.

"Better luck next time General. Now, I do believe there is the matter of two hundred Rupees."

"Damn you Spree! You could at least give me a chance to win my money back." Spree gave this some thought. He then picked up a dried pea, stepped up to the fifteen foot mark.

Cup.

Pea.

Fifteen feet.

He aims.

He shoots.

He scores!

The pea hit the rim, made several circuits around the inside of the cup and settled at the bottom.

"If you can do that, I'll give you your money back. If you can do it at twenty feet, I'll give you double. Fifty feet, and I'll triple it." Wong steps up to the fifteen foot mark. He picked a pea and turned towards the cup.

Cup.

Pea.

Fifteen feet.

He aims.

He... a pea lands in the cup.

"Hey! Who did that?" Wong asked. He turned to Spree who just shrugged and indicated behind them.

They turned and saw Jason Moon standing at the fifty foot mark. He approached the two men with a smile on his face. Spree thought he looked younger. He thought he knew why, but assumed Jason would put it down to Botox or plastic surgery.

"Triple the bet, I do believe. Assuming I heard right."

"No sir." Answered Wong. "It was triple your money back. Spree hadn't won any money from you." Jason turned to him. Still with the smile.

"Then I'll have to use the winnings from you as the denominator. I believe that was five lost bets of fifty, and none won. That's two hundred and fifty... er, what are you betting with?"

"Rupees sir." Spree answered this time.

"Rupees? Of all the currencies you could have gone for, you're using Indian Rupees?"

"No sir." Wong this time. "Sri Lankan Rupees. That's equal to one hundred cents, sir. Not one hundred paisa." Jason looked Wong in the eye. Smile still pasted on his face.

"I'm well aware of the Sri Lankan denomination. The fact still remains, that you owe me two hundred and fifty Rupees." Wong looked confused.

"Forgive me sir, but how is that? Spree made the bet, not I."

"You owe General Spree, two hundred and fifty Rupees. The General owes me, seven hundred and fifty Rupees. As that is more then two fifty, the money you give him will be given to me. So to save us all the bother, why don't you just give the two fifty to me, and the good General here can give me five hundred." Spree had already made this calculation and had the money in his hand. He handed it over. Wong mumbled something under his breath as he started counting out notes.

"What was that General Wong? Do you have a problem with this? If it would make you feel better, I could always take in consideration that the two of you were using this training field to play this silly game, while your men, who are actually doing their jobs, are currently tracking an M-Tron craft that is heading towards this very compound, and have the two of you court martialled." Wong immediately started grovelling. Spree, however, was not deterred. He held up a communications device that he had taken from his belt.

"Ninety degrees west, heading due east. Range, eight miles. Speed, surprisingly slow. Whoever it is, they're not in a hurry to get here. It's almost as though they want us to know of their presence. Like they're taunting us. At best guess, it's most likely to be a fighting class ship. An ASAU, or possibly even an ASAC. An M-Tron fighter, taunting us. It can only be the doing of one man." Jason pulled a gun from a holster on his back. He pointed it at Wong and fired.

"Conrad, Manké. My thought exactly." Spree looked down at the dead man.

"Why kill Wong?" He asked.

"Wong never did no white." He laughed at his little joke. "No. Wong is not my General. You are. The Japanese military have asked for him to return. It would seem the Independent Countries have decided to do just that. Stay independent. They are calling back their armies." Spree shrugged.

"They barely have a few hundred men each. We have thousands."

"There are thirteen Independent Countries, and forty nine factions. Each country has around three hundred men each, depending on how many factions there are in each country. All together they have a little more then four thousand men. We have seven thousand. That isn't

224

even twice their combined numbers. Meaning, my army has dropped by over a third of it's original size. Do the maths Spree."

"I have." Spree replied. "I count seven thousand Black Trons, and one M-Tron." He smiled. The smile was short lived as Jason told him,

"Don't forget that one man is Conrad Manké."

***

Conrad had gotten so fed up with the SIS computer, he had torn a panel off revealing her components and proceeded to crosswire the in feed to the primary and auxiliary command protocol boards. Then he located a few parts that allowed her to speak. One quick twist of a small restrictor separated it cleanly from the circuit board. The constant nagging and ticking off from SIS stopped immediately. He replaced the panel and accessed the internet.

"Now. Let's try this again. I want to watch TV. I'm gonna watch TV, and there is nothing you can do to stop me. Ha ha SIS. I got you!"

"You are in direct violation of rule three one three. Your on-board SIS unit is malfunctioning. Please return for maintenance."

"What the fff?" Conrad was looking around, trying to find out were the voice had come from. He was sure that resistor would completely disable her. Then as the voice repeated it's message, he remembered. He was wearing a personal SIS on his wrist. He had forgotten that the units could link with each other. He unstrapped the device from his wrist, opened the cockpit, and threw her out.

"Bon voyage!" He called after her. He closed the cockpit and resumed searching for a show.

"What are you doing?" Conrad froze. That definitely came from the ships speakers. Could the SIS unit repair herself?

225

"What do I have to do to shut you up?" He asked the unit.

"You could start by turning this ship around and returning home. You're deep in Black Tron territory, and I've detected several ships heading your way." Conrad thought she sounded funny, but couldn't put his finger on it.

"I have to keep going. We can't win while I'm alive. I always said I'd die for my country. I just hoped it wouldn't be alone."

"You're not alone Conrad. I'm here." That didn't sound right for a SIS unit. She was too emotional. Too human. Too... Conrad suddenly realized who it was.

"AICS! I thought you were the SIS unit. You know this thing is a pain in the arse."

"Hmm. It would seem you have done a little rewiring. You know, I designed the SIS for soldiers who follow orders. Not Commander Generals who can't stop messing with things.

"Coincidently, iPlayer is running your favourite show."

"Ooh! Star trek. Thanks AICS." He accessed the site and started running through the list of available programs. It didn't take long to find the one he was looking for.

"Are you sure you want to do this?" AICS asked.

"Of coarse I do. I mean, Star Trek! Hello."

"Don't play dumb with me Conrad. I'm not the SIS unit." Conrad sighed.

"It's not about what I want to do. It's about what I have to do. And yes. I do have to do this. For M-Tron AICS." When the super computers voice finally came through the speaker, it sounded sad. If Conrad hadn't have known better, he would have sworn it was the voice of a woman in tears.

"I understand Conrad. I will stay with you until the

end. I'm sure I'm going to get reprimanded for this, as I'm using a lot of up-link time. I've had to line up six satellites to keep in contact with you. But I won't let you go alone." This comforted Conrad a lot. He might be mad, but he wasn't stupid. He didn't want to die.

It still surprised him to hear AICS talk like that. It was strange to hear a machine speaking with such passion. To think, somewhere deep within that huge collection of boards, chips, drives, wires and neuro-technology, AICS was going to miss him. In fact, she was terrified of losing him. A tear rolled down Conrad's face.

"How many is 'several'?" He asked.

"Sorry Conrad. Do you mean literally, or in reference to something we said earlier?" Conrad allowed one of those rare moments to happen. He smiled.

"You told me there were several ships heading my way." He said.

"Oh yes. I count three hundred and fifteen OCT-F's; sixty two OCT-S's; twelve Double Pods and a Battle Pod." Conrad pondered for a moment.

"Is that all? Seems like an unfair advantage AICS. Maybe we should let them call in reinforcements before we kill them all."

"Perhaps if I disable the rear cannons. Would that help?" Conrad smiled at AICS's ability to pick up on a joke.

"Yeah. And slow the front cannons RoF* by twenty five percent. I recon it'll be about even then." They both laughed for a while. Then they were both quiet for a long time.

AICS eventually broke the silence.

"I know I'm not supposed to be able to, but I love you Conrad." Conrad didn't even think of joking.

*Rate of Fire

227

"I love you too AICS. Do me a favour."

"Yes, my love?"

"Keep talking to me. Please." AICS's answer was soft and quiet.

"Yes my love."

She kept her promise and spoke to him up to the point of battle. The ASAC was built to perfection, and Conrad destroyed many ships. AICS kept feeding him information. She was basically doing the SIS units job. But with Conrad's ability to spot trouble faster then a computer, AICS could better select the information that Conrad would need, better than the SIS unit ever could. She fed information, taunted the enemy and even came up with a few one-liners to make Conrad laugh. She didn't stop until the fighter had taken one too many hits, and the ship finally went down. She had called his name a couple of times. But the silence she got back, and the lack of life signs, told her only one thing.

Conrad was gone.

Chapter twenty six

The General had called a meeting. All the high ranking officers had attended. Aaron didn't know what it was about, but as he entered the Generals office and shook his hand, he couldn't help but notice the drawn, solemn look on his face. The General asked him to sit, and said not another word to him. Aaron was worried. He had never seen Barry looking so serious. Once all the officers had sat, including Edmund for some strange reason, General Man started the meeting.

"Hello all. For the next few moments we can forget about ranks, as I have some disturbing news for you all. This news also concerns Curator McKay. Hence the reason he is here.

"Now, what you are about to learn is… well it's hard for me to repeat. So if you'd all like to turn to the screen here, and AICS will tell you what she has told me." The face of AICS appeared on the screen. But before she could speak, a Colonel spoke up first.

"That damn machine is a menace! She spent over four hours using an open link to a vessel occupying enemy territory. And when we tried to disconnect the link, she disengaged the mouse and keyboard, and locked us out of our own computer system!"

"Your concerns have been duly noted, Wiseman. AICS, please continue." But once again, before she could speak,

"Why do you allow this machine to take such risks? If it had been the mistake of a human, I would understand. But to allow a machine to do this?" Aaron had stepped up behind the Colonel. Barry caught his eye and shook his head.

"Sit down Colonel! And with concern to your health, might I strongly suggest that you keep your fucking mouth shut!" Until now, the Colonel had been taking orders only from Edmund. Edmund was no military man, and so allowed the Colonel to make his own decisions. So the Colonel was in no hurry to back down.

"With due respect General, this is *our* military complex, and we would like it if this malfunctioning, over sized calculator, would keep out of-" Barry had gotten fed up. He made a quick motion with his hand, allowing Aaron to continue with his last train of thought. This had been to grab the Colonel in a Delta style head lock. This had cut off both the Colonel's airway and, more thankfully, the end of his speech.

Aaron sat the man down and released his grip just enough to allow the man to breathe.

"AICS is more human than you'll ever be." He hissed in to the man's ear. "So shut up and let her speak, 'cos you're offending her."

"Thank you Aaron." AICS spoke at last. "But what I did was risky and I accept the consequence of my actions. Also, technically, I am a machine." Aaron let the man go and returned to his seat.

"Not to Conrad you ain't." He said on his way. "And not to me either." Watching Aaron's behaviour, Barry assumed that he had already guessed what the terrible news was. He wasn't taking it well.

"The vessel in question," AICS continued, "as the good Colonel pointed out, was indeed in enemy territory. It was an ASAC sporting the colours of the Delta Commander, and was being piloted by your Commander General, Conrad Manké junior." This received a few shocked gasps. "What you are about to see is the ships log. All footage is from ships view. The sound was recorded by myself whilst in communication." She played the video. There were no cameras recording the inside of the ship, so all the footage was of the battle. But Conrad's voice was unmistakable. AICS had only muted the sound for one tiny moment: the moment she told Conrad she loved him, and his answer. Those watching thought it was from the ship being hit by plasma rounds. Barry knew better.

They watched the whole thing. At one point, the picture cut out, but you could still hear AICS and Conrad talking. Then there were some moments of static. The sound of Conrad's voice breaking through in spurts. As the words; fuck; going down and; had it, broke through the static, they all knew what had happened. Then there was an eerie silence. Then AICS's voice,

"Conrad. Conrad? Are you still there? Please Conrad! I'm not reading any life signs! Please Conrad, wake up! This isn't how it's supposed to end! Conrad!" Then in a voice so quiet as to be almost inaudible, "Good bye my love."

The room fell silent.

Then all of a sudden, all the officers were talking to each other. They seemed excited by something. They were actually happy about something. This had Aaron fuming. But not as much as Barry, who suddenly shouted in his deep booming voice,

"SHUT UP!!!" Silence fell upon the room once more. "You've just been told your President is dead, and this is how you behave? What the hell are you so excited about?" The Colonel spoke first.

"With due respect sir, we never got a chance to except Conrad as our President. His death is a great loss to us, and we don't mean to be disrespectful. But did you hear the way AICS was giving him information? If we hadn't have known better, we would have sworn there was a navigator in that ship with him. If we could take her apart-"

"Over my dead body!" Barry broke in, cutting the

Colonels sentence short once more. "AICS is the senior Communications Officer, and Tactician! You will defer to her superiority at all times! Even Edmund here is not privy to her actual whereabouts. So we will have no more talk like that! Do I make myself clear Lieutenant?" The Colonel looked a little confused for a moment.

"I, I'm a Colonel sir."

"And I'm a bloody General! With the power to demote anyone I see fit, Corporal!" The Colonel, or Corporal, got the point and sat down quickly. Barry continued. "Under section nine of the Presidential guidebook, Curator Edmund McKay is now officially the acting President of M-Tron. As you are all new to the idealisms of Delta Force, listen up. Sergeant Major Hammond is the highest ranked officer in Delta Force and is equal to that of a Lieutenant. Delta Force will defer to the Sergeant Major only. The Sergeant Major will defer to myself, the President and a Brigadier. As we don't have a Brigadier, that leaves me and Edmund. Unfortunately, an acting-President can not select a Commander General, so you are stuck with me. However, I do need an Air Force General. So... Captain Mallick. Where are you?" The Captain stood and saluted.

"I'm hear General." Barry handed him a wooden box. The box was identical to the boxes he and Aaron were given by Conrad.

"As you have the highest knowledge in Air Force procedures, I hereby raise you to the rank of Marshal. Air Force General." Mallick took the Generals hand and shook it. He tried very hard not to smile, but was failing miserably.

"Thank you sir."

"Don't sir me Marshal. We are, technically, of equal ranks now. Also, many of the men have better piloting skills then most. So I want you to stay after this meeting so we can discuss other Air Force personnel."

"Of coarse General." The officer formally known as Colonel stood up.

"Oh! I should have known you'd have something to say." Barry retorted before the man could speak.

"I have been in charge of this army for ten years! I demand some recognition!" He said. Barry clapped his huge hands together.

"Fine!" He said. "I will promote you. I hereby raise you to the rank of Lieutenant. Well done! You're a CO again! Now shut the fuck up, or I'll put you back to NCO and, this time, have you ejected from the room." The, er, Lieutenant sat down. "Now! Sergeant Major. You must be feeling lonely, as you're the only NCO in the room again."

"Yeah, why is he here again? I thought you said Commissioned Officers only." A Major asked. It was the newly appointed Marshal who answered.

"He is wearing the black pips of Delta, which means he represents them. There is no rank above Sergeant Major in Delta. And as all Delta ranks are superior to our standard ranks, he is equal to a Lieutenant. Which, as we know, is a CO."

"Thank you General." Barry said (a Marshal is a General of the Air Force, so calling him General is still correct). "Sergeant Major Hammond. How are your men faring?" Aaron shrugged.

"Well, they aren't exactly Delta, but they the best I got. Personally, I'd rate them closer to Alpha, Bravo or Charlie. But they'll run rings around this lot, so I'm happy enough."

"Remind me again why this man is the Delta commander. I thought he was originally from Bravo." Said the Major.

"He was trained as a Delta by Conrad Manké

himself. The only reason he ended up heading Bravo is because he and myself were both in line for Sergeant, but only one of us could be the Delta Sergeant. As I won the toss, I kept Delta. He got Bravo. Now, any more stupid questions or would you like me to demote you too?" The Major sat down. "Good. Lieutenant Harlem." The Lieutenant stood. "I was impressed by your actions and quick thinking the first day we arrived. So I'm promoting you too. Well done Major." The new Major saluted, took the box and shook Barry's hand. The old Major looked a little put out, but said nothing. "And if you can avoid the silly questions Major. I have a box for you too. As much as I know I'll receive some sour words from the Delta Commander, I'm raising you to Brigadier." The old Major stood, took his promotion and sat down again.

"I may not like you," Said Barry. "But you do know your stuff. Okay. We will be having a three minute silence at sixteen hundred hours, so unless you have some questions, meeting adjourned."

"I have a question." Said the new Brigadier. "Why can't we get AICS to navigate all our ships?"

"Because this would be a huge drain on her resources. Plus, our military network would be wide open for the enemy to hack our systems. However. You do have the next best thing. SIS. You have all been briefed on the SIS unit, and should have an idea of its capabilities. They were programmed by AICS herself and work almost identically to what you have previously witnessed. Of coarse, if you spent more time with your men and the machines they will be using, you would have seen this for yourselves." There were no more questions. So the officers all upped and left. Barry, Aaron, Mallick and the Brigadier were the only ones left.

"Can I help you Brigadier?" Barry said.

"He better watch it, or I'll help him out the door." Aaron sneered. The Brigadier shook his head.

"It must be a tradition for the Delta Commander to be a constant pain in the arse." He said without malice. "Conrad was the same. I met him a few times. I know you were both friends of his and I'm truly sorry for your loss. He will be missed by us all." He turned to the computer. "AICS. Might I have the co-ordinates of the Presidents last position. With the Generals permission, I would like to send a small unit to recover his body, so he can have a proper burial." Barry put a hand on his shoulder.

"Thank you Brigadier, but that won't be necessary yet. The enemy must not get a sniff of us until it's too late for them. Conrad died so we can have this chance. Let's not lay waste to his actions."

"Of coarse. General. Marshal. AICS." He said in a formal manner of departure. He turned to Aaron. "Commander." He said with a slightly different tone. Aaron gave him the finger as he walked out the door. Then he turned to the two Generals and said,

"I like him. He's cool." Barry gave a quick smile then turned to business.

"Listen. This raid is going to be mostly aerial attacks. So I'm going to be working very close by your side General." The General nodded. "Aaron. Do you think your boys are up to the task?" Aaron shrugged.

"In practice, they're pretty good. But as I said earlier, they're not like the Delta we used to know."

"But can they pull it off?" Barry insisted.

"Should do. But it'll be close. One mistake and we're screwed."

"Best not have any mistakes then."

"They're running the sim now. They are getting better. But I would like to know how much time we have left." Barry shifted his weight.

"Four days." Aaron and the Brigadier looked aghast.

"Four days?" Aaron asked.

"I know, I know. It isn't a lot of time, but AICS has calculated it as being our window of opportunity. Her calculations are pretty good." The two men nodded at this. "Okay. Four days.

"Then we end this war!"

Chapter twenty seven

The walls were too close to each other. They were cold and damp. And they were hard. There was no bed. Not even a blanket. They had not been kind to him. He hurt all over. He was blind in one eye and missing an arm. His legs had no strength in them. He was cold and damp like the walls. Only he was soft and bruised as well. He left small puddles of blood wherever he lay. He would lie wherever they would dump him. They would torture him for hours. They never asked questions. They never spoke. They never showed themselves. They just, hurt him.

He was so tired. He closed his eyes. Once again, he was visited by the dream that had frequented him so often.

.....

He was outside the principals office. He could hear two voices. The principal, and his father.

"You know what your son did is not tolerated at this school. The consequence of-"

"I understand the consequence! I'm a damn General! But you must understand, *he* is the *future* of M-Tron."

"General, with due respect, we can't have a pupil causing trouble like this. He had three classes using military tactics in his own personal war. He should be expelled."

"HE WILL NOT BE EXPELLED!! While this is a military school, I still hold jurisdiction! Do I make myself clear?"

"Yes sir."

"Good. Now send him in."

He was called in. He walks in with his head hung low.

"Junior. Come here. The principal informs me that you've been fighting. Is this true?"

"Yes sir."

"Why?"

"The bullies, they were causing trouble and picking on the other kids sir."

"You didn't just go and fight them though. Did you." The Principal interjected. "You organised an attack with your mates. This is grounds for expulsion."

"Principal! Junior will *not* be expelled! Leave us so I can talk to my son alone."

"Yes General." The Principal walks out of the room.

"Junior. Look at me. You organised an attack? How?"

"Like we're taught in class sir."

"You mean with military tactics?"

"Yes sir."

"You mean you used M-Tron military war tactics against M-Trons?"

"But..."

"But nothing Junior. You do not use your skill against your own kind. Do I make myself clear?"

"Yes sir. Are you angry?"

"Angry? I'm livid! Junior, you don't understand how powerful you are. Your skills I mean. Or how important you are to us. What am I to do?"

"I won't do it again. I promise."

"No you won't. I suppose you were just trying to help your friends. Is this true?"

"Yes sir." The General paused a moment.

"Actually, I already know this. I saw the tapes."

Junior is filled with a sense of shame. He looks at the floor and mutters quietly, "I'm sorry".

"What did you just say?"

"I'm sorry sir." He replies louder. The General sighs.

"This is a military school. The kids you are here with are going to be your personal army when you leave. You are the future. You are the future of M-

Tron. Don't let M-Tron die with you. You must learn to be the best, NO! the greatest in the world."

"But its so hard sir. I'm treated differently to the other kids. And… I'm afraid."

"No-one said war was going to be easy Junior. Everyone's afraid sometimes. Some of the most remembered war hero's spent most of there time believing they had lost the war. But they kept going in hope that their effort would somehow make a difference. And, usually it did. The rest of the time it just helped them die without fear. This is one of those times, and it will still be one of those times when *you* go to war."

"But I don't want to go to war. The world is such a beautiful place, so, why do we have to destroy it by killing each other?"

"Oh, Junior. No matter how beautiful mother nature makes the world, war and human greed always manages to fuck it up. This, unfortunately, is the law of man. I'd rather spend my time doing projects with my son then going to the office, thinking up new and better ways of killing people." the General becomes quiet. Almost as though he was speaking to himself. "Then trying to find the best way to win this war without losing to many troops." Then he readdresses his son. "Its hard you know. I'm not actually there, but I'm afraid."

"You're afraid?"

"Yes."

"Of what?"

"My soldiers. I'm afraid for them. My orders could lead them to victory, or, sentence them to death. I fear for the latter. Do you understand?"

"Yes sir."

"Go on. Back to class."

"Yes sir. Thanks dad."

Yet again his dream changes. Those familiar scenes of previous battles flashing in his mind, going round and round in his head. Round and round, scene after scene, faster and faster. Every time he saw himself taking life after life. The blood on his hands taunting him as it spread up his arms, across his body and over his face, suffocating him. Then, as it did before, it stopped. He was looking at his reflection in that damn mirror again. The reflection didn't look right. Then, right on cue, his reflection motioned for him to follow, turned round and started to walk away. He just stood there. He knew what was about to happen. His reflection turned back. It spoke those words again. It was his own voice, and yet, it sounded evil.

"Come on Junior, join me. We can be gods, you and I."

What was this other version of him supposed to represent? He caught himself trying to think on a conscious level. This meant he wasn't fully asleep. He used to have these, half awake but still dreaming experiences when he was a kid. He learnt very quickly that, if he got bored with the dream, he could wake himself at will. He tried to wake up, but nothing happened. He tried again. Still nothing. The reflection was standing there, waiting for him. "Come on Junior. What are you waiting for?" The reflection asked. Junior was panicking. Why couldn't he wake up? He tried again, and felt his real body shaking, but still he would not wake. His dream self looked down. He saw a gun. It was a large, silver handgun. Something about the gun was wrong.

He tried to shout, in hope he would wake himself that way. Nope. That didn't work either.

The gun. Something about the gun.

Then it hit him. That gun was his own custom built Glock, one of a pair, handmade with pure platinum. But

240

he had those guns made when he was nineteen. How could he be holding one at six? This dream was going crazy. He lifted the gun. "Junior?" His reflection said. "What are you doing?" He shot. Then again, and again and again until the mag was empty. His reflection was gone. His arm numb from the recoils.

He was scared.

He started to cry.

Then he was in his mothers arms.

"It's ok Conrad, it was just a dream. Don't cry."

***

Finally, the army was ready. Well, as ready as it was ever going to be. Barry still wished they could have had more time to prepare. They were getting on well with the new SIS units. The unit's AI system was supposed to learn their pilots abilities so it could better assist them. That was why each ship had a name etched in to it. They were meant for one pilot only. Every soldier had their own ship, and had to practice with their own SIS units. Thankfully, the SIS units could copy what they had learnt and send appropriate data to the personal SIS unit worn on the soldiers wrist and vice versa. So as one unit learnt, so did the other. This meant the units learnt faster. Unfortunately, they still needed more time to be capable of interacting with their user at the same level as AICS had done with Conrad.

Barry stood looking down at the men and women. They were putting on helms and entering their vehicles. Some were driving Mini-tanks in to the bays at the rear of the AUC's. Some were following behind on QMMHU's. Many were arming themselves as foot soldiers and entering the AUC's from the side entrance. Some were getting in to pilot the AUC's themselves. But thousands upon thousands of them were getting in to their seats to pilot the huge fleet of fighters. Barry had never seen so many ASAU's and ASAC's in one place before in his entire life. The fighter craft would be a little unstable on their attack run, as the underside of their great delta wings were laden with small bombs. Each ship was carrying six of them. Any more and they wouldn't fly at all.

The plan was to perform a drop bombing raid. The word 'drop' was in reference to the ships, not the bombs (although they were to be dropped also). AICS had finally managed to infiltrate the Black Tron communication and detection facilities, and was about to render their scanners inoperable. She would do this a moment before the fleet would appear on the Black Tron's radars. The fleet, at that point, would be in space and will 'drop' towards their targets. Mobile ground radar systems would still be operable, so they had to enter space to avoid them. The fleet would split up at key points to attack as many Black Tron specific military bases as possible. This would greatly reduce the enemy's ability to attack back. Of coarse, the enemy won't hang about. The sky would be full of enemy ships a few moments after the bombing run. Then all the M-Tron fighters, void of their heavy load, would be in attack mode and will shoot all enemy down. The key was to drop the payload first. While they were still carrying bombs, they were heavy and slow.

The whole thing would be done systematically. A fast, sudden, mass bombing raid first, followed by area specific dogfights. Long range fighters would stay at high altitudes to shoot down any OCT-S's trying to reach shooting distance, and to take out any fleeing enemy ships. The huge AUC's would be in key positions to use their heavy guns to force the enemy to disperse. This would cause a lot of mayhem. The position of the AUC's would also benefit the fighters as they could all use the AUC's massive radars, giving the fighters a larger scan of the battlefield. The AUC's had to be quick though, as they had to drop off the ground units. This was the AUC's main job. They were an Armed Unit Carrier, and were indeed carrying many ground units. If they were successful, the ground would be crawling with Mini-tanks, QMMHU's and soldiers in a matter of moments. The foot soldiers had even been issued with a few HC suits. The HC, or Heavy Combat, suits were huge, metal exoskeletons armed with four, high speed chain-guns and even a short range hover pack. The Mini-tanks were to search and destroy any military bases untouched by the initial attack.

Once the attack starts, Barry, in the huge command ship, had to quickly notify the members of the IC that they were only attacking Black Tron bases, and not their own. This was because Black Tron was not a country. Their military bases were spread amongst the Independent Countries, and as such, meant that the M-Tron fleet had to be careful when dropping their payloads. They didn't want to hit non Black Tron buildings. One Black Tron base was so deep in IC territory, they couldn't bomb it at all, for fear of killing innocent people. This base, typically, was the one Jason Moon would be stationed at. And this base was to be targeted by Delta. Aaron and his men were to attack this base with what was referred to as a soft attack. This meant they were to cause just enough damage to get their attention. Once the soldiers and craft stationed at this base were all launched, Delta was to fall back and lure them away from the base. Delta, however, was to be in two teams. Team one was to do the luring; team two was to infiltrate the base on foot once the soldiers had exited. Aaron was leading team two.

To honour Conrad, four ASAU's were to destroy the base in Scotland. Corporal McLain had been honoured to take this mission, as he had lost most of his family in the nuke attack. Of coarse, countless more lives were lost in other countries. Thanks to an old M-Tron contingency plan, a few billion lives were saved. However, this was only a handful compared to the lives lost.

After the nukes had fallen, M-Tron had tried desperately to rebuild it's armies. They had started with small divisions using old guerrilla warfare. As they became larger, they started to attack back more frequently. When the late General Conrad Jacques Manké became said General, the M-Tron army had grown quite large. His strategic skills and decisive victories had Black Tron on the retreat. In response, Black Tron had started building new weapons. The Octopods were their crowning glory. In fact, it was the design of the 'pod' itself that gave Black Tron their edge. Their ships were quick and cheep to build, and the pods allowed the pilots to return home after their ship had been destroyed. Black Tron weapons were less powerful then M-Trons, but their ships had more of them. Their ships were longer, and easier to shoot at from the side, but head on they had a small profile. They were fast, and despite Conrad's reserved judgment of them, they were surprisingly agile. M-Tron was growing, but Black Tron was growing faster. This was why the war lasted so long. It was also the reason for the late General's devastating plan. He had to cripple Black Tron, but in doing so he would lose his entire army. And so a new army had to be established in the underground bunkers. Secretly.

This was the dreadful secret Conrad had kept for so long. It wasn't the war that had sent him mad. It was the thought of losing his men. Although a Sergeant Major was still only a Non-Commissioned officer, as the Delta Commander and the son of the late General, he was privy to the plan. Only four others knew. The

President, General Harding (who had stepped up to take the late Generals position), Marshal Farrow and the Commander General [appointed by the President] Michael Gates. As the President had not been a military man, he had had to appoint a Commander General. Unlike Conrad who, once he held the title of President, could take on the role himself. This was sometimes referred to as a President General.

Barry was still thinking about his lost friend when the Marshal placed a hand on his shoulder.

"It's time Barry." It hadn't taken long for the two Generals to reach a first name friendship. The Air Force General, or Marshal, had a brilliant mind. His skill with aerial co-ordination was unfaltering.

Barry took a deep breath and let out a long sigh.

"For Conrad." He said.

"For the President." The Marshal returned. "And for M-Tron." Barry shook the man's hand and headed for the command ship.

"Are you sure you don't want me to go in your stead?" The Marshal called.

"No." Barry tossed over his shoulder. "I need you here to help co-ordinate the attack. If all goes to pot, it'll be up to you to continue the fight."

"Yes General. What do I tell the people?" Barry stopped and had to think about this one.

"About what?" He asked.

"About the President. About Conrad." Barry hadn't thought about it. The people didn't know about Conrad's untimely death. They thought he would lead them to victory and free them all from the underground. He was, after all, supposed to be the great saviour of M-Tron.

"Don't tell them yet." Barry said. "Wait until it's over. Then tell them he died fighting, for his people. Let him be a martyr. Let him be the Saviour. We owe it to him." The Marshal gave a solemn nod. Barry continued with his walk to the huge command ship. He got in and took his seat at the command station. AICS was waiting for him.

"I'm at your disposal Commander." She said.

"Thank you AICS. Your skills will be most needed and appreciated. Keep me informed of the Marshals orders, and keep your eyes on the battlefield." With the use of cameras, scanners and radars, AICS could see the entire battle all at once. Barry knew this would come in very useful. He didn't want to miss anything. He opened a com. line with the pilot.

"Ready to go?" He asked.

"Yes, sir!" Came the eager reply from the pilot.

"Then take us up Flight Sergeant."

"Wilco!"

"Yeah!" Said AICS. "Let's kick arse!"

Chapter twenty eight

He opened his eyes. A man was standing over him. He hurt all over and could taste blood in his mouth. The man was smiling. His face was in shadow, so couldn't be seen. But he knew he was smiling. He looked up at him.

"Who the fuck are you?" He asked the smiling man.

"I'm Jacques." He said. This name was familiar to him. He had heard it before.

"What do you want from me?" He asked. Jacques knelt down. His face stayed in the shadow.

"What makes you think I want anything from you?" He asked.

"I'm still alive aren't I? If you didn't want something I'd be dead." Jacques seemed to contemplate this.

"True."

"Well? What do you want?" The smile broadened.

"I want you to suffer, the way you made *me* suffer. I want you to feel my pain. I want you to know, once and for all, the true meaning of torture-"

"I do!" He broke in. "I've been shot, stabbed, electrocuted, beat up, drowned. I've had bits of wood shoved under my fingernails. Someone whacked my balls with a piece of two-be-four. I'm bruised all over and I can't even stand up. I've got a headache, my ribs are broke, I'm missing teeth," Jacques smile was getting larger by the minute. He was definitely enjoying this. "but all of that ain't nothing compared to LISTENING TO YOU BITCHING!!" The smile disappeared.

"So you want more?"

"No! For the love of god! I couldn't bear another minute of listening to you whinging!"

"I meant all the other stuff." Jacques said through

gritted teeth.

"Will you be talking to me?" He asked.

"No." Now it was his turn to smile. His mouth was covered with so many cuts and bruises it hurt like hell, but it was worth it.

"Oh, well, in that case. Bring it on!" Jacques stood up.

"The clone here wants more. Don't disappoint him lads." Jacques left and two Black Tron soldiers entered. He was lifted and dragged to the torture room.

"Get the rack ready Joe." Said the soldier on his right. The other soldier let him go and went to prepare the rack. He knew what to expect. The rack was lined with metal studs that would send high currents of electricity down his spine.

Something was pressed into his hand as the other soldier lent close. While Joe's back was turned, the other soldier whispered in his ear.

"Agent 247 at your service. Wait for the signal." That said he pushed him onto the rack and tied him down. Then he went over to Joe.

His arm was hurting, so he twisted it slightly, hoping to ease the pain. As he did so, the strap tying his wrist to the rack loosened slightly. Agent 247 hadn't tied it properly.

Suddenly, there was a booming sound and the whole place shook. Agent 247 got on the com. deck and asked what had happened. A voice said they were under attack. The tortured man quickly pulled his hand free of the trap and transferred the item in his hand to his mouth. A quick glimpse let him know it was a key. He put his arm back down and pretended to be to hurt to move. Joe spotted the loose bond.

"Terry! You didn't tie his wrist! Have I got to do everything myself!" He lent forward to tie it. Quick as a flash, Joe was hit in the throat by stiffened fingers.

248

Then a quick punch to the face had him on the floor. Loosening the rest of his bonds, the man turned to Terry, Agent 247. The man grabbed him and they struggled for a moment. Terry threw the man in to the corner of the room, then jumped on top of him.

"The camera can't see us here." He hissed. "You'll find your arm and eye next door in a trunk. The key will open it, assuming you haven't swallowed it." The man shook his head to say he hadn't. "Good. I'll pull you back in front of the camera. Knock me out. Good luck Conrad. Long live M-Tron." Before Conrad could say a word, Terry had him on his feet and pulled him in front of the camera. Conrad used a kung-fu move to knock Terry's arm away, then in true brawler fashion, he nutted the guy. Terry fell to the floor. Conrad ran to the door and opened it. He went through and found the trunk in the next room. He was breathing hard and trying desperately not to fall over. He was using all his strength to stand up. Why wasn't his legs working properly? No time to figure it out now. He spat the key from his mouth and opened the huge, wooden trunk. Inside he found his arm and eye, along with a note telling him how to reattach them. The note also said that Agent 247 had rebuilt the eye. It ended with 'hope you like the improvement'.

Conrad hadn't realised his robotic parts could be removed. His eye was so simple. It connected with a kind of reverse bayonet fitting. Except the pins were on the female side. He took a close look at the eye. It looked almost identical to the original. The difference was with the lens itself. His old eye had a single lens. This one had multiple lenses arranged in a concave or bowl shape. Conrad took a second to note the difference, but didn't have time to dwell on it.

Attaching his arm was a little harder. He had to activate the release mechanism with his mind.

Unfortunately, Conrad didn't know how to do this, and according to the note, the micro-chip in the back of his head that allowed him to do this, was temporarily disabled. The note had said that the rooms down here were being dampened with an EMP device. Only special machines could operate down here. And not many of those either. Conrad's micro-chip would reboot the moment he reached a higher level. Also in the trunk were his Glocks. Conrad hadn't taken any weapons with him as he had expected to die in the air and had no use for them. But for some reason, he couldn't leave his precious guns behind. He was real glad he hadn't. With the guns securely strapped to his waist, and his arm in his, er, arm, Conrad bolted for the exit. He was underground, so had to find some stairs leading up. He was surprised that he hadn't come across any more soldiers. Another boom and the ground shaking gave him an answer. They were too busy dealing with the intruders. One soldier did make an appearance. Conrad swung his metal arm like a club and knocked him out. The force also threw Conrad to the floor. He cursed his legs. Although he was also impressed by the fact he could walk at all. He was obviously using what was left of his leg muscles. They were not quite strong enough to move the heavy metal that had replaced his bones. They were also badly damaged. But they had just enough strength to be used in an emergency. He found some stairs and hobbled up them. A blink of light in his robotic eye told him he had left the dampening field, and that the tiny piece of computer was rebooting. He sat beside a wall and tried to get the arm to reattach. It wouldn't. He started to panic as he heard footsteps coming down the corridor. Lot's of them. A boot up sequence was scrolling in his eye.

"Come on!" He growled at his micro-chip. "Hurry

up!" He tucked himself in to a dark corner and waited as many soldiers ran passed him. They were in too much of a hurry to take notice of the silhouette lurking in the partial darkness. Conrad cursed his arm and tried to attach it again. To no avail.

***

The raid was going to plan. A few of the Independent Countries had responded to Black Trons plea for help. Some hadn't. The fight in the air looked very one sided. Aaron laughed at the fact it was their side being favoured. He and Delta's second team were watching as more Octopods were fleeing the military base. Team one had done brilliantly, and were luring the enemy fighters away from the base. Many foot soldiers pored out of the base a moment later. As soon as it was safe to do so, Team two left their hiding place and went for the entrance. Their mission was simple. Find Jason Moon. Kill him.

Door open, Aaron took his men inside. It was dark inside. Plasma shots must have knocked the lights out. They started their search. The place was a maze. They found a huge bay where several Octopods had previously occupied. They found rooms full of bunkers. Soldier sleeping quarters. Then they found the offices. Jason Moon had to be close. They met no one. The place seemed deserted. Room after room and no sign of the enemy.

Then they found him.

At the end of a richly decorated corridor was a room with huge, gold doors. Aaron almost laughed. Of coarse the pompous old git would be here. He was sitting behind the desk. His hands on top with his fingers knitted together. Aaron led the men in. The further they went, the more Aaron felt that something was wrong. Why was he just sitting there? The men were all in. Aaron pointed his PEEP at Jason's head.

"Got you, you coward!" Jason smiled.

"No, Commander. I, got you." The desk disappeared. Jason, the chair he was sitting on, the rich décor. All vanished. Then so did the walls. They were in a room twice the size as it had first seemed. The fake walls had been hiding a large group of Black Tron soldiers. Half on one side of the room, half the other. The door with which they had come through had also disappeared. They were trapped.

An image of Jason reappeared. This time, he was standing by the far wall. He seemed pleased. He took a couple of steps forward and smiled.

"Sorry Commander. But when I see Delta ships retreating, I automatically assume a trap. Delta's eighth rule; Retreat *is* an option. You can kill more if you live longer. However, that rule was supposed to be; retreat over *defeat* is an option. In other words, Delta only run away when they are no longer able to win. There were more then enough Delta fighters to take on my ships, so why retreat? No reason. Unless..." He indicated the M-Tron soldiers. "See what I mean?"

"Well done arse-licker! Now what?" Aaron snapped at him.

"Now I give the order to- arrggh!" The image of Jason suddenly lifted half a foot into the air. He was clutching at something around his neck. Aaron took a closer look and saw something metal. It looked almost like five silver hooks. Four sitting side-by-side and the fifth coming around from the other side. Almost like... Almost like... Fingers.

Fingers!

That could only mean one thing. But it couldn't be. He was dead. Then a new person entered the holographic field and was seen by all in the huge room.

"Hello girls. Miss me?" Aaron could only smile at the image. His old friend looked hurt and quite battered, but god was it good to see him.

"Conrad you old bastard! I knew you couldn't die." Conrad smiled, an actual smile.

"Never my friend. Now." He turned to the gasping man in his iron grip. "Tell your men to drop their weapons or I'll break your fucking neck! And after what I've been through, I strongly suggest complying!" Jason waved at the men.

"Drop... your... weapons." He managed. The soldiers did as was ordered. Aaron and his men swung towards the enemy and raised their own guns.

"Okay Conrad. You can kill him now." Aaron called. There was a pause. Then nothing. Aaron turned to see why he hadn't heard the sound of bones breaking. Conrad was still standing there. Jason was still in his grip. Conrad seemed to be struggling with some deep emotion. Aaron could see the rage on his face. Conrad wanted to kill him, but couldn't. The anger drained away and he sat the man on a seat.

"Conrad? What are you doing? Kill him!" Conrad shook his head.

"No." He said. "That won't end the war. I'll not make a martyr out of him."

"You're a... wise man... clone." Jason said, still gasping and drinking in great lungfuls of air. Conrad slapped him across the back of the head.

"I'm not a fucking clone!" He said through clenched teeth. "Now listen closely. I'm going to call my men off."

"What?!?" Exclaimed Aaron. Conrad ignored him and continued speaking to Jason.

"And you're going to do the same. Because, if you don't, I'm going to snap you like a twig." Then he turned to Aaron. "Commander. Get on the blower. Don't tell them I'm alive yet."

"Yes, sir. Er, why?"

"Send them home of coarse."

"No, I meant, why don't tell them about you?"

"Oh." Conrad said a little sheepishly. "I may not make it back. Don't ask questions, just do as I've asked." Aaron shook his head in disapproval, but contacted Barry anyway.

"Sorry old friend." Aaron told the General when he got a reply, "But I'm gonna have to use the old Delta override command and ask you to send everyone back to base. I've got a good reason. I'll debrief you when we get back." Being on the front line, and being privy to top secret information, at times of great need a Delta Commander can issue an order to the General. The General could still refuse, but it was always a wise move not to.

"Okay Aaron. Is there a threat?" Asked Barry.

"No. All okay. Mission is over. I'll debrief you at HQ."

"Okay." The line went dead.

"That means you too Commander." Conrad said. Aaron was about to argue, but saw the determined look in Conrad's eye. They turned and left.

***

In Jason's true office, Conrad was getting comfortable. He had poured himself a drink from Jason's drinks cabinet, and was sitting in Jason's favourite chair.

"Wow! This is comfy. I should get a chair just like it for my office." He taunted. He put his feet up on the dead officer laying on the ground. Jason eyed the corpse. "Yeah, sorry about him. Didn't want him sneaking up behind me while I was wringing your neck."

"Think nothing of it Conrad." Jason said, remembering not to call him 'clone'. "He wasn't very useful anyway." He had been actually.

"Well," Conrad cooed, "He's pretty useful now."

Jason wanted to kill the man. But he steadied his nerves. They were quiet for a moment while Conrad drank his scotch, and Jason sipped at his whisky. Then, suddenly, Jason laughed. Conrad eyed him.

"What's so funny?" He asked. Jason laughed for a moment longer before replying.

"I've been trying for years to have you captured and brought before me. And when I finally give up trying, you walk in here of your own accord. You have to see the irony there." He laughed some more. Conrad thought about it and found it funny also. The M-Tron president and the Black Tron president. Sworn enemies. Sitting in a room together, drinking and laughing. This thought came to them both and had them laughing even more.

"You know," Conrad said through a fit of laughter, "any one coming in here is gonna wonder what the fuck is going on."

"Oh god yeah!" Jason roared back, clutching his side in hysterics.

The laughter lasted almost an hour. Then it slowed to rhythmic chuckling.

"So what now?" Asked Conrad.

"What do you mean?" Asked Jason in return. Conrad rode out a chuckle before answering.

"I mean, are you going to kill me now, or torture me some more?" Chuckle.

"Why? Were you enjoying Jacques company?" Chuckle, chuckle.

"Not when he was talking. That was the worst kind of torture." This brought about another short burst of laughter.

"My men will be here soon." Chuckle, snort.

"Then we can let them decide?" More laughter. "No, no… seriously. I only stayed so my men could get away. What *are* you going to do with me?" Chuckle.

"I could always let you go." This had them roaring with laughter.

"Oh please! My sides are hurting!" Conrad blurted.

"Do you want to know what's really funny?" Jason asked, giggling.

"Sure. What's that?"

"I'm being serious." Conrad nearly fell off the seat with laughter.

"You're being serious! Ha haa!"

"No. Really. I'm going to let you go. I'm actually not joking." Conrad's laughter started to falter.

"What? Why?" Jason let his own laughter die out with Conrad's.

"Because I like pitting my wits against you. I've never had an opponent like you. Believe it or not, I wouldn't know what to do if I didn't have a great warrior like you to fight." Conrad's face finally took on an air of seriousness.

"Oh my god! You really *are* letting me go." Jason's face also went from happy to serious.

"Yes. I am"

"You know, it's a shame we weren't on the same side. You'd make one hell of a partner." Jason nodded.

"I thought the same thing about you. But if we were on the same side, who would we fight?"

"Good point." Jason went to the oversized fireplace and pulled on a statue sitting on the mantle piece. A secret door beside the hearth opened up.

"Go that way. When you reach the water, turn left and keep going."

"I can't figure you out Moon." Jason gave a snort.

"Good bye Conrad. We'll meet again." Conrad ducked under the low doorframe.

"Good bye Jason. Oh, and you'd better hope we don't meet again."

"Why is that?"

"'Cos if we do, I'll kill you."

Chapter twenty nine

Aaron and Barry had fallen out with each other. After they had returned to base, Aaron had told Barry about Conrad. The shock of hearing that he was alive was bad enough. Barry had been so excited to know that he would see his friend again. Then Aaron told him that Conrad stayed behind. Barry worked it out right then and there. Conrad had sacrificed himself again.

It had been over a month since the raid. Conrad never showed up. They had to proclaim him dead once more. This caused an argument between the two friends. Aaron and Barry hadn't spoken to each other for three weeks.

The people had all gathered in the great park on level three. This was the top level. Curator Edmund was standing on the huge dais. Many screens showed the man's face. He was clearly distressed at having to give this news. The people were all waiting to hear him speak. He hesitated.

"Ladies and Gentlemen." He said, nervously in to the microphone. He caused a little feedback and had to cover his ears for a moment until the squealing had stopped. A sound man gave him a thumbs up sign to say the problem was fixed. Edmund tried again.

"Ladies and Gentlemen. I have some grieving news." The faces of the people was a match for his own. At the mention of bad news, they had all become very saddened. "The battle is won, but the war is not over." This received a few shouts from the crowd and even several 'boos'. "Jason Moon still lives and so does Black Tron." The crowds angry shouts and booing became louder. "And worse of all. Conrad Manké is dead." The crowd fell silent. Not a sound. They all looked up at Edmund with haunting eyes, pleading for this not to be true. A tear rolled down Edmunds face.

For many years these people had been clutching at straws. The only straw to clutch was the belief in the great Saviour. He was their hope. Their shining star to freedom. And he was dead. The world suddenly seemed empty and pointless. They all saw their freedom slipping from their grasp. The straw was gone.

"Conrad died at the hands off-" A hand on his shoulder cut him short. A voice whispered in his ear.

"Conrad died at the hands of no-one. There isn't a mother fucker on this planet that can kill me." Edmund lifted his eyes and saw the people staring in bewilderment. He turned and came face to face with the President of M-Tron. Edmund almost cried with joy. Conrad took the mic from him and addressed the crowd.

"The world outside is still polluted with radiation. But there is much land that is free from pollution. With the right equipment, we can start reducing the radiation forever. To do that, we need you. If you are all willing, and if you are all prepared to work, we can leave this place now, and return to the surface." The people gave a roar of excitement. "But you must help us to rebuild. For rebuild we will. The cities will be alive again! The skies will fill once more! The roads will be busy again! M-Tron will RISE! And you are going to help us raise it! For if we all pull together, we can do anything! Black Tron has been raised to the ground! We have decimated them! It will take them a long, long time to rebuild. And when they do, and when they come calling, WE WILL BE WAITING FOR THEM!!" Edmund started to say something, but it was drowned out by the crowd. Barry and Aaron had come up and were shaking Conrad's hand. Edmund gave up trying to talk to the crowd. He went and shook Conrad's hand also.

***

The people couldn't just leave the underground bunker like that. They had organised themselves into work details and each shift would go out on an AUC and work the lands. With the use of special chemicals, they started neutralising the radiation. It would take decades to clear it all, but for now they were trying to chase it back to make enough room for the people to leave the underground for good. Several AUC's at a time would carry workers to and fro, protecting them from the radiation as they left the giant airlocks in the mountainside. Conrad got his ship back and went to work fixing it. He was also reunited with his personal SIS unit. Much to his distaste.

As the people went about rebuilding M-Tron, Conrad couldn't help but wonder… Why did that slimy bastard let him live? 'Oh well' thought Conrad, 'too late to dwell on it now'. A shape caught his attention in the corner of his eye. Not long ago, this would have been a blind spot for him as it was the corner of his robotic eye. But Agent 247, whoever he was, had rebuilt it. Conrad now had a panoramic view of the world in his robotic eye that was almost exactly the same as having a real eye. He looked up at the cause of the shadow. A small boy of about nine years looked down at him.

"Can I help uncle Conrad?"

"Uncle? How long have I been an uncle? When I see your father I'll kick him in the testis." Zach sat beside him.

"What's a testis?" He asked. Conrad smiled and gave the boy a hug.

"Do you know what a twenty four mill spanner is?"

"Yes uncle Conrad."

"Good. You'll find one in the toolbox. See if you can get that plasma inducer apart."

"Yes uncle."

"And stop calling me uncle."

"Yes uncle."

He was almost tempted to ask Zach if he wanted the watch he was wearing. It was a lovely watch. Told the time perfectly.

But only at half past three.

**

Spree was sitting on the small chair in Jason's office. Jason was sitting in his favourite chair. Spree put his drink down and decided to ask the burning question.

"Why did you let him go? I thought you wanted him dead." Jason slowly sipped his own drink.

"I do. And *I* want to kill him." Spree seemed confused.

"So why didn't you?" Jason placed the glass on the great oak desk.

"Because I want him to suffer first."

"I don't understand."

"I'm going to kill Conrad at a time when he is powerless to stop me. I want him to remember that first day. I want him to remember me and what he did to me. Then I'm going to kill him. And he will watch as I do so." Spree was really confused now.

"Sir? I think you've gone mad." Jacques leapt over the desk and grabbed the man by the throat lifting him clear in to the air.

"Madness runs in the family Spree! Remember that!" Jacques put him down roughly and returned to where he had sprung from.

"I may be mad Spree." Jason continued. "But I'm not stupid. If I kill Conrad now, his army will rise and kill us all. I won't make a martyr out of him. We don't have enough soldiers left to fight now. If I had killed him, I would have signed our own death warrant. Let Conrad have his fun. It won't last long. Soon, none of this will ever have happened. History will be rewritten.

261

"Then I'll be a god Spree."

"Yes sir." Spree said, rubbing his throat.

"The holo-projector worked wonders by the way. The Utopian soldiers were easily fooled. Which is good, or they might have found Jacques little toy down there."

"Yes sir."

"Well. I believe you have work to do?"

"Yes sir."

"Then get on with it. We have a lot to prepare."

"Yes sir." Spree made to leave.

"Oh, and Spree."

"Sir?"

"Don't ever make Jacques cross again. Or he'll kill you."

"No sir."

www.ingramcontent.com/pod-product-compliance
Lightning Source LLC
Chambersburg PA
CBHW031211260626
47169CB00007B/2009